Praise for the Downward Dog Mystery series

Karma's a Killer

"Tracy's Weber's *Karma's a Killer* delivers on all fronts—a likably feisty protagonist, a great supporting cast, a puzzler of a mystery and, best of all, lots of heart. This book has more snap than a brand-new pair of yoga capris. Pure joy for yoga aficionados, animal lovers…heck, for anyone who loves a top-notch mystery."

—Laura DiSilverio, national bestselling author of
The Readaholics book club mysteries, two-time Lefty finalist
for best humorous mystery, and Colorado Book Award finalist

"Crazy, quirky critters and their odd yet utterly relatable human counterparts make *Karma's a Killer* an appealing story. But when you add the keep-you-guessing mystery with both laugh-out-loud one-liners and touching moments of pure poignancy, the result is a truly great book!"

—Laura Morrigan, national bestselling author of
the Call of the Wilde mystery series

"Yogatta love this latest in the series when Kate exercises her brain cells trying to figure out who deactivated an animal rights activist."

—Mary Daheim, author of the Bed-and-Breakfast
and Emma Lord Alpine mysteries

A Killer Retreat

"Cozy readers will enjoy the twist-filled plot."

—*Publishers Weekly*

"[Kate's] path to enlightenment is a fresh element in cozy mysteries."

—*Library Journal*

"Weber's vegan yoga teacher is a bright, curious sleuth with a passion for dogs."

… bestselling author
…nd Claws Mysteries

"An engaging mystery full of fun and fascinating characters and unexpected twists."

—Linda O. Johnston, author of the Pet Rescue Mystery series

"Fun characters, a gorgeous German Shepherd dog, and a murder with more suspects than you can shake a stick at. *A Killer Retreat* is a must-read for cozy fans!"

—Sparkle Abbey, author of the Pampered Pet Mystery series

"Whether yoga instructor Kate Davidson is wrestling her hundred-pound dog, her new love life, or trying to solve a murder, *A Killer Retreat* is simply a killer read! Witty, fun, and unpredictable, this is one cozy mystery worth barking about!"

—Shannon Esposito, author of the Pet Psychic Mystery series

"Weber's second yoga mystery, *A Killer Retreat*, is as delightful as her first. Readers will love the setting, the complex mystery, and the romance of Kate's second adventure…Enjoy!"

—Susan Conant, author of the Dog Lover's Mystery series

Murder Strikes a Pose
"*Murder Strikes a Pose*, by Tracy Weber, is a delightful debut novel featuring Kate Davidson, a caring but feisty yoga teacher…Namaste to Weber and her fresh, new heroine!"

—Penny Warner, author of *How to Dine on Killer Wine*

"[T]his charming debut mystery…pieces together a skillful collage of mystery, yoga, and plenty of dog stories against the unique backdrop of Seattle characters and neighborhoods. The delightful start of a promising new series. I couldn't put it down!"

—Waverly Fitzgerald, author of *Dial C for Chihuahua*

"Three woofs for Tracy Weber's first Downward Dog Mystery, *Murder Strikes a Pose*. Great characters, keep-you-guessing plot, plenty of laughs, and dogs—what more could we want?"

—Sheila Webster Boneham, award-winning author of *Drop Dead on Recall*

KARMA'S
A
KILLER

KARMA'S

A

KILLER

....

A DOWNWARD DOG MYSTERY

....

TRACY WEBER

MIDNIGHT INK
WOODBURY, MINNESOTA

First Edition
First Printing, 2016

Book format by Bob Gaul
Cover design by Kevin R. Brown
Cover illustration by Nicole Alesi/Deborah Wolfe Ltd.

Midnight Ink, an imprint of Llewellyn Worldwide Ltd.

This is a work of fiction. Names, characters, places, and incidents are either the product of the author's imagination or are used fictitiously, and any resemblance to actual persons living or dead, business establishments, events, or locales is entirely coincidental.

Library of Congress Cataloging-in-Publication Data
Weber, Tracy.
  Karma's a killer: a downward dog mystery/Tracy Weber.—First edition.
    pages; cm.—(A downward dog mystery; 3)
  ISBN 978-0-7387-4210-6 (softcover)
1. Yoga teachers—Washington (State)—Seattle—Fiction. 2. Murder—Investigation—Fiction. I. Title.
  PS3623.E3953K37 2016
  813'.6—dc23

33614056456741   2015028417

Midnight Ink
Llewellyn Worldwide Ltd.
2143 Wooddale Drive
Woodbury, MN 55125-2989
www.midnightinkbooks.com

Printed in the United States of America

*To my mom, Marcia. Your support of
my writing means the world to me.*

ACKNOWLEDGMENTS

First of all, I'd like to thank every reader who has contacted me to tell me that they enjoy my work. Each email, Facebook post, and letter makes my day. Without you, I'm not sure I'd have the fortitude to continue writing.

Karma's a Killer has a special cast of people I want to acknowledge.

My yoga students continue to listen to my grumblings, join in my cheering, attend my events, and support my writing in more ways than I could ever have hoped for. Special thanks to Katie West, who addressed and mailed a seemingly infinite number of packages to my street team members, and Katie Burns, who proofed the manuscript before I submitted it to Midnight Ink. Thanks also to my agent, Margaret Bail, editors Terri Bischoff and Sandy Sullivan at Midnight Ink, and freelance editor Marta Tanrikulu, who all continue to give me invaluable help and feedback.

Special thanks go to Michael Westerfield, author of *The Language of Crows*. Michael graciously answered my many questions about crow behavior. His insights about crows raised as fledglings and released to the wild were invaluable. Of course, if there are any errors in this work—about crows or anything else—they are completely mine.

My husband, Marc, and my real-life Bella, Tasha, continue to be the lights of my life. Anything I accomplish is only possible through their love and support. Marc gets extra kudos for designing and maintaining my author website. Tasha gets credit for introducing me to her crow friends and fueling my fascination for these intelligent, underappreciated creatures.

Finally, thank you to all of my street team members. These dedicated individuals spread the word about my writing, pass out my bookmarks, and make me smile on days that otherwise seem glum. The best part of writing has been connecting with all of you.

ONE

"I can't believe I let Michael talk me into this. The man is obviously nuts."

I reached out my arms and slowly turned a complete circle, trying to fully take in the deafening chaos around me.

Under different circumstances, *I* probably would have been the one referred to as crazy. I was, after all, muttering to myself while spinning like a slow-motion top. But today, nobody seemed to notice. The soccer fields of Seattle's Green Lake Park undulated with a buzzing, beehive-like swarm of people.

And their dogs.

Lots and lots of dogs.

All blocking the path to my destination.

A golden retriever pulled toward me from the front, practically dislocating the shoulder of an acne-scarred teenager. Behind me, a yapping Chihuahua flashed piranha-like teeth at the backs of my ankles. To my right, a geriatric woman tried, unsuccessfully, to restrain an adolescent bull mastiff that was seemingly intent on saying hello to, well, to everyone.

And that was just the start.

Each time a potential path opened, it was quickly obscured by a new member of the dense canine stew. I almost squeezed between two roughhousing pit bulls, but I got distracted by a huge Rottweiler head attached to six-inch-long wiener dog legs. A Rott-wiener? Was that even physically possible?

By the time I shook off the image, the momentary opening had disappeared.

The closely packed crowd shouldn't have surprised me. Over two thousand people had registered for Paws Around Green Lake, today's 5K dog "fun" walk. Twice as many as my boyfriend, Michael, had anticipated when he agreed to organize the fundraising event. I should have been happy for Michael, and I was. I was even happier for DogMa, the no-kill animal shelter that would receive the day's proceeds. Or I would have been, if those same two thousand bodies hadn't stood between me and my destination.

If only I'd brought my hundred-pound German shepherd, Bella, with me. My treat-motivated tracker dog would have beelined it straight for the food vendors, parting the crowd with me flying like a kite behind her. But Bella still didn't like other dogs, or most bearded men for that matter. I could never have inserted her into this canine carnival—not without risking a multiple-dog homicide—and it was too warm on this uncharacteristically sunny spring day to leave her in the car, even if I'd parked in the shade.

So here I was, on my own.

I took a step back and assessed the event's layout, trying to simultaneously decipher an entrance and plot my escape. The normally empty field had been marked off in sectors. The northernmost end held a multicolored assortment of receptacles marked *garbage*, *recycle*, *pet waste*, and *compost*. Where the dumpsters left off, a golden line of stacked straw bales began, outlining the fenced area allocated to Dale's goat petting farm.

To the south stood a stage, a registration desk, several food vendors, and the roped-off area I would later use as a makeshift yoga studio. The rest of the perimeter was lined with about two dozen tent-covered booths. My goal, should I choose to accept it, was to find the booth assigned to my yoga studio, Serenity Yoga.

Okay, Kate. You can do this.

I plugged my ears to block out the din, lifted my heels, and stood on my toes in a tennis-shoed Tadasana, trying to see over the masses.

Maybe if I jag to the right, dive under that banner, and—

"Whoa!"

The Chihuahua sank his teeth into my pant leg and yanked. I flailed my arms and tried—unsuccessfully—to stay balanced. My left foot got tangled in the fur-covered piranha's leash; my right hand connected solidly with his owner's coffee cup. The lid flew across the field. Hot, dark brown liquid spilled down my shirt.

"Hey!" she snapped. "What are you, drunk?"

I opened my mouth to apologize, but the supermodel-thin woman didn't give me a chance. She snatched her dog off my pant leg, ignored the hot liquid soaking my chest, and pierced me with an ice-pick-sharp glare.

"Watch where you're going, you big oaf. You could have hurt Precious."

My ears zipped right past the word "oaf" and landed solidly on "big." Who was she calling big? I'd lost almost twenty pounds in the six months since my misadventures on Orcas Island. Even *I* had to

3

admit that my five-foot three-inch body had finally landed on the thin side of normal.

But that didn't stop me from feeling insulted.

My body reacted before my mind could control it. Anger-laced adrenaline zapped down my spine. My fingers curled into tight fists. My teeth clenched together so hard I was afraid I might shatter a molar.

Every fiber of my being wanted to lash out, which wasn't surprising. I'd struggled with my Hulk-like alter ego since my first two-year-old temper tantrum. But I was trying to change—to better embody the yoga principles I believed in.

My father's voice echoed inside my head: *Don't do it, Kate. Not today. You don't want to create a scene today.*

Three years after his death, Dad was still right. Today's event was important to Michael—too important to risk ruining. Besides, I had vowed not to lose my temper anymore. If I'd learned anything on Orcas, it was that bad things sometimes happened when I got angry. Sometimes people got hurt.

I shuddered.

I couldn't let myself think about that.

Instead, I took a deep breath, consciously relaxed my jaw, and forced my lips into a smile.

The Chihuahua's owner thrust her empty cup in my face. "You owe me a new mocha."

Honorable intentions be damned. I seriously wanted to punch her.

My only alternative was to retreat.

I tossed her a five-dollar bill, took three large steps back, and bumped into the teenager attached to the golden retriever. "I'm sorry." I turned right and tripped over the bull mastiff. "Excuse me." I stumbled and "excused me'd" and "I'm so sorry'd" my way through the crowd, toward the water. I finally burst onto the path and bolted past the Green Lake Community Center to my new destination: a large, T-shaped wooden dock. The clamor faded to silence.

Empty. Thank goodness.

The scarred wooden dock was normally occupied by local fishermen, but for the moment, it was mine. All mine. The crowds, noise, and limited parking had kept everyone but the dog walkers away from Green Lake today.

I stood at the dock's southernmost end, as far away from the pandemonium as possible. For several long, lunacy-free moments, I found peace. I stared at the lake, smelled the crisp, clean scent of the water, and took slow, soothing breaths. Hypnotizing light jewels rippled off the lake's surface. The boards underneath my feet gently swayed. My nervous system rebalanced, forcing my inner demon back into her lair.

When I finally felt ready, I touched my palms together in the prayer-like Anjali Mudra, bowed my head to reconnect with my center, and turned back toward the soccer fields.

Bummer.

If anything, they looked even more chaotic. I couldn't deal with all of those people. Not yet.

Perhaps a short visualization practice would help.

I sat cross-legged on a relatively goose-dung-free spot, closed my eyes, and touched my fingertips to the wood's warm, rough surface. The sun melted my shoulders; a cool breeze pinked my cheeks.

I mentally transported myself to the beach near the soccer fields. Soft, white energy floated above the water and spilled over the lake's borders. The fog-like mist expanded, filling the grassy area. It stilled the crowd, creating more space. In my mind's eye, I reached out my hand. The field still wasn't empty, but at least it was permeable. I could sift through the crowd, untouched. I took a deep breath, lifted my right foot, and—

Angry whispers interrupted my meditation.

"No one asked for your opinion."

I opened my eyes and turned toward the sound. Two quarreling women huddled near the shore, hidden from the soccer fields by a half-dozen bright yellow paddleboats. Their hushed voices carried across the water as clearly as if they were using a megaphone.

I considered ignoring them, and frankly, I should have. *The Yoga Sutras*—yoga's key philosophical text—might not have *explicitly* condemned eavesdropping, but I was pretty sure the teachings considered it bad karma. Still, I was curiously drawn to their conversation. Something about them felt oddly familiar ...

I shaded my eyes from the sun and tried to make out their faces. Both women were dressed completely in black: black long-sleeved T-shirts, deep black jeans, black tennis shoes. The only touches of color were the bright orange flames embroidered above each woman's left breast.

The woman speaking was about my age—early to mid-thirties. She cradled a stack of picket signs in one arm and gesticulated wildly with the other. The sign on the top said *Apply the HEAT* in bold red letters. Her fingernails matched her deep black outfit, except for the middle fingernail of each hand, which was painted blood burgundy. Long, curly dark hair bounced off her shoulders with every emphatic shake of her head.

"You have to choose, Dharma. Either you're one hundred percent on board, or you're out. Which will it be?"

The second woman, obviously named Dharma, didn't answer immediately. She was small—about my height and maybe five pounds heavier—and at least ten years older than her friend. She wore black wire-rimmed glasses, and her gray-streaked brown hair was tied back from her shoulders in a single long braid. When she spoke, she sounded exasperated, as if she'd repeated this argument many times before.

"You've clearly lost all perspective, Raven. This protest doesn't make any sense. We have more important issues to deal with. Why don't we go after factory farming? How about animal experimentation? Heck, I'd rather go back to Brazil and try to preserve what's left of the rain forest. Why beat up innocent, sensible pet owners?"

"Innocent? What's *innocent* about slavery? Do you have any idea how many of these so-called innocent slime bags abandon or euthanize their pets every year?"

Dharma leaned forward earnestly. "Which is precisely why we shouldn't go after a no-kill shelter like this one."

Go after a shelter? Were they planning to protest DogMa? Today? I kept listening, hoping that I'd misunderstood.

"I told you before: stop propagating that lie," Raven growled. "There's no such thing as a 'no-kill' shelter. If anything, DogMa and other shelters like it are 'low-kill.' Don't be fooled by all of their pretty promises. These people are frauds, and I'm going to expose them."

I couldn't make out Dharma's grumbled reply, but her tone didn't sound friendly.

Raven held up her hands. "Back off, Dharma. I don't need your help, but I won't stand for your insolence. I'm taking this place down with or without you. Trust me; these hypocrites at DogMa are going to burn." Her voice turned low and threatening. "And if you get in my way, I might have to fry you, too."

Dharma flinched and glanced warily over her shoulder. "Watch what you say, Raven. Someone might take you seriously."

Raven snorted. "Yeah, well, maybe they should."

Dharma's mouth opened, but she didn't respond, at least not at first. After several long, tense moments, she shook her head, almost sadly.

"I'm sorry, Raven, but this has gone far enough. Eduardo talked me into coming on this ill-conceived road trip, but we never agreed to violence. I'm out." She turned and started walking away. "We both are."

"I wouldn't be so sure about Eduardo."

Dharma froze. Her entire body stiffened. When she slowly turned around, her expression was tight, as if her thinned lips and hardened eyes had been carved out of stone.

Raven's lips lifted in a cruel-looking grin. She crossed her arms and leaned back against the paddleboats. "Sweetheart, you can leave any time. The sooner the better. I never wanted you here to begin with. But trust me, Eduardo's not going anywhere. By the time I get through with him, he'll be finished with you, too."

The older woman exploded.

She howled and shoved Raven into the boats, using significantly more force than I would have expected from someone ideologically opposed to violence. Raven's face hit the edge and she fell, splitting open her lower lip. Picket signs scattered in every direction.

Dharma scooped up a sign, snapped its wooden handle in two, and waved the jagged edges at her friend.

"I'm warning you—leave Eduardo alone, or you'll be the one who burns." She jabbed the wooden stake at Raven's chest for emphasis. "In hell."

Raven's response seemed more amused than frightened. She licked the blood from her lower lip, stood, and slowly clapped.

"Well done, Dharma. Well done. We'll make an anarchist out of you yet."

Dharma gaped at her hands, as if surprised to see them grasping a weapon. A strangled cry escaped from her throat. She took two large steps back, threw the broken sign to the ground, and stumbled away, sobbing. A moment later, she disappeared into the crowd.

Raven mumbled several words I couldn't decipher, gathered the rest of her signs, and sauntered off in the opposite direction. I lost sight of her midway through the parking lot.

I stared after her, torn. Whatever Raven was up to, it couldn't be good. Part of me wanted to stop her. But how, exactly, was I supposed to do that? Commandeer her picket signs? Tie her to a bicycle rack with my shoelaces? Yell the word "cat" and hope the dogs took care of the rest? I considered trying to find one of Green Lake's bicycle patrol officers, but what could the police do? The fight was already over, and picketing, though disruptive, wasn't illegal.

A confident female voice called out over the loudspeaker. "Dog walkers, welcome to Paws Around Green Lake, DogMa's first annual furry 5K fun walk. Pick up your leashes and gather your treat pouches. Let the walk begin!"

I glanced at my watch. Ten o'clock. I should have opened my booth an hour ago.

The crowd's human-canine duos trickled toward the trail and started jogging, walking, sniffing, and marking their way around the lake. If the women I'd witnessed were still planning to protest, they'd likely do it during the post-walk celebration. I had plenty of time to find Michael and help him plan for the threat.

I hoped.

TWO

I LOOKED FOR MICHAEL at the registration desk, but he'd already left, likely searching for me. A smiling, braces-wearing teenager handed me a printout of the day's schedule, confirmed that the roped-off area had been set aside for the class I'd teach later, and pointed me toward Serenity Yoga's booth.

Now that the walk was underway, the field was gloriously empty; the path to my lonely, tented table completely clear. I hesitated, tugged by conflicting priorities. A savvy business person would have set up her booth hours ago. On the other hand, I was already late, and I was eager to see my friend Dale. What difference would another five minutes make?

I turned and headed in the opposite direction, toward the goat petting farm. I still couldn't believe that Michael had convinced Dale—self-proclaimed goat rustler and attorney at law—to make the four-hour trip from Orcas Island to Seattle for today's event, but I was happy he did. I hadn't seen Dale since he represented me last fall, and I missed his back-hills country charm. Besides, I still owed him a lifetime's worth of yoga lessons for getting me out of that murder charge. It was time to start paying my bill.

I glanced around the enclosure, looking for my friend's distinctive gray beard. Dale had truly outdone himself. Over a dozen floppy-eared Nubians happily napped, grazed, and otherwise entertained themselves in a thirty-by-thirty chain-linked square. The perimeter was papered with a variety of goat-related signs: *The Best Kids Have Hooves*, *Don't Get My Goat*, and *Home Is Where the Goats Are* among them. Every color of the goat rainbow was represented: black, brown, gray, white—even two cute little white-on-black-spotted kids that looked like reverse-image Dalmatian puppies.

The enclosure was lined with straw bales strategically placed so that exhausted parents could rest while two teenaged volunteers taught their children how to safely interact with the playful animals. The teen boys—one blond, the other brunette—had matching brown eyes, square jaws, and short, stocky builds. If they weren't twins, they were at least brothers.

I saw pretty much everything I would hope for in a goat petting zoo: laughing children; curious, friendly Nubians; a dense carpet of wood shavings; even an obstacle course containing makeshift ramps, old tires, oversized wooden spools, and empty five-gallon water containers. The only thing missing was Dale.

After five minutes, I gave up and headed for my booth. On the way, I stopped at the tented table for Michael's pet supply store, Pete's Pets.

Tiffany, my nemesis and Michael's employee, acknowledged my arrival with a bored-looking yawn. She snapped her chewing gum, glanced down at her cuticles, and frowned, a sure sign that she was in a better mood than usual. To be fair, I wasn't paying much attention to her, either. I was too distracted by the colorful retail area Michael had created in the ten-by-ten space around her. Unlike

Serenity Yoga's empty tent and bare table next door, the Pete's Pets booth was filled with rhinestone-studded collars, bright yellow tennis balls, and a huge variety of dog treats ranging from organic freeze-dried meat cubes to individually wrapped dog cookies to five-foot-long bully sticks.

Tiffany finished her visual manicure and acknowledged my presence. She pointed at the six-inch brown coffee stain decorating my front.

"Nice shirt."

I glanced at a barely visible blemish on the side of her nose.

Nice zit.

I immediately felt bad for the uncharitable thought. Patanjali's *Yoga Sutras* clearly advocated neutrality toward evil, and my thoughts toward Tiffany were anything but neutral. But in my defense, it wasn't my fault. At least not completely.

Tiffany and I had started our immature rivalry a year ago, the day she began working at Pete's Pets. Michael, for whatever reason, liked her. Bella—the traitor—did too. Neither Tiffany nor I agreed with Michael's taste in friends, but Bella was more discerning, and she'd decided that Tiffany was her best cookie buddy. So for the sake of the pup, Tiffany and I had put down our verbal weaponry and declared an uneasy truce.

A truce that dissolved three weeks ago when she broke up with her latest boyfriend.

Since then, she'd started wearing her jeans a size or two tighter; the neckline of her shirt, three inches lower. She'd invested in a push-up bra and dyed her hair a new ultra-platinum shade of blonde. And on more than one occasion, I'd caught her twenty-one-year-old gaze wandering to my boyfriend's well-muscled behind. Not that I blamed her; Michael's backside was impressive when viewed from any angle. But that particular backside was mine. All mine.

Tiffany pulled out a nail file and started sharpening her claws. "Your booth is next door." Her bored vocal tone telegraphed her thoughts: *Dismissed.*

For once, I took the high road. I showed my teeth in a fake submissive grin and backed away to check out the rest of the vendors.

Serenity Yoga's booth stuck out like the answer to an IQ test question: "What doesn't belong here?" The vendors surrounding my table were all animal-related. Pete's Pets was on one side, Precious Life Wildlife Center on the other. The rest of the booths showcased an assortment of animal organizations ranging from dog training centers to pet daycares to do-it-yourself dog washes. Brightly colored banners, sparkly leashes, and a smorgasbord of dog treats all vied for human and canine attention. Somehow I didn't think I'd be getting a run on my booth.

The dog walkers were still meandering their way around Green Lake, so after I covered my empty table space with informational flyers and freshly printed class schedules, I did a little wandering myself, next door to visit Precious Life Wildlife Center.

A tiny, seventy-something woman organized educational materials at her table. A large black crow tilted his head and watched me curiously from a cage on the chair behind her.

I smiled and waved at him. "Hi buddy."

The woman glanced up, then returned to organizing her flyers. "That there's Blackie."

Upon hearing his name, the crow walked to the edge of his cage and cawed. The woman made clicking noises with her tongue, reached into her pocket, and produced a peanut. "You want this, baby?" She gave him the peanut and turned to face me.

"I think he likes you." She smiled and wiped her hands on her tunic. "Any friend of Blackie's is a friend of mine."

On a good day I barely topped five-foot-three, but I still had to look down to meet the wiry woman's gaze. A flower-print blouse and pink polyester pants peeked out from under her blue medical tunic. Her paper-thin skin seemed fragile, and her face sported more wrinkles than a Shar Pei puppy. But her smile—especially when she talked to that bird—radiated an almost childlike humor.

She held out a red, swollen hand. "I'm Judith Ferguson. Nice to meet you."

I hesitated before squeezing it, afraid I might hurt her.

"Don't worry hon, you won't break me. The chemicals I use are hard on my hands. Old age ain't any easier." She smiled. "But I manage just fine." She gave my hand a firm shake. "You still haven't told me your name."

"Oh, sorry. Kate Davidson."

"Well, Kate Davidson, it's nice to meet you." She picked up the crow's cage and carefully set it on the table.

I leaned down and stared through the bars.

"He's gorgeous."

I'd never paid much attention to crows. Up close, Blackie was much bigger than I would have imagined, and the word "black" didn't come close to describing the color of his dark, glossy, almost iridescent feathers. What surprised me the most about him, though, were his eyes. They sparkled with keen intelligence and what I swore was a dry sense of humor.

I reached my hand toward the cage.

"Can I touch him?"

"Go ahead. He won't bite."

I poked my index finger through the bars and stroked Blackie's soft feathers. "He's amazing," I said. "I've never known anyone with a pet crow."

Judith's expression grew stern. "You still don't. Blackie's not a pet. He's a patient."

I flinched, surprised by her suddenly brusque tone. "I'm sorry. I didn't mean to offend you."

Judith frowned for a moment, then she closed her eyes and sighed. "Sorry. I shouldn't have grumped at you like that. Unless you're involved in animal rehab, you wouldn't know. But the distinction is important. I'm a certified wildlife rehabilitator, and I have to be careful."

She gestured toward Blackie's cage. "Corvids, even tame ones like Blackie, are considered migratory birds. They can't be kept as pets. According to the government wildlife bureaucrats, animals like Blackie have to either be fully rehabilitated and released or euthanized." She shook her head. "There's no middle ground. If word got out that I was keeping Blackie as a pet, they might revoke my license."

That sounded ridiculous to me. "You wouldn't really lose your license over a crow, would you?"

"A single crow? Probably not, but I can't risk it. A friend of mine's center got shut down a few months ago."

"What if he couldn't survive in the wild?"

"Then, according to law, I'd have to euthanize him." She handed me a flyer titled *Handling and Helping Injured Wildlife*. "This answers most of your questions."

I scanned the page. "I had no idea the laws were so strict."

"You don't know the half of it, honey. Some of the rules I'm supposed to follow make me mad as a honey badger. Nobody who works in this business *wants* the animals they help to live in captivity. But when it's either that or death?" She crossed her arms. "Choosing to end some-one's life should at least warrant a discussion, don't you think?"

I did, actually.

"In any case," Judith continued, "that's my soapbox, not yours. As far as Blackie, here, he's one of the lucky ones. He's fully recovered now, and he'll get to go back into the wild."

"What happened to him?"

"He got caught by a dog here at Green Lake." She pointed to a featherless spot near his neck. "See that bald spot there? That's where the dog bit him. Broke his wing and everything." She shook her head. "Makes no sense to me why they can't keep those buggers on a leash."

I agreed with that, too. Bella and I were constantly dodging friendly but out-of-control dogs here at the lake, in spite of Seattle's supposedly strict leash laws.

"At least the guy had enough decency to get Blackie some help. Most people would have left him behind to die."

I shuddered. The thought of letting an injured animal suffer made my stomach churn.

Judith kept talking. "To tell you the truth, I'm still surprised Blackie made it. A sane rehabilitator would have euthanized him on the spot." She grinned. "But as my husband says, sanity's never been one of my weaknesses. Blackie still had so much life in his eyes. I had to help him."

She leaned toward the cage and nestled her face in its wires. "You're Momma's miracle boy, aren't you?"

She waited for the crow to touch his beak to her nose, then stood up and pushed a glass jar across the table. "We're taking donations today, if you're interested in helping. We mainly need money, but anything helps: cages, crates, towels, blankets, food … You name it, we pretty much need it."

I pulled a twenty-dollar bill out of my pocket and tucked it inside.

Judith gave me a brisk nod. "Thanks."

Blackie made a chattering noise, as if trying to get our attention.

"He seems tame," I said.

"He's been that way since the beginning. I figure somebody raised him from a fledgling and released him. He probably grew up with a dog, which would explain why he didn't have the smarts to fly away from the mutt who caught him. Hopefully he learned his lesson and will do better today."

"Today?"

"Today is Blackie's big day. I'm going to release him so he can go back to his corvid family. I'll sure miss the little bugger, though." She placed her palm tenderly on the side of the cage. "You'll never forget your mommy, will you?" Her eyes grew wet. "He won't, you know. Crows have amazing memories. Blackie here will be my friend for the rest of his life. Play your cards right, and he'll be yours, too."

I smiled. "And how would I do that?"

"Hold out your hand."

I did as instructed—I had a feeling no one intelligent ever argued with Judith—and she placed several unsalted peanuts in my palm. She nodded toward the cage. "Go ahead now, feed him."

Blackie cawed and marched to the edge of his cage. I gingerly wove a peanut through the bars, hoping I wasn't about to lose a finger. Blackie took it, hopped a few inches away, and cracked open the shell. In less than a minute, he hopped back to the edge of the cage and cawed at me again, clearly asking for seconds.

"You can give him another one. He won't get fat."

I gave him a second peanut. He hammered the shell with his beak and liberated the two nuts within.

Judith narrowed her eyes and looked at me shrewdly. "What's your angle, anyway?"

"What do you mean?"

"I'm supposedly here to teach people how to handle injured wildlife. Truthfully, I'm hoping to scrounge up donations. She gestured with her chin toward Tiffany and the Pete's Pets booth. "Your friend over there is selling overpriced dog food. But I can't figure out where you fit in. What's a yoga studio doing at a pet rally?"

I pointed toward the main event stage. "My boyfriend organized the fun walk." I mentally crossed my fingers and hoped that would end the conversation.

Judith eyed me expectantly. "And?"

I should have known I wouldn't get off that easily. I glanced around to make sure no one was listening, then leaned forward and mumbled.

Judith frowned and cupped her hand around her ear. "What's that? You'll have to talk a might louder than that, honey. I'm seventy-five. My hearing has gone south with the rest of my body."

I sighed, steeled my shoulders, and forced myself to say the words at full volume. "I'm teaching a Doga class."

"Doga? What in the heck is Doga?"

I tried not to flinch. "Yoga for dogs."

Judith shook her head in apparent disbelief. "Well, now don't that beat all? Yoga for dogs…" Her voice trailed off.

To be honest, I wasn't all that sure about Doga myself. My breath-centered style of yoga required mindful connection of movement and breath—a skill that was challenging for most *humans* to master. The thought of Fluffy or Fido inhaling while lifting his paws seemed, well, ludicrous.

But when Michael flashed his gorgeous blue-green eyes and asked me to teach Doga as part of the closing ceremonies for today's event, I couldn't say no. So I'd done some research, set my ego aside, and here I was.

Teaching Doga.

At best, I would show the (hopefully small) class a few human-assisted dog stretches. At worst, I'd become the new laughingstock of the Seattle yoga community. If I got super lucky, Raven's protesters would stage a sit-in and block the entrance to my yoga space, making the entire point moot.

Which reminded me, I needed to find Michael and warn him about the protesters.

I was about to do exactly that, when a sound startled me from behind.

THREE

"THERE SHE IS!"

Dale Evans, my white-bearded, goat-rescuing attorney from Orcas, waved furiously from the edge of my booth. Michael stood behind him, grinning from one gorgeously crinkled eye to the other. I'd never met the two women standing between them, but even they looked amused.

Dale wore his normal outfit: worn jeans, baseball cap, suspenders, and dark brown work boots. His bright red T-shirt featured a cartoon cowboy riding a bucking-bronco-like goat. The caption read *Chief Goat Wrangler*. Bandit, his black-and-white Jack Russell terrier, jumped up and down at the end of his leash. The matching red bandanna he wore read *Wrangler's Assistant*.

Dale lifted me off the ground in a tight hug. I hugged him back, turned my face away, and tried not to think about the millions of multilegged microbes swarming from his face to mine.

It didn't work.

No matter how often I assured myself that Dale's facial hair was perfectly hygienic, being anywhere near his long white beard gave me the willies. My best friend Rene teased that pogonophobia—the irrational fear of beards—was a clear sign of mental illness, but it didn't matter. No matter how much I loved Dale—no matter how much I loved *any* bearded man, for that matter—I couldn't stomach face-to-fur contact. Even thinking about it made my skin crawl.

Dale set me back on the ground, took a step back, and held me at arm's length. "Let me get a good look at you!" He ignored the dark coffee stain decorating my chest, narrowed his eyes, and frowned.

"Miss Katie, I do believe you've lost weight."

"Thanks." I smiled.

He didn't smile back. "It wasn't a compliment."

From anyone else, the words would have stung, but I knew he meant well. Dale was never one to worry about social niceties. He narrowed his eyebrows and examined me again with almost fatherly concern.

"You doing okay?"

I pasted on a fake smile and lied to my friend. "I'm doing great."

Time to change the subject before he probed any deeper. I turned away and motioned for Judith to join us.

She tossed another peanut to Blackie, grabbed a handful of flyers, and ambled next to me.

"Everybody, I'd like you to meet Judith."

Dale flashed Judith a hairy-faced grin and tipped his baseball cap. "Good day to ya, ma'am."

He winked at me, implicitly asking me not to break his cover. Dale loved playing the part of a southern-born goat farmer. His friends all knew that the good-old-boy persona was a pretense, but we went along anyway. Who were we to spoil his fun?

He handed me a crumpled paper bag. "I brought something for Bella."

I opened it and inhaled the pungent aroma of goat cheese. "These smell amazing!" I pulled out a goat-shaped cracker.

Dale stopped my hand an inch away from of my mouth. "Not so fast, Miss Kate. I baked those for Bella, not you. They're flavored with chicken broth."

I reluctantly dropped the delicious-smelling morsel back into the bag. Chicken broth wasn't part of my vegetarian diet.

Dale grinned and gestured toward Michael. "Seems kind of silly to bring Bella cookies now that you both live with a pet store owner, but I figured these were a special treat."

"She'll love them, Dale," I replied. "Thank you." I pointed toward the goat area. "Hey, where were you earlier? I looked for you over by the petting farm."

"A couple of 4-H kids from the island are managing the rescue during their spring break. I conned them into running the petting zoo, too. They get community service credit for school and a few days off from working on their daddy's farm. I get a week's vacation to harass my old Seattle friends." He nudged me with his elbow. "That includes you, Missy Kate. Bandit and I are going to take you up on those yoga classes you promised us."

"Hey, you two," Michael interrupted. "Catch up on your own time." He winked to let us know he was kidding. "Kate, I want you to meet these two ladies." He started with the woman on his right. "This is Maggie Phillips, the founder of DogMa, the shelter we're all here to support."

Maggie was attractive, probably in her mid-thirties, with gorgeous auburn hair and intelligent, dark brown eyes. I instantly liked her, though I questioned her fashion choice, especially for a day devoted to dog walking. Her four-inch heels sank into the grass with every step, and her dark blue jacket and slacks ensemble seemed specifically designed to pick up every stray strand of dog hair. Ten minutes with a German shedder like Bella, and she'd turn into a human lint roller.

She carried a cup of coffee in one hand and a pen, clipboard, and key ring in the other. She set the clipboard and keys on the table to shake my hand, but she held tightly to her mug. We Seattleites take our caffeine pretty seriously.

Michael continued the introductions. "Sally is Maggie's assistant."

Sally stiffened.

Maggie quickly corrected him. "'Assistant' doesn't quite cover it. Sally is our bookkeeper, office manager, volunteer coordinator, and adoption counselor. She even fills in as a veterinary technician and dog walker when needed. She does pretty much everything that needs doing at DogMa, and then some. I'm the face of the organization, but Sally's the true hero."

Sally looked less like a hero, more like a wounded warrior. She was at least thirty pounds overweight, and her face had the sallow complexion of someone either seriously ill or several years overdue for a long vacation. Sagging skin under her eyes suggested that she was in her late sixties, but I had a feeling she was at least a decade younger. She stood with a slumped, almost defeated posture and wore serviceable clothes—a T-shirt and brown khakis—that were suitable for hiding a variety of animal indiscretions.

Sally remained silent as Maggie continued talking. "I wanted to come by and thank you in person. Everyone's so excited about your Doga class."

I cringed before I could stop myself, but nobody seemed to notice.

"We're hoping that the more you relax people's bodies, the more they'll open their pocketbooks. DogMa seems to be bleeding money lately. Most suppliers aren't nearly as charitable as Michael. He's a real treasure."

Michael's face reddened. He supplied all of the shelter's pet food at cost, but he preferred to keep his generosity private. It was one of the many things that I loved about him.

"It's nothing, really," he said. "Helping abandoned animals find good homes benefits everyone, especially pet food stores like mine."

"You might be right," Maggie replied, "but that doesn't stop our other suppliers from price gouging. Our costs have risen dramatically over the past year, and we've been forced to make cuts wherever we can, including laying off employees. Without successful events like today, we'd either be forced to shut down or take in significantly fewer animals."

"Hopefully that won't ever happen," Michael said. "The good news is, unless something goes wrong, we should far exceed our donation goals today. We had over two hundred drop-in registrants this morning. That brings us to almost twenty-three hundred walkers." He looked out toward the lake. "And the weather turned out great."

He was right. The day was uncharacteristically warm for April in Seattle. The projected sixty-five degree high would provide plenty of warmth for the walkers without overheating their canine companions. Even better, water-loving dogs could go for a technically illegal but almost always tolerated dip in the lake without being exposed to the toxic algae that polluted it in late summer.

Michael frowned and pointed to the coffee stain between my breasts. "What happened to your shirt?"

"Believe me, you don't want to—"

A metallic crash stopped me mid-sentence.

"End animal slavery!"

We all gasped in unison and whipped toward the sound. Judith yelled, "Hey, stop! What are you doing?" Even Tiffany ran over to check out the commotion.

Blackie's cage lay open on the ground. He stood next to it, looking confused. A teenage girl waved her arms and stomped her feet, trying to scare him away. "Go on, fly! Be free! Animals should never be prisoners!"

I'd never met the young woman who was yelling, but I recognized her outfit: black jeans, black boots, long-sleeved black T-shirt decorated with an orange flame emblem. The jagged ends of her purple-black hair brushed against multiple silver ear-piercings. Black lipstick and eyeliner highlighted the matching jewelry in her left eyebrow and lower lip.

The Goth Girl kept yelling, sounding frustrated. "Go on, you stupid bird, fly! You're free!"

Blackie cocked his head right, then left, then right again, as if paradoxically confused, entranced, and annoyed by the oddly adorned female. He tried to approach her; he tried to make friends; I'm pretty sure he asked for a peanut. Each time he hopped closer, she shooed him away, calling him names and ordering him to take flight.

He finally took her advice. He flapped his wings and soared—away from his supposed freedom and straight to Judith's shoulder.

The whole episode was laughable, at least at first. Blackie clicked, preened, and nuzzled Judith's ear, looking happy and completely at home. Goth Girl yelled, waved her arms, and tried to scare him away from afar. "Get out of here before that evil animal terrorist traps you again!"

Judith turned toward Goth Girl and shouted, "Shut your trap, you little punk! You'll scare him."

Blackie ignored them both. He let out a loud caw and flew from Judith's shoulder to my table, where he landed next to Maggie's clipboard. He cocked his head forward and stared, transfixed by her shiny keys.

"Blackie, no!" Judith yelled.

Her words had no effect. Three quick hops later, Blackie leaned down and picked up the key ring.

Judith snatched Bella's bag of dog cookies, grabbed a large handful, and threw. Miniature goats rained to the ground in a five-foot radius.

"Look, Blackie! Treats!"

It almost worked.

Blackie paused, distracted by the yummy-looking morsels littering the grass. For a split second, he dropped the keys.

Judith lunged, faster than I would have thought possible for a seventy-five-year-old woman with obvious arthritis. But before she could reach him, Blackie picked up the key ring again, looped it securely around the bottom half of his beak, and took flight, carrying his treasure off into the distance.

Crows cawed from every direction, as if celebrating his victory. A half-dozen dropped down to clean up the home-baked plunder. By the time I looked back at Blackie's cage, Goth Girl had disappeared.

"Well, it was worth a try," Judith said. She reached up and wiped beneath her eyes. "He's gone for good now."

"I'm so sorry," Dale replied.

"It's okay. Not how I wanted to release him, but at least he's finally home with his buddies, where he belongs."

She pointed a claw-like finger toward Blackie's empty cage. "As for that little Miss Vampira that scared him off, I'd like to wring her scrawny neck. Someone should teach her—and the rest of her kind—a lesson in manners."

"She was right," Tiffany retorted. "Birds *shouldn't* live in cages." She locked eyes with Michael, as if expecting his agreement. "We don't even carry bird supplies at Pete's Pets. Michael says keeping pet birds locked up in cages is cruel. And that crow's cage was *tiny*."

Judith's jaw clenched. Her hands formed swollen-jointed fists. "I wasn't keeping him as a pet, you little..."

Dale grabbed Judith's arm, I assumed to prevent her from cold-cocking Tiffany. Michael cringed and gave Tiffany a be-quiet-now look. Sally stood quietly on the sidelines, shaking her head. Maggie, on the other hand, didn't seem to notice much of anything. She stared off into the distance, eyes wide, mouth open.

"Um, you guys, where did that crow take my keys?"

Judith shrugged. "I'm sorry, hon, but I have no idea. I'm sure he has some hidey-hole nearby where he keeps his treasures, but you'll never find it. I've never found anything he stole from me, anyway. Jewelry and keys are his favorites."

Maggie closed her eyes and pinched the bridge of her nose. "Great. Just what I needed. One extra hassle." She looked at her watch and frowned, as if mentally calculating. "My spare keys are at DogMa, and there's no time to get them before I have to start the closing ceremonies." She turned to Sally. "Looks like I'll need you to stick around through cleanup today after all. When we're done, you can give me a ride back to the shelter."

Sally's shoulders tensed. "But you promised that I could leave at noon. I've already worked almost sixty hours this week. I haven't visited Frank at the rehab center since Thursday."

Maggie's tone invited no argument. "I'm sorry, but I have to insist. The van and its contents are too valuable to leave parked here overnight. You can see Frank tomorrow."

Sally's face turned so red I was afraid her hair might ignite, but she didn't argue. I hated to interrupt them with more bad news, but I had a feeling that a few misplaced keys wouldn't be DogMa's biggest problem today.

"The van might be the least of our worries," I said.

I filled everyone in on the conversation I'd overheard between Dharma and Raven down by the dock. When I started, Maggie's eyes flashed with what looked a lot like fear. By the time I finished, her expression had morphed into anger. She grabbed Sally's arm. Hard.

"Did you know they were planning to protest today?"

Sally jerked away. "Ouch! That hurts! No, of course not. How would I have known?"

Maggie peered at her assistant through narrowed eyes. "We'll talk about this later. Right now, we need to figure out what they're up to and stop them before they ruin everything."

The two women rushed off before I could find out what Maggie meant.

FOUR

MICHAEL LEFT TO FIND Maggie and see if he could help stop the protest. Forty-five minutes later, the last of the dog walkers finished their loop and started streaming into the main soccer field for the post-walk shenanigans. Like it or not, it was showtime.

I placed a sign on Serenity Yoga's table saying that I'd be back in an hour and headed off with Dale and Bandit for my likely-to-ruin-my-reputation-forever Doga class.

Dale jolted to a stop at the entrance to my makeshift yoga studio. His lips frowned. His nose wrinkled. Even his whiskers quivered in disgust. "What in tarnation is that smell?"

The question was rhetorical. Anyone who'd ever cleaned up after a dog with a bellyache knew that stench. Believe me, it wasn't Nag Champa.

I pointed to the three-foot-tall, overflowing garbage can positioned inside the entrance. The sign taped to the front bore Tiffany's unmistakable handwriting: *Dog Waste Only*. The smell was so rancid that even Bandit gave it a wide berth.

Dale looked the container up and down, as if mentally measuring it. "It looks pretty heavy. Do you want me to try and move it?"

I waved my hand through the air, resigned. Tiffany had won this round. "Thanks, but don't worry about it. Go inside and find someplace to sit—preferably upwind."

If Tiffany had intended to scare people away from my class, her prank was a grave error. That waste receptacle was like a dog-owner magnet. Dozens upon dozens of tired-looking dog walkers made their way to the doggy-doo can, deposited their bio bags, and continued straight into my practice area. Suffice it to say that the crowd gave the phrase "dog pack" a whole new meaning.

Having that many dogs in such a small space couldn't possibly be a good idea, but I didn't have another alternative. I eased my way to the front and tried to assess the crowd's mood. My audience included most of the dogs I'd seen earlier, as well as quite a few new ones.

A growling Doberman gave the stink-eye to a scruffy black terrier. The mastiff I'd seen earlier rolled to its side and groaned, almost crushing his ancient female owner. The piranha-Chihuahua barked at me from the arms of his owner. The Rott-wiener used all of its strength to keep its massive head up.

My only hope was to get this over with as soon as possible.

I cupped my hands around my mouth and yelled over the din. "Okay everyone, find a space to sit and please ask your dogs to lie down beside you. We don't have any yoga mats today, but the grass will work fine. We'll get started in a few minutes."

Dale and Bandit claimed a spot in the middle of the front row. A frighteningly large number of people arranged themselves behind them. I should have been pleased at the turnout. After all, what fun is teaching a class if no one attends? Still, when Michael convinced me to participate in this circus, he'd sworn I'd have at most a handful of students. From what I could tell, all twenty-three hundred walkers—and twice that many dogs—had decided take me up on my offer.

I closed my eyes, took several deep breaths, and gave myself a mental pep talk.

It's okay, Kate. You can do this. Forty-five minutes tops and it will all be over. After all, how bad can it...

I made the mistake of opening my eyes. My stomach dropped to my toes.

... be.

Pretty darned bad, evidently.

A middle-aged, heavyset woman elbowed her way to the front and squeezed in beside Dale. One look and I knew I was in trouble. I wasn't worried about her outfit, though her black spandex pants were three sizes too small and she wore a bright pink baseball cap with long, fuzzy rabbit ears. I wasn't even worried about her attitude, though she'd rudely elbowed and pushed and grabbed her way through the crowd to claim the best spot. I was worried about her bag. Or rather the creature that peeped out over the top of it.

A huge, white, floppy-eared bunny.

Bandit took one look at the twitching-nosed creature and froze. His ears perked up; he leaned forward, every muscle fiber in his fifteen-pound body tensed on high alert. Dale sat beside him, eyes closed, oblivious to the impending disaster.

This would never do.

I approached the obviously insane woman with a cautious smile and pretended to assert some yoga teacher authority.

"Hi, I'm Kate. I'm the yoga teacher today. I'm sorry, but I can't allow a rabbit in this class. It will be too distracting for the rest of the animals."

Bunny Lady nestled the rabbit up close to her chest. He wiggled his nose curiously from between her bulbous breasts. "Alfalfa's not frightened of dogs. He'll be fine."

Alfalfa wasn't the one I was worried about. "That may be true, but I'd be more comfortable if you and the rabbit waited outside. It's for everyone's safety."

Bunny Lady's lips thinned to a scowl. She squeezed the poor trapped bunny tightly against her chest and drummed her fingers against his side. A huge diamond ring decorated her left ring finger.

"My husband and I are two of DogMa's biggest contributors. I wrote them a check for ten thousand dollars an hour ago. Do you honestly think that it's wise to refuse me service?"

The answer was no. As in no-win. If I threw Bunny Lady out of the class, she would inevitably take her frustrations out on DogMa. If I let her stay, the dogs might do worse.

She mistook my silence for assent.

"As I thought." She lifted her lips in a fake smile and pretended to be benevolent. "Don't worry, dear, it will be fine."

I hoped she was right.

I sat at the front, stared across the crowd, and tried to get my bearings. After multiple years of experience, teaching yoga to humans was easy. I could quickly and intuitively assess *human* yogis' needs at the beginning of each class. Could I do the same with canines?

Might as well give it a try. I closed my eyes and visualized the dogs I'd seen enter the yoga space. The mastiff could use an energizing practice with back bends and flows designed to build vitality. The Chihuahua would benefit from a relaxing practice to address his anger management issues. Maybe I could teach some neck strengthening exercises to that poor Rottie mix.

Dale cleared his throat to get my attention. All around me, dogs and their owners were fidgeting. It was time to begin, whether I was ready or not.

I pulled out the Tibetan chimes I'd brought with me, rang them three times to focus attention, and then stood up so my voice would project through the crowd. "Before we start, I need to set some ground rules."

I pointed at the empty space beside me. "Notice that I didn't bring a dog today. That's for a couple of reasons. First, I'm here as your teacher, not a participant, so I need to focus all of my attention on you. But more important than that, my crazy pup—though I love her dearly—doesn't like other dogs. She prefers private Doga." I grinned, waiting for the crowd's response.

They stared back at me in silence, obviously confused by my joke.

"You know, like private yoga."

Nothing.

"A single student?"

Not one appreciative twitter.

"It was a joke."

Dale let out a halfhearted sympathy laugh. I moved on.

"Second, this isn't a dog-training class. In fact, if your partner isn't already well trained, she shouldn't attend." I looked directly at the Bunny Lady. "For Doga to work, the dog needs to focus on its handler without distraction." I smiled to take the sting out of my words. "Now would be a great time to leave if this class isn't right for your pet."

Two people stood and led their canines toward the exit. The bunny and his owner weren't among them.

I pointed toward the vendor area. "If your dog gets completely out of control, take him to the Pete's Pets booth and ask for free dog treats." I didn't try to suppress my smirk. "Be sure to tell Tiffany that Kate sent you."

Complete silence. Not a smile in the area.

So much for my stand-up comedy routine.

"Well, okay then. A couple of additional thoughts. Doga is actually partner yoga, with a little assisted stretching for Fido thrown in. It has been shown to help with behavior issues, particularly separation anxiety. If you practice consistently, you and your dog can develop a stronger, more meaningful bond."

The more I spoke, the more I realized that, in spite of my reservations, I actually believed what I was saying. I always felt better after I practiced yoga with Bella. Happier. Why wouldn't the reverse be true? I wasn't sure Bella fully understood yoga's connection of body, breath, and mind, but she definitely benefited from my calm, post-yoga energy. And—whether they fit the true definition of yoga or not—assisted stretches and passive range-of-motion exercises helped mitigate arthritis and other orthopedic diseases common in dogs.

I gave the class an encouraging smile and began.

"Let's get started. Put your dog in a down-stay in front of you."

Dale snapped his fingers, made a sweeping motion with his right hand, and pointed to the ground. Bandit flopped down and stared at him adoringly. The rest of the dogs wiggled, whined, and generally voiced their protests, but most of them eventually lay down in front of their owners. So far so good.

"Place one hand on your abdomen, the other on your dog. Close your eyes and notice your breath." The humans all complied, which was evidently the opportunity the canines had been waiting for. The Doberman leveled a hard stare at the terrier. The Chihuahua showed me his teeth. Bandit crawl-walked toward the rabbit and drooled.

"On second thought, keep your eyes open and watch your dog, but continue lengthening your breath." The owners opened their eyes. Many seemed surprised to see their dog focusing elsewhere.

"Breathe in calming energy with every inhale," I continued. "With every exhale, send that same calming energy to your pet."

The Chihuahua's owner rolled her eyes at my woo-woo imagery, but the Doberman stopped goading the terrier and Bandit turned back to Dale, which were my primary goals.

After several lengthened breaths, I asked the class to come to hands and knees. "Keep your dog in a down-stay but hold onto his leash, just in case. Place your hips on your heels, reach your arms forward, and rest your forehead on your dog."

The positioning took more shuffling than I had anticipated, but the class eventually found the right place. "With each inhale, come to hands and knees. With each exhale, fold back and bring your hips to your heels again in Child's Pose. Touch your forehead to your dog."

The mastiff closed his eyes and sighed in pure pleasure. The Chihuahua tolerated two repetitions before it jumped up, shook its entire body, turned, and barked at the Bunny Lady. His beady little eyes stared hungrily at her pant leg.

Time to shift tactics.

"Tell you what—let's come to standing and try some balance postures instead." I looked pointedly at the Chihuahua's owner. "If your dog is small, pick it up and hold it in your arms."

I asked the class to watch as I demonstrated several variations of Tree Pose. "Shift your weight to your left foot and place the sole of your right foot on your left inner thigh."

"Are you kidding me?" the elderly woman asked.

I smiled. "Or you can keep the toes of your right foot on the grass for balance. There are three options for your dogs. Option one is to keep your dog in a sit next to you. Option two—for those of you with small dogs—is to cradle your pup in your arms. If your dog is tiny, you can try option three, which is to reach your arms up like this, holding your dog overhead." I pantomimed holding a tiny dog between my palms and lifting it up.

Bunny Lady, of course, chose option three.

She grasped Alfalfa between two chubby palms and thrust him up to the sky. Alfalfa didn't appreciate his new view. He squirmed, he lurched. I would have sworn that he frowned. When that didn't get Bunny Lady's attention, he thrashed his body weight forward while forcefully kicking two bunny-sized feet back, straight into her nose.

"Hey!" she yelled.

To be fair, Bunny Lady gave that balance pose one valiant effort. She weebled and wobbled and wove and warbled. For an insane, hopeful moment, I thought she might remain standing. But the piranha-Chihuahua couldn't withstand the temptation. He spied her flapping pant leg, dove from his owner's arms, and chomped onto the fabric.

Bunny Lady yelled, "Get it off of me!" and dropped both Alfalfa and his leash.

The terrified rabbit skirted away from the falling monolith. Dale somehow managed to hang on to Bandit, but that didn't stop the other terrier. The little black monster slipped his collar and tore after Alfalfa. The Doberman broke free and chased after them both.

All of Green Lake seemed to erupt in an explosion of barking, chasing, howling, and lunging as hare and hounds zipped through the crowd, ducked under the rope, and tore across the main soccer field toward the hot dog stand. Bouncing cellulite, flopping bunny ears, and deep-throated growls ripped through the air. And that was just from the Bunny Lady.

The animals collided in front of the condiment table.

Innocent bystanders dove in all directions, some trying to escape the melee, others trying to stop it. I stared in horror at the Tasmanian Devil–like vortex of fur, teeth, ketchup, and hotdog buns. When the food stopped flying, a triumphant-looking teenager cradled the bunny; an angry-looking, ketchup-covered man wrestled the terrier. Michael, having come from lord only knows where, held onto the collar of the still-lunging Doberman.

Michael was the first to arrive back at my yoga area. He handed the Doberman's leash to its handler, who apologized and quickly skirted off into the crowd. The terrier's owner ran to the food truck and ineffectually dabbed napkins across the shirt of his dog's rescuer.

The rabbit-carrying teen arrived last. Bunny Lady marched up to him imperiously, her rabbit-ear hat askew like a poorly fitted toupee. She grabbed Alfalfa from the teen without so much as a thank you.

I should have felt bad, and honestly I did. But that didn't stop me from getting the giggles. I bit my lower lip and tried not to laugh.

Michael didn't look amused. "Kate, what in the hell happened here?"

Bunny Lady spoke directly to Michael, but she pointed an accusing finger at me. "This…" She paused as if unable to spit out the words. "This so-called *dog trainer* let those vicious mutts chase my rabbit out of yoga class."

Michael's face turned so red it was almost purple. He gaped at me. "You allowed a *rabbit* in class with that many dogs? What were you thinking?"

"It's not my fault. I—"

"Not your fault?" Bunny Lady yelled. "You're supposed to be a dog trainer!"

"No, I'm not. I'm a yo—"

Michael tried to shush me, but he was too late.

Bunny Lady almost burst an aneurysm. "You're not a dog trainer? No wonder you're so incompetent! You had no business representing yourself as an animal expert."

"I didn't. I—"

She didn't give me a chance to finish. "You'll be hearing from my lawyer about this." Her lips wrinkled as if she'd bitten into a not-so-fresh carrot. "And the owners of those vicious dogs will be hearing from Animal Control!"

My face burned with embarrassment and unspoken retorts, but I couldn't think of a single reply. At least not one any self-respecting yoga teacher could utter in public.

Fortunately, Maggie and Sally arrived before I could say something I'd later regret. Maggie rushed up to the agitated woman and placed a calming hand on her shoulder.

"I'm so sorry about this incident, Mrs. Abernathy. Is Alfalfa okay?" The bunny cuddled deep inside his owner's ample bosom, appearing none the worse for wear. "Please don't be angry, especially not with the dogs. Chasing after prey is their nature. Would you be mad if a cat chased a mouse?"

"Well, no ..."

"And Kate is just a volunteer yoga teacher."

I bristled at the word "just," but Maggie's eyes begged me to remain silent. "She isn't one of the trainers at the shelter. In hindsight, dog yoga obviously wasn't the best idea. Maybe next year we can arrange for a rabbit show."

Maggie must have been some sort of Bunny Lady whisperer. With each soothing assurance, I could feel more of the agitated woman's anger melt away.

"I promise you, this won't happen again," Maggie finished.

We all waited for Bunny Lady's response. After what felt like a century, she sighed and adjusted her hat. "Well, as long as Alfalfa wasn't hurt, I suppose I can let it go this time."

Maggie smiled, I assumed in relief more than pleasure. "Thank you, Mrs. Abernathy. That's very kind. If you come with me, I'll have one of our volunteer veterinarians examine Alfalfa." She turned to me. "Kate, I think we've had enough Doga for today." She faced the crowd and raised her hand. "Everyone, thanks for your understanding. Please—"

We never heard the end of her sentence.

FIVE

The shouts that drowned out Maggie's words were impassioned, if a little misguided.

"Break down the cages!"

"Close the dog warehouses!"

"Animal ownership is slavery!"

Over twenty people, all wearing black shirts with the orange flame insignia, cut a swath across the grass, waving picket signs and yelling at top volume.

Two teenage girls held onto opposite ends of a banner that read *Humans for Ethical Animal Treatment. Turn up the HEAT!*

Raven—the woman I'd seen arguing behind the paddleboats earlier—marched next to them, holding a sign in one hand and a leash attached to the neck of a handsome, thirtyish, olive-skinned man in the other. Eduardo, I assumed. I shaded my eyes with my hand and examined the object of Raven and Dharma's confrontation.

Even from a distance, I could understand Eduardo's appeal. With broad shoulders, deep cocoa eyes, and wavy black hair that curled under his earlobes, this man would easily make more than one woman's heart go atwitter. His one glaring fault was the sandpaper-thick layer of dark stubble covering the lower half of his face. No amount of shaving would keep that beard-in-the-making under control. Even thinking about it made my skin itch.

His dark leather jacket and matching motorcycle boots contrasted hypocritically with the sign that he carried: *Animals Are Sentient Beings, Not Possessions!* His face wore a trapped, agonized expression, though that might have been part of the show.

I scanned the area behind him, looking for Dharma and Goth Girl. I didn't see either.

The dog walkers stopped talking, stared at the ruckus, and scowled. No one seemed to be having fun anymore, which was probably the protesters' intention. A short, rail-thin young woman stomped away from the picket line, knocked a hot dog out of a child's hand, and yelled, "Meat is murder!"

Michael pulled out his cell phone. "That's it. I'm calling the police."

Maggie closed her eyes and sighed. "I can't believe she's actually going through with this."

"You know them?" I asked.

She shuddered, but her eyes never left the protesters. "Never mind. It doesn't matter. Sally, take Mrs. Abernathy to the pet first aid tent and ... " Her voice trailed off. She glanced left and right. "Where on earth did Sally go?"

The Bunny Lady wrinkled her nose, ill humor back in full force. "Sally wandered off a few minutes ago, which is exactly what I should have done. You obviously don't have control over this fiasco." She slipped the rabbit into her bag and stomped several feet away before turning back to spit out two final sentences. "Don't bother cashing that check I gave you earlier. I'm putting a stop payment on it as soon as I get home!"

Maggie cradled her face in her hands. "Can this day get any worse?"

She shouldn't have asked.

The words had barely escaped her lips when Dale's head jerked up. "Do you smell that?"

I did. I would have recognized that smell anywhere. Gasoline.

I heard a loud swoosh, punctuated by a louder explosion. New, significantly more frightening, words rang out across the field.

"Fire! Somebody help! The dumpsters are on fire!"

Dale's face turned as white as his beard. "Oh no! The goats!"

"I'll grab the fire extinguisher!" Michael yelled.

Michael and Maggie ran toward the registration desk, while Dale, Bandit, and I tore off to the goat petting zoo. Picketers and dog walkers scattered in every direction.

By the time we rounded the corner, the fire was already spreading. Hot yellow flames licked from the dumpsters to the loose hay that surrounded the petting area. Within seconds, the entire line of straw bales had ignited, creating a flaming, Hades-like fence.

The teenage volunteers had already rushed the children outside the fenced area, but the goats were still trapped, huddled together in the corner farthest away from the fire. Michael skidded to a stop behind me a few seconds later. He blasted the straw bales with the extinguisher, but the fire was spreading too fast. He may as well have been spraying the Towering Inferno with a garden hose.

Dale tossed Bandit's leash to a gawker. The blond teenager held the gate open while his brother, Dale, and I scrambled inside. Michael kept spraying the extinguisher, holding the flames back as best he could.

The goats refused to move.

"Force them to the entrance," Dale yelled.

I channeled my inner Goth Girl, waved my arms, and yelled, "Go, you stupid goats! Run! Get out of here!"

The three of us screamed and clapped and pushed and stomped until the terrified animals bolted from the enclosure and charged onto the field, straight past the onlookers, who were too transfixed by the flames to do anything but watch.

Dale gathered the final fear-frozen spotted kid in his arms and carried it away from the flames. Sirens wailed in the distance.

"Get the truck," he said to the blond teen. He handed the baby goat to the other.

It seemed like a century passed, but it couldn't have been more than a few minutes before firemen started dousing the area with cold water. Dale kept a watchful eye on his skittish herd, which was huddled several hundred feet away. A few people broke off from the crowd and tried to approach them.

"Stay back!" Dale yelled. "Just block them from the road. And for land's sake, don't chase them."

Michael came up behind us. "Shouldn't we try to round them up somehow?"

Dale's expression was grim. "They're too riled up. Give them a few minutes to calm down. They'll come to me." His voice didn't sound confident.

The blond teen drove a livestock truck onto the field and parked. He jumped out of the cab, opened the back, and pulled down a wide ramp. Dale grabbed a metal pail from inside and filled it with grain from a five-gallon bucket.

"Hope this works," he muttered. He walked halfway to the goats, vigorously shook the metal bucket, and yelled "Grain!" at top volume.

As if in one motion, twelve goat heads turned. After a split second's hesitation, the entire herd galloped toward Dale, bleating happily about their unanticipated snack. I couldn't help but smile.

Dale greeted each goat with a vigorous neck scratch, a handful of grain, and a murmur of encouragement. He shook the bucket, made clicking noises with his tongue, and slowly backed up to the truck. Forty-eight hoofs clanked up the ramp and followed him inside.

A minute or so later, he jumped down from the truck, slid the ramp back into place, and closed the door behind him.

"That's a pretty cool trick," I said.

"Amazing what a little bribery will get you." The sparkle returned to his eyes. "If I waved a paper bag and yelled 'scones,' you'd come running faster than they did."

I couldn't argue with that.

He turned to the teens. "Boys, I think that's about enough excitement for one day. I'll figure out what to do with what's left of the fencing. You two take those critters on home now. I'll call you tonight to make sure they settled in okay." He slapped them each on the shoulder. "You done good. Your daddy'd be proud of you." The boys' smiles spread across their entire faces.

"Now remember, you're in charge of the rescue until next Friday," he added. "Feed these guys some extra treats the next couple of days to help them settle down." He winked. "I suspect you'll find something a little extra in your paychecks, too."

As the two grinning teens drove off, Dale, Michael, and I returned to the fire line. Maggie had evidently found Sally, because the two hovered near the edge of the crowd, watching the firemen douse out the remaining hotspots.

Maggie shook her head disconsolately. "I guess I should go make an announcement. This event is officially over. What a disaster."

"It could have been worse," Sally replied.

"I don't see how. We lost Mrs. Abernathy's support, and now everyone's leaving before I could give them my final pitch. You know we needed this money."

"There are worse things than losing a few donations, you know. At least no one was hurt."

Maggie sighed. "You're right. Of course you're right." She chewed on her lower lip. "If we're lucky, we might not get sued."

Sally didn't reply.

"Did anyone see who started the fire?" Michael asked.

"Not that I know of." Sally pointed toward the booths. "But it had to be the demonstrators. Maybe one of those two over there."

My eyes tracked her finger straight to Serenity Yoga's booth. A black-clad woman with Dharma's long braid was rifling through the information on my table. The handsome, dark-haired man I assumed was Eduardo was chatting with Tiffany at Pete's Pets next door.

Tiffany's smile was wider than a shark's at a chum factory. She played with her hair and leaned forward to touch Eduardo's arm. He scanned the crowd, obviously looking for something. I got the feeling he was only pretending to listen to Tiffany.

"Isn't that the guy who was wearing the dog collar?" I asked. "He couldn't have set the fire. He was demonstrating—on-leash, no less —when we heard the blast."

"You're both jumping to conclusions," Dale countered. "The fire might not have anything to do with the protest. For all we know, some kid tossed a lit match into that dumpster. That's for the police and the fire chief to figure out."

"Maybe," I replied. "But I'm going to have a chat with them." I glanced at Michael. "Want to come with?"

Michael and I headed across the field, fully intending to question the two protesters. But by the time we arrived at our booths, they had vanished.

SIX

I looked for Dharma and Eduardo as long as I could, then scooted off to pick up Bella from my friend Rene's house. From there, I drove directly to Greenwood to meet with Alicia, my private yoga student. She'd barely entered Serenity Yoga's lobby before I started telling her about my crazy morning. I didn't normally discuss my personal traumas with students, but I was surprisingly rattled about the day's events. Besides, Alicia was more than a student. She was also my landlord. She owned the mixed-use building that housed Serenity Yoga, the PhinneyWood Grocer, Pete's Pets, and the apartments above them. Beyond that, she was rapidly becoming one of my closest friends.

As I finished my story, Alicia slipped off her shoes and slid them under the bench in the lobby.

"So you never found out if the protesters were involved in setting the fire?" she asked.

"No, and it's driving me crazy. I wanted to question Eduardo and Dharma, but we couldn't find them before I had to leave to get Bella."

I pointed at the coffee stain still decorating my shirt. "I didn't even have a chance to go home and change clothes."

"Why were you so interested in talking to those two?"

I paused before replying. Her question was reasonable; I just didn't know how to answer it.

"I have a funny feeling about them."

"What do you mean?

"I can't say why, exactly, but Dharma seems familiar. Like maybe I've seen her on the news or something. And Eduardo was acting strange, too. Why would someone so adamantly opposed to animal ownership make nice with a pet store employee?" I poured a glass of water from the studio's water cooler, took a long drink, and shared the rest with my thirsty schefflera tree. "According to Tiffany, they took off in a hurry right before Michael and I got there."

"Do you think they saw you coming?"

"Maybe, but why would they care? Neither of us knows them." I absently chewed on my thumbnail. "Something just feels off. And get this: I read the propaganda Eduardo left with Tiffany. HEAT is a vegan animal rights group based out of Sacramento."

Alicia's eyes widened. "Sacramento? Why would a group from California protest an animal shelter in Seattle?"

"Beats me. I would have grilled him about it, but Tiffany was so starstruck by his deep baby browns that she didn't think to ask." I shook my head. "That girl is so gullible. Now she's decided to go vegan. I swear she falls for anything that walks upright and has an extra appendage, if you know what I mean."

Alicia smirked. "Come on, Kate, go easy on her. She's young. Besides, I seem to remember a certain yoga teacher who spent the night with a local pet store owner—on their very first date, no less."

I ignored Alicia's teasing. Her words were true, but my situation was entirely different. I'd fallen for Michael well before that first date, whether I'd been willing to admit it to myself or not. Tiffany, on the other hand, had a long history of questionable taste in men.

"Dharma took some of my flyers, but that's not surprising. After all, that's why I put them on the table." I shrugged. "Honestly, if I hadn't known that those two were protesters, I wouldn't have thought twice about their behavior. The way Tiffany describes it, they were just browsing."

"You know, Kate, you might be reading too much into their actions. Contrary to your recent experiences, not everyone who acts out of the ordinary winds up being a criminal. Maybe this Dharma person likes yoga."

"And her friend?"

Alicia shrugged. "I know neither of us is fond of Tiffany, but she is pretty cute, in a singles-bar-trash sort of way. Men like that." She took off her jacket and hat. When she turned back around, she wore a big smile. "Notice anything different about me?"

My mouth dropped open. "Wow, Alicia, your new haircut looks gorgeous!"

Next to Rene, Alicia was the most attractive woman I knew. She somehow managed to make T-shirts seem elegant, and when she smiled, it radiated through the entire room. Still, I couldn't quite get over how her new hairstyle transformed her. The chin-length cut fell in wisps around her face, and the new blonde highlights complemented the honey tones of her skin. She looked young, happy, confident, and, most importantly, healthy.

Alicia shook her head vigorously and smiled as every strand fell back into place. "Thanks. My stylist convinced me to cut off the chemo curls. Between the new cut and the return of my eyelashes, I feel like a new woman."

Alicia was a survivor of stage IV malignant melanoma. When she was diagnosed, her doctors didn't expect her to last more than a few months, but they underestimated her ability to fight. Twelve months after her last treatment and a few weeks past her thirty-fourth birthday, she was still in remission.

We moved into the yoga room. Alicia grabbed a blue Mexican blanket for knee padding, rolled out her mat, and sat cross-legged on the floor. I lit a candle for ambiance, rang my Tibetan chimes three times, and asked her to deepen her breath. After coaching her through a few gentle poses to help her connect her mind with her body, I led her in the first of several Sun Salutes.

She performed them almost effortlessly, cycling through Head-to-Knee Pose, Downward Dog, Upward Dog, and Cobra Pose. Her biceps bulged as she held a core-strengthening Plank Pose before lowering her body an inch from the floor and hovering, seemingly weightless, in a perfectly straight Chaturanga. I couldn't help but admire her resilience. Ten months after literally fighting off death, she was stronger than most of the yogis I knew, including myself.

We continued through a standing sequence with twists, squats, and balance poses, and eventually finished with some delicious-looking seated forward bends. After leading her through a luxuriously long Savasana—yoga's pose of quiet rest—I rang the chimes three times again to signal the end of class.

"Start by wiggling your fingers and toes, maybe yawning and stretching. When you're ready, roll to your side, then slowly press yourself up to sitting."

Alicia placed her palms together at her heart. We finished by saying the word "Namaste," which loosely translates as "the light within me acknowledges the light within you." When she opened her eyes again, her skin seemed to glow.

"That was amazing, Kate. Thank you." Alicia rolled up her mat, gathered her belongings from the reception area, and handed me a check. "I need to do some work in the office, so I'll leave through the garage."

I grabbed my keys and walked her to the studio's back entrance. "See you on Wednesday at our normal time?"

"Deal."

I opened the door, but Alicia stopped, unwilling to take the first step. "That's disgusting!"

Dozens of bird droppings decorated the steps to the parking garage. Similar splotches painted the handrails.

"Sorry. I noticed it on my way in, but I didn't have time to clean it up." I pointed at the Road Warrior–like assortment of chicken wire, netting, and metal spikes that Alicia had installed above the back entrance. A gunmetal-gray pigeon roosted comfortably between two metal spikes. "Looks like your newest bird-deterrent didn't work any better than the others."

Alicia scowled. "I'm getting really sick of that flying waste generator. The apartment residents have started complaining, too. But every time I come up with a new plan to keep him out, he figures out how to overcome it. I swear that bird is smarter than I am." She paused. "I know we've talked about this before, but . . ." Her voice trailed off.

I shook my head emphatically. "Absolutely not. I don't want you to use anything that isn't completely humane. It's my studio's entrance that he's messing up, so I should have the final word. I don't want him harmed."

She sighed. "Okay, fine. I'll get maintenance to pressure-wash the cement. Again." She trudged toward the office, mumbling words never uttered by the Dalai Lama. At least not in front of his yoga teacher.

Contented cooing filtered down from the ceiling.

I lifted my eyes to the feathered menace and scowled. "You don't have to be smug about it." I double-checked to make sure that the studio door had locked behind me and skirted around the mess toward my car. Time to give Bella a bio break.

Figuring out where to leave Bella during the workday was always a dilemma. When I originally fostered her, I tried letting her hang out at the yoga studio. What a disaster. She'd made it her life's work to chase intruders and junk mail–wielding psychopaths—aka customers and mailmen—out of the building. Doggy daycare? Perish the thought. Bella would have to be the only four-footed creature on the premises. Ditto for leaving her with Michael at Pete's Pets.

The problem was compounded when Michael moved in with me and we started remodeling my tiny two-bedroom house. If we left my overly territorial German shepherd alone with the contractors, we'd come home to find construction-worker body parts scattered all over the yard.

Besides, Bella—though perfectly content when guarding the back seat of my ancient Honda Civic—suffered from significant separation anxiety when left home alone. I couldn't blame her. Her first owner had tied her up to a stake in his yard; her second left her locked in a crate the night he was murdered. Keeping Bella in my car wasn't the most politically correct alternative, but according to her vet and her trainer, it was the safest, as long as the car remained cool. So I'd begged Alicia to rent me one of the resident parking spots inside the building and checked on Bella every couple of hours. The back-seat solution wasn't perfect, but it worked for the time being.

I clipped on Bella's leash, glanced around to make sure no off-leash dogs or bearded men were nearby, and let Bella out of her mobile home away from home. She hopped to the ground, did a quick happy dance, and pulled me through the garage's exit toward the large outdoor parking lot shared by the businesses.

Bella stopped at the entrance to Pete's Pets and nudged the door with her nose, clearly hoping to go inside and bond with her cool friend Tiffany. I could have sworn I saw the question *Where's the Cookie Lady?* dance across her pretty, deep brown eyes.

"Sorry, sweetie. Michael and Tiffany aren't here. The store is closed today because of the event at Green Lake."

I dragged my disappointed canine buddy away from the door, turned toward the front entrance of Serenity Yoga, and froze. A woman with a long braid loitered outside the entrance, holding one of my pamphlets.

What was Dharma doing outside of my yoga studio?

Up close, I could tell that Dharma was older than I'd originally thought, likely in her early fifties. Deep creases surrounding her eyes hinted at too much sun exposure and too little sunscreen. She wore minimal makeup, but then again, she didn't need to. Her face was naturally attractive. In her youth, she had probably been stunning. Instead of the solid black outfit she'd worn earlier, she was dressed in jeans, tennis shoes, and a light blue sweater.

My skin prickled with the same apprehensive sense of déjà vu I'd felt earlier, as if this woman and I were somehow connected. I knew her, but how? I closed my eyes and tried to remember, but nothing pierced through the fog.

When I opened my eyes, Dharma was staring at me. She raised her hand in a tentative wave. Bella moaned, relaxed her ears, and slowly swished her tail, clearly inviting her closer.

"Stay, sweetie," I whispered.

I watched, feeling uneasy, as Dharma moved toward us. When she was three feet away, Bella broke her stay, wiggled up to her, and nudged her hands.

Dharma kneeled next to her and gently rubbed her ears. "Some big scary guard dog you are."

Bella leaned into Dharma's touch, entranced by her new stranger-friend. She gave Dharma several warm, sloppy kisses and offered her paw. I was so taken by the ease of their friendship that several moments passed before I realized that Dharma was paying attention to Bella—at least in part—to avoid looking at me.

"Excuse me, but do I know you?"

Dharma froze, mid-scratch, and lowered her hand. She stood and tentatively reached out her fingers as if testing the burner on a recently turned-off stove. A smile touched her lips, then faltered. "Yes, you do. My name is Dharma. I knew you when you were little."

Every cell in my body reacted to this stranger's words. My stomach clenched, my throat constricted. Nerve endings tingled along my spine. My mind whirled, trying to connect the disparate pieces in some way—any way—other than the truth. I knew the term 'dharma'; it was the Sanskrit word for "duty." And, of course, Dharma was this stranger's name. But that wasn't what felt familiar. Somewhere deep in my subconscious I had to have known who Dharma was, but I didn't want to—I couldn't—accept it.

Bella sensed my inner turmoil. A low sound rumbled deep in her throat. She backed slowly away from Dharma and stood in front of me. Stranger-friend or not, if Dharma meant me harm, she'd have to go through Bella first.

"Easy, girl," I said automatically. "This is our friend." I wasn't sure I believed it.

Dharma took several steps back, but she didn't break eye contact.

I wanted to flee. I wanted to go home. I wanted to jump back in bed, pull the covers over my head, and live the rest of my life blissfully unaware of this woman's existence. But I couldn't. A ten-ton weight had fallen from the sky and pinned my feet to the earth. My heart got crushed somewhere beneath it.

"You might not remember me anymore," Dharma continued. "When you were a little girl, I went by Daisy. My last name is Carmichael now, but for a very short time, it was Davidson."

I couldn't delude myself anymore, no matter how much I wanted to. I knew *exactly* where I'd seen Dharma's eyes before: every morning in the bathroom mirror. I opened my mouth to reply, but the sound that emerged was an unintelligible hybrid of a squeak and a croak.

The no-longer-a-stranger-and-certainly-no-friend tentatively smiled.

"It's nice to see you after such a long time, Kate. I'm your mother."

SEVEN

"You lied to me. You told me that your mother was dead."

Rene's voice was significantly louder than I would have preferred, given the circumstances. Every coffee drinker within a twenty-foot radius halted mid-sip and craned their necks in our direction. The barista even stopped steaming my soy milk to peer at me over the espresso machine.

At least someone found my life entertaining.

Dharma had left after dropping her emotional bombshell. She claimed that I needed time alone to think, which was proof positive that the woman knew nothing about me. Stewing in solitude would have eaten a hole in my stomach.

That is, if it didn't outright kill me.

Before Dharma had gotten out of the parking lot, I'd run to the studio, called Rene, and begged her to meet me across the street for an emergency girls' date at our favorite coffee shop, Mocha Mia. Now, forty-five minutes later, I stood at the counter, trying to look inconspicuous while Rene alternated between browbeating me and adding items to her characteristically complex and calorie-laden order.

I muted my voice, hoping our audience would lose interest. "I already told you. Dharma is *not* my mother. At best, she qualifies as an egg donor." I looked pointedly at the barista. "Let's talk about it after we sit down."

The barista took the hint. Sort of. She turned her back to our conversation and poured my drink into one of the café's diverse collection of second-hand mugs. Her choice for today was a cream-colored ceramic mug with the caption *Happy Mother's Day.*

Classic.

I spied an empty table by the window. "I'll save us a seat. Try to leave some food for the rest of the neighborhood."

I tucked a dollar in the tip jar and wove through Mocha Mia's eclectic collection of mismatched chairs, scarred wooden tables, and Tiffany-style lamps. The garage-sale decor usually amused me, since it so closely matched the not-quite-up-and-coming vibe of my studio's neighborhood. Greenwood was famous for aging antique shops, trendy art galleries, and crumbling, dive-bar-like restaurants whose patrons started the day drinking rotgut whiskey with a caffeine chaser. Walking past the bus stop any time after noon gave the term "breath of fire" a whole new meaning.

Today, however, Mocha Mia's eclectic decor seemed like a painful symbol of my own jumbled life. After two years of self-imposed solitude, I'd finally scrounged up enough hope to build a future with a man that I loved, only to have it darkened by shadows from my past. If every life had a purpose, mine was obviously to be the butt of some karmic practical joke. Frankly, I wasn't amused.

I absently stirred my coffee and stared across the street at my yoga studio, wishing I could cancel my evening Yoga Nidra class. I had no desire to teach. I didn't even want to be seen in public. I wanted to slink home, hide in the closet, and not come out until Dharma left town. Instead, I picked at the unappetizing whole wheat bagel on my plate and shredded my napkin into hundreds of tiny pieces, waiting for Rene and hoping—praying, even—that she would somehow come up with the magic words that would put Dharma's revelation into perspective.

Rene waddled from the checkout counter to the table, carefully squeezing her hugely pregnant body through the crowded café while balancing a double-sized slice of eight-layer chocolate decadence cake, a bagel, two packets of cream cheese, and a decaf double fudge mocha.

I added an extra packet of Splenda to my soy latte, just for the indulgence.

Rene thumped her pastries onto the table and scowled. "You know, I'm beginning to get annoyed with that barista. What is this, a restaurant or a comedy club?" She pointed an accusing finger at her mug. "I mean really. *Hungry Hippo?*"

I suppressed a grin. The waitress's antics seemed significantly funnier when they were directed at someone else. "Well, you said you wanted a double extra grande. Maybe that's the biggest mug they had." I paused for effect. "Besides, it kind of fits."

Rene swatted me with her napkin. "Keep it up, funny girl. I'm here to do *you* the favor, remember?" She slid her fork through eight layers of chocolate flavored calories, lifted it to her mouth, and chewed, wearing an expression so sensuous, it was likely illegal in most southern states. "Oh my lord, that's good." She laid the fork back on the plate, careful not to disturb the heart-shaped caramel swirls the barista had drawn along its edges.

"That should give me enough strength to get to the bathroom and back." She looped her shoulder bag over the back of her chair.

"I'll be back in a minute. Remember, I've got dibs on your story. Don't you dare tell it to anyone else before I get back."

Like that was a big risk.

She gestured to the collection of plates, napkins, condiments, and silverware that she'd accumulated on her side of the table. "And don't even consider touching my food, especially the cake. I have that fork mark memorized."

The scary thing was, I believed her.

She returned five minutes later, still grumbling. "I swear, I can't go ten minutes without peeing these days." She slowly lowered her rear to the chair. "Oomph!"

I bit my lip to keep from smirking. "Geez, Rene. How will I ever get you back up?" I pretended to scan the restaurant. "Maybe I should rent a crane."

Rene ignored my teasing, picked up a butter knife, and slathered pineapple cream cheese all over her jalapeño cheddar bagel.

"Rene, that's disgusting."

"It's not my fault," she replied, pointing down at her belly. "The girls want what the girls want. And I have to eat more. Doctor's orders. She says I'm not gaining enough weight. Besides, I had to give up caffeine and alcohol. I've got to fuel myself somehow."

Now that she mentioned it, Rene *did* look awfully thin for a woman six months pregnant with twins. Her belly was growing, sure, but the rest of her body was still a highly toned size four.

"Not gaining enough weight? Are you and the twins okay?"

"Chill out, Kate. I'm fine. I'm sure it's all those smoothies Sam keeps forcing down my throat." She turned to the side and pretended to gag. "I tell you, it's not natural for humans to drink anything that green." She took a huge bite of bagel and continued talking as she chewed. "Thank goodness I talked him into going to that conference

59

in Tokyo. Now maybe I can eat in peace." She licked a wad of pine-apple-encrusted cream cheese off of her lower lip.

"The doctor says the girls look perfect." She dropped the oozing concoction onto her plate and wiped her hands on a napkin. "Ooh, hang on, I'll show you. Sam and I sprung for a 3-D ultrasound a few days ago." She rooted around in her purse and pulled out two brown-and-black photos. "Kate, meet Twin A and Twin B."

I stared down at the sickeningly cute faces of my future tormen-tors. The one on the left clearly had Rene's evil grin. The one on the right seemed to be rubbing her palms together, already plotting her strategy. No doubt about it, I was in trouble.

"They're gorgeous, Rene," I said honestly. "I can't wait to meet them."

Rene wiggled happily. Her deep brunette hair bounced off her shoulders. "I know. Aren't they adorable? I wish I knew whether or not they're identical, so I could start planning their outfits."

"But you already have four dozen dresses!"

"I bought a few basic items, sure, but I haven't even considered accessories."

I rolled my eyes.

"Seriously," she continued. "It's more complex than you think. If the twins are identical, their outfits will be especially important. Do I dress them alike, match their hats and booties, or make them en-tirely unique?" She shuddered. "And the hair bands I've found so far have been simply atrocious."

"They're babies, Rene. Not runway models."

She looked down and softly patted her belly. "Don't listen to her, girls. It's never too early to start building good fashion sense." She pointed at the coffee stain still splashed across my shirt. "You don't want to end up being a slob like your Aunt Kate."

I swiped the air with an imaginary sword. "Touché."

Rene grinned. "Ooh—and I found the cutest Roberto Cavalli leopard-print bottle holders. They only had one color, though." She paused and pursed her lips. "You don't think the twins will mind if their bottles holders match, do you?"

I groaned and covered my face with my hands.

"See? It's complicated. It would be so much simpler if we knew whether or not the girls are identical."

It was easier to concede the point than keep arguing. "When will you know?"

"The doctor can't be sure based on our sonogram. She said we might not even be sure after they're born. In that case, we'll have to do a DNA test." Rene took a huge bite of cake, smearing a thick chocolate mustache across her upper lip. "I'll tell you one thing, though. Identical or not, my sweet little parasites have both inherited my metabolism. In the first trimester they stole my beauty; now they're snarfing up all of my food. Ever since I got over the morning sickness, all I can think about is eating."

So what else was new?

She pointed to my coffee cup. "But enough about me, Ms. Mother's Day. Let's get back on topic. We're here to discuss Mommy Dearest, not my food-sucking progeny. You've had a tough day, so I'll forgive you this time. But admit it—you lied to me. You told me your mother was dead."

"First, stop calling her that. I didn't have a mother. A mother doesn't take off when her child is a toddler, then drop by unannounced thirty years later because she happens to be in the neighborhood."

Rene remained silent.

"Second, I didn't lie to you; I simply skirted the truth. The last time I saw Daisy, Dharma, or whatever her name is, I was barely three. After that, she was too busy saving the world to spend time

61

with me." I couldn't keep the resentment out of my voice. "As far as I was concerned, she was dead."

"That doesn't seem fair," Rene chided. "And bitterness doesn't suit you. Seriously, why didn't you tell me about her? I thought we shared everything."

I couldn't explain my relationship with Dharma to myself, let alone anyone else, but I had to try.

"Honestly, Rene, it didn't seem important."

Rene leaned back and narrowed her eyes, clearly skeptical. "What kind of kid thinks her mother isn't important?"

"You're right. When I was young, I *did* care. I wanted to see her so much that I ached." I swallowed to clear the tightness in my throat. "I dreamed about having a mother. I made up fairytales to justify her absence. When I got old enough to understand that none of my stories were true—that she'd simply abandoned me—I got mad. Anger was less painful than feeling rejected. When the anger died down, all I had left was indifference." I shrugged. "By the time you and I became friends, it didn't seem relevant."

Rene arched her eyebrows.

"Or that's what I told myself." I took a long drink of my luke-warm latte.

"Does Michael know?"

"Not yet, and don't you tell him, either. He'd just insist on having some sort of family reunion."

"I thought you promised not to keep secrets from him anymore."

"I did, and I won't. I'll tell him all about Dharma just as soon as she leaves town." I frowned. "Trouble is, she wants to get together."

Rene's reply was uncharacteristically soft. "What are you going to do?"

"I have no idea. Ignore her and hope she goes away? Invite her over to bake cookies? Go to the Greenwood Spa and get matching mani-pedis?" I tossed what was left of my napkin onto my plate. "Part of me wants to tell her to leave Seattle and never come back, but I can't. I keep thinking about George."

"Your friend that was killed last year? What does he have to do with your mother?"

"George deserted his daughter when she was a child, too. I know he screwed up, but he was a good man, and when he finally reached out to his daughter, she turned him away." Tears burned the backs of my eyes. "I don't blame her. That's my first impulse, too. But if she hadn't, George might still be alive. How can I do the same thing?"

"What did you tell her?"

"Nothing. I froze. I stood there like an idiot with my mouth hanging open. Dharma told me to think it over and let her know. She's coming back tomorrow after my Flow Yoga class." My lower lip trembled. "Why did she have to come back now? I haven't seen her in almost thirty years."

Rene stalled for time by taking a long drink of her mocha. "I hate to say it, but you should prepare yourself to be disappointed. She probably wants something from you."

"Like what?"

"Maybe she needs money. Isn't that what long-lost relatives usually come looking for?"

"If she's come to harvest the money tree, she's going to be sorely disappointed. It's been completely picked dry. Michael and I have put every penny into the kitchen remodel." I pushed my uneaten bagel to the side. "With my luck she needs a new kidney."

Rene reached across the table and took my hand. "How can I help?"

63

"Honestly, I don't know. I'd hoped that talking with you about it would make me feel better, but nothing has changed. Every time I think about Dharma, all I feel is anger. I can't let myself get angry anymore. After Orcas …" I looked down at my hands.

"Kate, you didn't cause Monica's death."

I looked up. "I know that."

I wasn't lying, simply avoiding the truth—again. Monica's murder wasn't the death on Orcas that plagued me. Not the only one, anyway. I still felt responsible for the other fatal accident that weekend. If it *was* an accident. My angry outburst may not have caused *Monica's* death, but it set in motion the events that led to another.

A familiar churning agitated my stomach. I had to do better—to *be* better, not just for myself, but for Michael, Bella, and anyone else I might hurt. My angry outbursts had already caused more than enough suffering. And, as *The Yoga Sutras* asserted, future suffering should be avoided.

Refusing to cross emotional minefields—like opening up to your estranged mother—might be a good start.

"Kate, are you listening?"

I jumped at the sound of Rene's voice. "No, sorry. I tuned you out for a second."

"I said you should meet with your mother and tell her how you feel. Go ahead and get angry with her. Yell if you want to. Tell her how much she hurt you. You've kept way too much bottled up inside lately. Releasing some of those pent-up emotions might do you a world of good."

Rene meant well, but I couldn't risk it. Not again. The collateral damage might be too high.

I smiled, looked my friend straight in the eyes, and lied. "I'll think about it, I promise."

EIGHT

THE REST OF THE afternoon was blissfully uneventful. I went back to the studio at five-thirty to check on Bella, only to find an empty car and a note from Michael saying that he'd taken her home with him. I left a vague message on Michael's cell phone telling him that I'd be home late because I had some "things" to do at the studio. After a year together, Michael could read me almost as well as Rene. Until I was ready to tell him about Dharma, my best strategy was avoidance.

I plastered on my most soothing smile and greeted the fifteen stressed-out yogis who came for six o'clock Yoga Nidra—the comforting meditation sometimes called the Divine Sleep. Truthfully, I taught that class completely on yoga teacher autopilot. Physically, my students and I shared the same space. My body sat at the front of the room, shadowed by flickering candles; my voice filtered through the darkness, creating a soft, spoken lullaby; but my mind never entered the building. It remained out in the parking lot, staring into those eyes so uncannily like my own. What could Dharma possibly want with me after all of these years? And was I even remotely capable of giving it to her?

Fortunately, my students didn't seem to notice my mental distraction, or if they did, they were kind enough to not say anything. Yoga students were lovely that way. I said goodbye to the last straggling practitioner, locked the door behind her, leaned against it, and sagged to the floor.

Dad's voice scolded from inside my head. *Get it together, Kate.*

In a few minutes, Dad. I promise.

I allowed myself twenty minutes to wallow in self-pity, then forced myself to take action. I symbolically cleared my mind by cleaning the yoga studio. I scrubbed the sink and the toilet. I vacuumed the lobby. I swept and reswept the already clean hardwood floor. I pinched the brown leaves off my jungle of house plants and fertilized the orchids. I folded and stacked the blankets, organized the blocks, and wound up the yoga straps. None of it mattered. No matter how orderly I made the space surrounding me, my mind still whirled in a disorganized mess. I laid out my mat and tried practicing some focusing, breath-centered asanas, but my mind and my body refused to connect.

Even Buddha must have had an off day every now and again.

I gave up and trudged to the front desk. If I was going to be miserable no matter what I did, I might as well do something I hated. I'd already cleaned the bathroom, so bookkeeping would have to do.

Next to paying the quarterly taxes, bookkeeping was my least favorite business activity. Immersing myself in the numbers always reminded me how vulnerable Serenity Yoga was financially. I wasn't exactly immune to financial challenges. Any Girl Scout raised by a single-parent cop earned her coupon-clipping badge at a very young age. But that didn't prepare me for the realities of being a small business owner. Steady paychecks—not to mention frivolous benefits like health insurance and disability leave—were luxuries I'd lost when I opened the studio three years ago.

Part of me—probably the delusional part—knew that Serenity Yoga would eventually make it. The first person I'd hire on that glorious day would be my very own bookkeeper. Until then, performing the odious task when I was already in a bad mood would have to do.

I spent the next 173 minutes immersed in number-crunching torture. I budgeted the next six months' rent payments. I paid every bill and entered every petty cash receipt. I created a monthly budget for candles and cleaning supplies. At midnight I finally gave up and drove home.

The lights were off when I pulled into the driveway, so I assumed that Michael had already gone to bed. I tiptoed up to the kitchen entrance, silently inserted my key, and eased open the door.

To the obvious aftermath of a tornado.

I looked around the kitchen remodel, taking in the day's devastation. The smell of freshly cut wood tickled my nostrils. Sheets of white plastic covered every window and doorway, plunging the room into dreary grayness. The tiny amount of counter space that hadn't yet been dismantled was covered with power tools, bright orange extension cords, and a thick layer of grime.

Seriously? Every day?

When Michael and I agreed to combine households in my tiny Ballard bungalow, I knew that we'd have some issues. Michael hated my secrecy; I was annoyed by his messiness. We were both trying to meet each other halfway, but after five months of cohabitation, I had a feeling that I'd have to learn to accept Michael's housekeeping deficit disorder. That was okay. I had plenty of flaws of my own. Like not telling my partner about my not-so-dead mother.

Our first couple of months went surprisingly well.

Then we started the remodel.

What began as a relatively simple bathroom remodel had somehow morphed into a major house expansion that included fencing my yard, redesigning both the kitchen and downstairs bathroom, and adding a two-person office next to the guest bedroom. The escalating price tag made me distinctly uncomfortable, but Michael was paying for it with the money he saved in apartment rent each month.

Part of me felt crazy for taking on such a huge project with a man who only held the title of "boyfriend." The other part knew that marriage license or not, Michael would be stuck with me for the rest of his life. Our relationship had already withstood my crazy commitment-phobic neuroses and a murder accusation. I figured it could withstand anything.

I hadn't counted on the stresses of construction.

All sixty-seven days of it, so far.

The single clean spot in the kitchen was the tiny, well-organized space on the table I'd claimed as my own. That four-foot-square area contained two dog bowls, an assortment of measuring cups and spoons, and the blender I used to grind and prepare Bella's special diet. She suffered from an autoimmune disease called Exocrine Pancreatic Insufficiency (EPI), which left her unable to digest food on her own. Her meals had to be prepared in a highly customized way that included grinding, adding water and enzymes, and waiting a minimum of twenty minutes while the disgusting-looking concoction "incubated."

Michael knew better than to let anything disturb my Bella food-preparation rituals. The last time he distracted me while I was mixing her food, we ended up with a sick dog, a terrible night's sleep, and a blow to the skull (mine, not Michael's). Neither of us planned to repeat the experience.

I pressed through the plastic sheeting covering the doorway and entered the living room. As Michael had promised, the living room and upstairs bedroom were mainly untouched by the construction. If you didn't count the continual layer of dust that somehow seeped through the plastic or the Jenga-like piles of boxes, furniture, towels, and kitchen appliances stacked in every available space.

I pulled a bottle of Merlot from the wine rack, filled a semiclean glass with liquid tranquilizer, and chugged it down. Eight ounces of twelve-percent alcohol hit my stomach at the same time, leaving me warm and deliciously woozy. Another pour and two swallows later, I headed upstairs.

Michael snored softly on one side of the bed; Bella snored loudly on the other. I carefully wove my body between them, relishing their warmth and wondering, not for the first time, what I'd done to be lucky enough to deserve them. I laced my fingers through Michael's, then rolled my back to him and wrapped my arms and legs around Bella. She groaned and leaned into my touch.

I lay there for at least a hundred years, trying not to think about Dharma, breathing in Bella's sweet scent, and willing myself to fall asleep. I could only hope that—as *The Yoga Sutras* promised—sleep would allow my spirit to return to its source, so that maybe, just maybe, I could find peace.

———————

When I woke up the next morning, Michael was gone.

He left a note on the nightstand: *You need to call the construction company. The contractors left the kitchen door open yesterday.*

Again? That was the third time they'd left the house unlocked this month. How was it that highly skilled men—who could focus long enough to cut two-by-fours to within an eighth of an inch without losing a finger—didn't have the brain capacity to lock a door behind them?

Michael's note ended with, *Sorry I fell asleep before you got home. Everything okay?*

Excellent question. Was it?

Bella interrupted my musing with a single sharp bark.

"You're right, sweetie. We should definitely go for a walk after breakfast."

I'd deliberately misunderstood her. Bella's demand-bark always meant *Feed me. Now.* Still, her vocalization gave me the excuse I'd been looking for. I couldn't explain why, but I was curiously drawn back to the dock at Green Lake—the first place I'd seen Dharma. Maybe visiting it would give me more clarity.

As soon as Bella finished her breakfast, we hopped into the car and drove straight to the soccer fields.

I had the perfect plan. By nine, the before-work exercisers would have completed their three-mile loop, leaving the dock relatively empty. I would sit on the wooden platform, touch my fingers to its rough surface, and try to tap into Dharma's energy. If I connected with her essence, I might be able to intuit her agenda—or at least understand my own. If nothing else, Bella would get the first of her half-dozen bio breaks for the day.

I parked near the Green Lake Community Center, clipped on Bella's leash, and allowed her to drag me toward the water. My feet stopped near the cement tulip planters.

Bella's stopped, too.

Something was wrong.

Three police cruisers and a gray coroner's van were parked on the trail. The area surrounding the paddleboats and dock had been blocked off with yellow crime-scene tape. A large crowd loitered and whispered outside it. Bella pricked her ears forward, raised her hackles, and stepped between me and the uniformed officer containing the gawkers. A low growl rumbled from deep in her chest.

I placed my fingers between her shoulder blades. "It's okay, Bella. This has nothing to do with us."

My words weren't convincing, even to me. Deep inside, I knew that whatever was happening, it had *everything* to do with us. I considered retreating back to my car, but curiosity-laced foreboding pulled me, step by wary step, toward the water. I wrapped Bella's leash tightly around my wrist and stood with the spectators.

I spoke to the young Asian jogger beside me. "What happened?"

She pointed to a trio of gray-haired men huddled near the patrol cars. "See those fishermen? They found a woman in the water. I think she drowned."

Drowned?

Tiny hairs all along the back of my neck prickled. No one swam in Green Lake until the water warmed up later in summer. I stood on my toes and craned my neck to see over the crowd. Two men in dark blue uniforms lifted a female body and placed it on a wheeled stretcher. She wore a black T-shirt with an orange flame emblem.

My heart froze in my chest.

Could it be Dharma?

My eyes jerked to the clear plastic bags covering her hands. The body's fingernails were black, except for the middle ones, which were painted blood burgundy. My heart started beating again, thudding a steady rhythm of guilty relief.

Thank God.

It wasn't Dharma; it was Raven.

The man at the top of the stretcher turned, and I finally saw Raven's face. Guilty relief turned into gut-wrenching dread.

If Raven had drowned, how did she get that deep red gash across her forehead?

I lowered my heels, grabbed Bella's collar, and slowly backed away. "Come on, sweetie. Let's go."

No doubt about it. Dharma's and my meeting this afternoon had just gotten significantly more complicated.

———————

I arrived at the studio in time to teach a mindless rendition of my ten-thirty Flow class. I obsessed about my upcoming meeting with Dharma. Did she already know about Raven's death? If not, how was I—a virtual stranger—supposed to tell her? After what felt like ninety years, the ninety-minute class was finally over. I said goodbye to my students, stared out the window, and waited for Dharma to arrive.

And waited.

And waited.

Three hours and two group classes later, I said goodbye to the Mom and Baby instructor and told her that I'd take care of the afternoon's cleanup.

I should have been happy. I wanted the whole Dharma situation to go away quietly, and apparently it had. So why was I still standing here, pining next to the window like a teenager who'd been stood up on prom night?

Whatever Dharma was doing, it was, as always, more important than me. I grabbed my jacket from behind the chair, unlocked the filing cabinet, and pulled out my purse. It was time to go home and figure out what to tell Michael.

I was three steps away from the desk when the phone rang.

"Serenity Yoga, this is Kate. How can I help you?"

A mechanized voice answered. "This is a collect call from the King County Jail." Then Dharma's voice came on the line. "Kate, it's Dharma. Please pick up." The mechanical voice continued. "Will you accept the charges?"

Every part of my body constricted. Unyogic or not, I wanted to say no. If Dharma was a guest at King County's correctional facility, it could only be for one reason: Raven's death. In the past year, I'd already been mixed up in two murders too many. I had no desire to get sucked in again. Especially not for a stranger who'd walked out on me three decades ago.

I took a deep breath, fully intending to tell the robot voice no. To tell Dharma that she should call someone that she actually knew. Someone she cared about. Someone who cared about her. But then I flashed on my last image of George: dirty clothes, whiskey-laden breath, worried eyes. George adored his daughter even though he'd abandoned her. Given the opportunity, he might have proven it.

"Yes, I'll accept the charges."

"Thank goodness you answered, Kate. Thank you." Dharma's voice sounded shaky, frightened even. Almost hysterical. Not at all like the woman I'd met the day before.

"What happened, Dharma?"

Delusional Kate hoped that Dharma's answer would be a surprise. Maybe she'd been arrested for some minor pet-activist crime, like chaining herself to an Animal Control vehicle or stealing some poor unsuspecting pit bull from inside its own yard.

"Kate, I—" Her voice caught. "I can't say it. I can't even believe it." When she spoke again, her voice was so soft, it was almost a whisper. "Kate, I need you to come see me. I've been arrested for murder."

NINE

FOR THE RECORD, TELLING your boyfriend that your not-as-dead-as-you-might-have-implied mother has been arrested for murder doesn't go over well. At least it didn't in my case.

Michael was still fuming the next morning. He road-raged his way through downtown Seattle's Monday morning traffic, gripping the steering wheel so hard that his knuckles turned white. His jaw trembled. A small vein pulsed high on the side of his forehand. His face glowed so red I was afraid he might have a stroke.

"Explain this to me again. You told Rene that your mother was alive and in town when?"

"Saturday."

"A full day before you told me."

"It was less than a day, Michael. More like twenty-two hours."

Michael's look would have soured milk.

"I swear, I wasn't going to hide it from you forever. I was planning to talk to you after Dharma and I met yesterday, but as you know, I never saw her." I cringed and tried to look innocent. "It could have been worse. I didn't tell you about Dharma right away, but at least I didn't lie to you."

"Only because you didn't get the chance. You came home so late on Saturday night that ... " His shoulders, already tense to begin with, shot up to his ears.

Busted.

He slammed the heel of his hand against the steering wheel. "*That's* why you came home so late, isn't it? You were avoiding me."

"Michael, I—"

"Enough, Kate," he interrupted. "I don't want to hear it." He reached over and cranked up the radio's volume, clearly ending the conversation.

The safest response was to let him sulk in silence. I didn't have a good explanation for my behavior, anyway. Michael was right. I'd already kept way too many secrets from him. I knew he'd calm down eventually; Michael wasn't the type to hold a grudge. I also knew that each time he caught me in an evasion—and each time he blew his stack at me for shutting him out—it chipped away at the foundation of our relationship. If we were going to work as a couple, we'd have to figure out a compromise.

I glanced at Michael's anger-rigid body. Necessary or not, today wasn't the day to begin negotiating a peace treaty.

Instead, I stared out the passenger-side window, watched the skyscrapers go by, and made up fairytales about Dharma's arrest. Imagined scenarios were all I had to work with. Other than telling me she'd been accused of killing Raven, Dharma had refused to discuss the charges against her unless I came to see her in person. She claimed that her lawyer warned her not to talk on the jail's phone system, but I suspected that the decision to hold back was hers. Information was the only bait she had to lure me into her lair.

At first, I was torn. Dharma should be making nice with her lawyer right now, not her estranged daughter. But my old nemeses—curiosity and guilt—drew me toward Dharma like a mosquito to a bug zapper, with the same likely outcome. Within minutes of hanging up the phone, I was back on it with John O'Connell, my father's old partner at the Seattle Police Department, begging him to expedite my background check so I could secure a coveted spot on Dharma's approved visitors list.

All of which led to this—me having to endure the silent treatment from Michael as we drove to the King County Jail for the first of two weekly visiting times. I had a gazillion questions for Dharma, and I intended to get answers to all of them. Two prime examples: *Why do the police think you killed Raven?* And, more importantly, *Did you do it?*

Twenty minutes later, Michael and I opened the double glass doors of the King County Jail, passed through the metal detectors, and submitted to a brief and minimally invasive pat-down. We signed in at the front desk and handed a bored-looking officer our photo IDs. She scowled over the top of her glasses at Michael.

"You're not on the inmate's approved visitors list."

Michael's mumbled response was unintelligible, which was probably a good thing. There were children in the room, after all.

I smiled and did my best impersonation of a trustworthy yoga teacher. "We were hoping to go in together. Can't you make an exception?"

"Listen, Ms. . . . " She peered down at my ID. "Ms. Davidson." She wrinkled her nose as if the name were somehow distasteful. "There is only one way your friend here is getting into the jail today, and it is *not* as a visitor. Would you like to accompany him?"

I sensed it was a rhetorical question, so I didn't answer. I turned to Michael as she handed him back his driver's license. "Don't take it personally, Michael. I didn't tell Dharma about you, and—"

Wrong answer.

"Of course you didn't," he growled. "But I'll bet you told her all about Rene."

I hadn't, actually, but now wasn't the time to argue.

He shoved his wallet into his back pocket. "I'll wait in the chairs with the rest of the chauffeurs."

I turned back to the police woman/receptionist. "I guess it will be just me."

She recited the rules in a perfect monotone.

"Thirty minutes maximum per visit. The clock starts as soon as the inmate sits down. No cell phones, keys, or other personal items. Inappropriate attire, profanity, or disruptive behavior will not be tolerated. Shoes must be worn at all times."

"Seriously? Who goes inside a jail barefoot?" As a yoga teacher, I spent most of my workday in bare feet. But tiptoeing shoeless through a space that housed prostitutes, drunks, and IV drug addicts? Well, that seemed like a poor hygiene choice, even to me.

Officer Friendly gave me a droll look and continued. "Any attempt to smuggle in contraband materials will result in expulsion and further sanctions." She pointed to the crowded waiting area. "Have a seat and wait until your name is called."

I turned away from the desk and stared across the dismal room. Screaming children, exhausted-looking mothers, well-dressed professionals, broken-hearted grandparents. All loitered together in the suffocating space, waiting for the chance to spend thirty no-contact, monitored minutes with their loved ones.

I claimed the orange plastic chair bolted to the floor next to Michael, closed my eyes, and tried to numb myself to the energy around me. Like many yoga teachers, I had become highly attuned to energy. I wasn't psychic, simply sensitive to the subtle energies of people and places. Sometimes horrifically so. This room was one of the worst. Anxiety, anger, hopelessness, and depression rippled through the air, as suffocating as the heat waves rising off a Death Valley freeway.

I'd spent more than a few hours at the West Precinct with Dad, but the closest I'd been to this side of the American justice system was my arrest on Orcas. At the time, I'd thought nothing could feel as claustrophobic as the baby-vomit-green inquisition room they'd used to detain me.

I was wrong.

This was worse.

Much worse.

I passed the next several minutes emptying my pockets. Cell phone, change, keys, and dog treats all went into my purse, which I set on the floor next to Michael. He refused to make eye contact, so I spoke to the side of his head.

"I'm sorry you didn't make Dharma's visitors list, but I'm glad that you're here. I couldn't have faced coming alone." I placed my hand on his forearm. "You know I adore you, right?"

Michael continued looking forward. "I love you, too, but I'm still angry. You shut me out. Again."

"I know." I didn't promise that it would be the last time; lying would have made the situation worse. I interlaced my fingers with his and we waited in silence.

Officer Friendly droned out several names. Mine was among them. She pointed to an elevator. "You can go up now."

Michael squeezed my hand. "Be strong. I'll be here when you get back."

I smiled. "If you haven't picked up a better girlfriend."

He gripped my hand tighter. "I mean it. I'll always be here for you. No matter how hard you try to push me away."

I believed him. I'd be there for him, too. I backed toward the elevator and winked. "Then I guess you're stuck with me, buddy."

The other visitors and I rode the elevator upstairs in silence. When the door opened, we walked together, expressions grim, like a herd of cattle en route to the slaughter. Our shoes clicked a syncopated rhythm down the stark, hospital-like hallway. The stench of disinfectant-laced body odor permeated the air.

A grumpy-looking male officer directed us to a fluorescent-lit room, which was divided in two by a Plexiglas wall of half-enclosed phone booths. Each booth contained a wooden, bar-stool-like chair that was bolted to the floor and a black phone receiver affixed to a metal partition. A sign across the top of the divider read *Keep hands in plain view at all times*. I considered asking Officer Chuckles what I could possibly pass to a prisoner through bulletproof plastic, but I opted to sit in the uncomfortable seat he assigned me and wait quietly instead.

Dharma and several other female prisoners were escorted through a door on the opposite side of the partition. She sat on the stool across from me and picked up her handset.

"Thank you for coming."

Granted, I didn't know Dharma well, but I doubted that she'd ever looked worse. A bright red rash had erupted across her forehead. Her formerly braided hair hung in greasy-looking clumps, and the pale skin under her eyes was accented by dark purple half circles. Dharma hadn't just aged in dog years since I'd seen her last; she'd aged in dog decades.

She gave me a tentative smile. "Did you have any trouble finding parking?"

"Really? That's what you want to spend our thirty minutes talking about? Parking?"

Dharma flinched at my response. She took off her glasses, closed her eyes, and slowly rubbed the bridge of her nose. When she looked up, her eyes were wet.

"You're right, Kate. We have much more important things to discuss." She slid her glasses back on and gripped the receiver. "I'm sorry about missing yesterday. I'm sorry about … everything. When you were a baby—"

I held up my hand in the universal *stop* sign. "Not now, Dharma." I took a deep breath to steady my emotions. "We can talk about the past later. Let's focus on now. You don't look well. Are you doing okay in here?"

"This isn't summer camp, but I'll survive. It's better than the Juarez jail I was stuck in for six weeks." She shuddered. "The worst part is the food. Jail isn't exactly vegetarian friendly."

Dharma was vegetarian, too? It shouldn't have surprised me. She was, after all, an animal rights activist. Still, it hadn't occurred to me that Dharma and I might have a lot in common. The insight felt dangerous. Keeping a healthy distance would be significantly more challenging if I actually liked her.

She kept rambling, whether from nervousness or guilt I couldn't tell. "There was some sort of desiccated meat patty on my plate this morning. I gave it to my crazy-eyed roommate and traded my reconstituted eggs for the heroine addict's apple. No one wanted the watered-down orange drink. I would kill for a cup of coffee." She looked over her shoulder, as if expecting an espresso cart to magically appear.

"Enough about the accommodations, Dharma. Why do the police think you killed Raven?"

Dharma's lips tensed. "I don't want to talk about my arrest, Kate."

"Then why am I here?"

"I need you to do me a favor."

A favor? Seriously?

Thirty years' worth of bitterness spewed from my throat.

"A favor? You disappear from my life for three decades, then con me into visiting you in jail just so I can do you a favor?" I stood up, preparing to smash down the phone and leave Dharma behind once and for all. But not without getting in three final words: "Go to—"

Dharma jumped to her feet and slammed her palms against the partition. "Stop!"

The officer behind Dharma grabbed his walkie-talkie and took three quick steps forward, ready to call in reinforcements. Officer Chuckles appeared behind me.

Dharma's eyes locked on mine. "Please, Kate. Please. I'm begging you. Don't leave."

Two overwhelming sensations hit me at once. The first was staggering empathy. Not with Dharma; not even with my murdered friend, George. With George's daughter. I finally understood why she was so hostile to George the day he tried to make amends. Some wounds—especially those inflicted in childhood—couldn't be bandaged. Not even stitched. Sometimes, in order to save the patient, you had to cut off the limb.

I almost walked out the door. I *should* have walked out the door. But I couldn't. The second sensation froze me in place.

Connection.

To Dharma.

In spite of the bulletproof wall separating us, in spite of the other gaping visitors, in spite of Officer Chuckles's glaring stare, I felt Dharma's energy.

She was trapped. She was terrified. She was vulnerable.

She might even be innocent.

And she needed my help.

The insight into Dharma's psyche hit me like a blow to the sternum. Bitter or not—morally justified or not—I was supposedly a yogi. Yogis showed active compassion whenever they saw suffering. Telling Dharma to go to Hades while marching out of the room would never pass muster. I had to choose: I could live by my values, or I could walk away. I couldn't do both.

I slowly sat down and motioned for her to do the same. The two officers backed away.

"Okay, Dharma. I'm listening."

"I need you to go to my motel and pick up my belongings."

"Your belongings?"

"It's not much. I only brought one suitcase. It's all worthless to anyone else, but if I don't get out of here soon, the motel will get rid of it. My attorney says I can sign a release and they'll give you my key card. Can you please go to the motel, pack up my stuff, and keep it for me?"

"Why don't you call your boyfriend Eduardo?"

I was fishing, of course. I suspected that Eduardo and Dharma were a couple, but I didn't know for sure.

Dharma's lips thinned. "How do you know Eduardo?"

I didn't lie, but I didn't tell her the whole truth, either. "I don't. He chatted up someone I know after the protest. She was staffing the pet food booth. Evidently, he made quite an impression."

Dharma sighed. "Eduardo and I broke up on Saturday night. I found out that he's been cheating on me with Raven. For months."

She leaned up to the plastic partition, as if being closer provided her the illusion of privacy. "Kate, I don't know who to trust anymore. One of my friends from HEAT is likely the killer. And anyone who *didn't* kill Raven probably thinks I did. I need someone I can count on."

I stared at Dharma, not sure that I fully believed her story or that I wanted to get involved, even if did. I flashed on *The Yoga Sutras* again. Some days I hated Patanjali.

"What makes you think you can count on me? You don't know me."

"I know you better than you think, and I knew your father better than you'll ever understand. You won't let me down. You can't. You weren't raised that way."

She was right.

I sighed. "Okay. I'll do it."

Dharma smiled.

I held up my index finger. "On one condition."

Dharma closed her eyes, whether in relief or resignation, I couldn't tell. "What's that?"

"You have to be straight with me. Why do the police think you killed Raven? Is it because of the fight you had with her Saturday morning?"

Dharma's face paled. "How do you know about that?"

"You two weren't nearly as stealthy as you thought."

She shook her head. "I don't want you involved in all of this ugliness, Kate. That's what my attorney is for."

"I mean it, Dharma. That's my condition. If you want my help, you have to answer my questions. I already know that you and Raven had an argument less than twenty-four hours before she was murdered, and you admitted that she was sleeping with your boyfriend. You definitely have motive, but the police need more than motive to make an arrest."

Dharma swallowed. "They have other evidence."

I remained quiet, waiting for her to continue.

"You might not know it to look at me, but I have a pretty bad temper."

I frowned. That was the second thing Dharma and I had in common. Dad always said that I got my short fuse from Mom. He must not have been joking after all.

"I confronted Eduardo after my argument with Raven, and he admitted that they'd been having an affair." Her lips tightened. "I was furious. I mean, I'm not stupid. The man was almost twenty years younger than me. I never expected exclusivity. But with *Raven*? She'd been acting crazy lately. Eduardo was more fed up with her than I was. I decided to have it out with her once and for all, so I called her and told her we needed to talk. She said to meet her at eleven back at Green Lake, on the dock near the paddleboats."

"Wait a minute. Eleven o'clock at night? At Green Lake?" The park was always deserted after dark.

"I know, it surprised me, too. But Raven had been acting strangely the last few weeks. I figured skulking around in the dark must be part of her new anarchist image. I met her where she asked, but when I told her to leave Eduardo and me alone, she laughed. She called me a miserable old has-been." Dharma's face flushed. "We had a bit of a scuffle, and my billfold must have fallen out of my jacket pocket. The police found it on the dock, near Raven's body."

"That's not good."

Dharma looked down and worried the skin at the edge of her thumbnail.

"No, it's not. But that's not the worst of it."

My stomach churned. "What *is* the worst of it?"

Dharma rolled up her sleeve. A long, red welt bisected her forearm. "When I got home, I noticed this scratch. Raven probably has my skin underneath her fingernails." She lowered her arm and looked down at her lap. "And she might have bumped her head when I pushed her."

"You pushed her?" My voice came out louder than I intended.

"Yes, but she was still alive when I left, I swear!"

I reached up my hand to rub my forehead. This wasn't good. Not good at all. Hopefully Dharma hadn't blabbed this whole story to the police. I was no lawyer, but—

Oh no.

I dropped my hand back to my lap and gaped at the handset in horror. Dharma's lawyer had warned her not to talk about the case on the phone. Did that include the handset in the visitors' area?

"Dharma, you need to stop talking."

Either she didn't hear me, or she chose not to listen. "Kate, you have to believe me. I wouldn't kill anyone. Not even Raven. She drowned. Some poor fisherman found her floating by the dock. She smashed her head when she fell, but—"

"Dharma, be quiet!"

The whole room froze in echoing silence.

I lowered my voice and whispered into the handset. "Listen to me. I heard you." I gestured with my eyes toward the guard. "But you have to stop talking. Now."

Dharma's mouth dropped open, but she said nothing. Her complexion turned stone gray.

I peered into Dharma's eyes. I tried to find guilt. I tried to find subterfuge. I tried to find *anything* I could use as an excuse to leave this whole nightmare behind. All I saw was confusion. And isolation. And fear.

"This attorney of yours. Is he any good?"

Dharma hesitated. "I assume so. I only spoke to him for about fifteen minutes. He was assigned to me by the court."

"Your attorney is a public defender?"

"Kate, I'm an activist, not part of the social elite. I don't have money to hire my own attorney." She tried to smile, but her lips never made it past a grimace. "He's young, but they wouldn't have given him a murder case if he weren't adequate." She swallowed. "He says I should consider taking a deal."

Officer Chuckles interrupted. "That's it, everyone. Your thirty minutes are up. The next visiting hours are on Thursday."

Dharma got out one more thought before they made her hang up the phone. "Kate, when you pick up my belongings, make sure you get the wooden box. It's important to me."

I laid my palm against the plastic that separated us and smiled, trying to give her some form of comfort. "I will. I promise."

And I would. But first, I had to hire her a better attorney.

TEN

I BARELY RECOGNIZED THE man who pulled into the studio's parking lot five hours later, but I would have known that rattletrap orange Plymouth pickup anywhere. Dale's feet barely touched the ground before I wrapped him in a huge, heartfelt hug.

"Dale, I'm so glad you're still in town. Thank you for agreeing to meet with Dharma. It means the world to me." I stepped back and took in his new outfit. "Look at you, all dressed up like that. You look like a real lawyer."

I wasn't kidding, either. The Dale I'd had for an attorney wore flannel shirts, suspenders, and goat-dung-encrusted work boots. This Dale wore a dark blue power suit, a yellow-dotted navy tie, and black dress shoes so shiny I could have used to them to touch up my makeup. His beard—which was usually scraggly, unkempt, and littered with straw—had been trimmed short and looked so clean that I almost didn't get nauseated looking at it. He looked, in a word, powerful.

A single thing marred his impeccable appearance: the fine, white dog hair covering his suit jacket. I pointed to a particularly large clump in the crease of his right elbow. "I see you brought Bandit with you."

Dale's lips lifted in a huge grin. "Of course I brought Bandit. I can't go anywhere without that little monster." His words sounded cranky, but his voice held nothing but affection.

As if he knew we were talking about him, Bandit jumped on the pickup's dashboard and began scratching at the windshield. White fur puffed around him, creating an indoor fur blizzard. His brown eyes flashed with pure mischief.

"Let me grab him and we'll go inside to talk."

Dale continued talking as he clipped a leash on Bandit's collar. "We're lucky the boys are on break this week and can look after the rescue. I was planning to hang around Seattle for a couple more days anyway. Checking in on your momma's case will give me an excuse to visit my old stomping grounds."

I flinched at his easy use of the word "momma."

"Her name's Dharma."

"Fine, Dharma then. But where I come from, young'uns don't call their parents by their first names. Seems a might disrespectful."

Dale stopped, suddenly serious, and placed his hand on my forearm. "Kate, you know I'll do whatever I can to help, but I need to know something. Are you sure Dharma is innocent?"

I paused before answering. The question was important. Dale acted like a country bumpkin most of the time, but it was just that—an act. Before Dale had traded in his briefcase for a farmer's cap and work boots, he'd been one of Seattle's most formidable defense attorneys. He gave up criminal law after one of his clients murdered a woman—three days after Dale got him out of jail for assaulting her.

My arrest last fall was the first criminal case Dale had taken in almost seven years. I knew he'd worked on other criminal cases since then, but like Perry Mason, Dale made it a point to fight for the innocent.

I flashed back to my visit with Dharma that morning and what I'd felt in her energy. "I can't guarantee anything, Dale. I don't know her well enough. But yes, I think she's innocent."

He responded with a single nod. "Good enough. Let's go talk inside."

We walked across the parking lot toward the studio. I still couldn't believe Dale's transformation.

"Where'd you get the fancy clothes? I almost didn't recognize you."

"It's like I told you before, Kate. Things work differently in Seattle than they do on Orcas. If I'm going to play big-city attorney again, I need to dress the part." He grinned. "I bought the monkey suit at Northgate on the way over. I don't look half bad, do I?"

"You look great."

I opened the studio's front door, flipped the sign from *Open* to *Closed*, and told the teacher staffing the desk that she could take the rest of the day off. Dale sat on the bench in the reception area and gestured for me to sit beside him.

He handed me a paper bag. "I brought a few more of those cookies for Bella, since the crows got most of the first batch."

I opened the bag and inhaled the pungent aroma of goat cheese. "Keep baking these and you might convince me to stop being vegetarian."

I filled Dale in on everything I'd learned during my jail visit with Dharma while he plucked fine white dog hairs off his suit jacket. At the end, I admitted that the conversation might have been a mistake.

"You two talked about all of that in front of the guards? Are you nuts?"

The answer was undoubtedly yes, we were both certifiable. But I suspected Dale already knew that.

"I don't know what we were thinking. Dharma's attorney warned her not to talk about the case. I guess we got carried away."

"She's already hired an attorney?"

"If you can call it that. She met with a public defender. A young one. I'm afraid he might be in over his head."

"Wouldn't surprise me. I certainly was when I started out at the PD's office. What makes you so sure she wants to hire someone different?"

I shrugged my shoulders. "I'm not, but I have to try. She's going to need better than some overworked kid who just passed the bar exam." I bit my lower lip. "Dale, you should know—Dharma doesn't have any money."

He smirked. "Seems to be a family trait."

I couldn't come up with a snappy retort, so I reached down and rubbed Bandit's ears.

Dale slapped his hands on his thighs and stood. "We can work out the money issues later. First, we need to figure out which lawyer's going to be alpha. I'll head downtown and make a few phone calls. Maybe I can finagle that young pup who's representing Dharma into getting me a visit." He squeezed my upper arm and dropped the red-necked façade. "Don't worry, Kate. If she wants my help, she'll get it."

He stood up and handed me Bandit's leash. "Now, I shouldn't be gone longer than a few hours, so you entertain Bandit. I'll pick him up and fill you in later this evening."

I looked in the cute pirate-dog's beady brown eyes and saw nothing but trouble. "You're not taking him with you?"

"Kate! You should know better than that. I can't possibly leave him alone in the truck."

I looked outside at the overcast rainy day. "It's cool outside, and you can park in one of the downtown parking garages. He'll be perfectly safe."

"Bandit would be safe enough all right. But what about my truck? The last time I left him alone, he ripped a hole clean through the upholstery. That truck's a classic! Besides, Bandit would much rather spend time with you."

As if plotting his future misconduct, Bandit cocked his head, scratched his left ear, and sniffed at the carpet. I could only hope that he wasn't planning to lift his leg on the statue of Ganesh that guarded the yoga room's entrance.

Dale's smile didn't look sincere. "Bandit won't be any trouble at all." He paused. "As long as you don't leave him alone. Or let him get bored." He backed toward the door and looked at me with what I swore was an expression of sympathy. "Have a great time, you two!" He jogged across the parking lot, jumped into his truck, and sped off.

Bandit sniffed every square inch of the lobby, not seeming worried in the slightest that his human had abandoned him. I glanced at the desk clock, then down at the wiggling monster. "Okay, kid. Looks like it's you and me until my class starts at six. Think you can behave and let me get some work done for the next couple of hours?"

Bandit chose not to commit.

I tied his leash to my desk and returned the first of the studio's long list of phone messages. Bandit busied himself by sharpening his teeth on my desk. No problem, I could deal with that. I opened the drawer, pulled out one of Bella's favorite chew toys, and firmly gave the command "sit." Bandit remained standing, at least in the seconds his feet touched the floor. The rest of the time he levitated, yipping at full volume and trying to snatch the toy from my hand.

"Fine, you win." I handed him the toy, which of course ruined the game. He started digging in the carpet, obviously determined to bury the toy somewhere in China, or at least far out of the reach of any yoga teacher stupid enough to try and reclaim it.

Perhaps ignoring him would do the trick. I looked away from the little he-devil, dialed the second number, and tried, unsuccessfully, to speak loudly enough to be heard over the barking. No problem there, either. I could always spend the next hour responding to the day's deluge of emails. Bandit might be more stubborn than I was, but I was smarter. I could outthink any canine. Well, any canine except Bella.

Or so I thought.

Forty-five migraine-inducing, suicide-ideation-causing minutes later, I gave up, grabbed the little monster, and carried him down the sidewalk for a visit with Uncle Michael at Pete's Pets.

The sucker (oops, I mean, my amazing life partner) actually looked happy to see the little black-eye-patched demon. I felt bad for not giving Michael adequate warning, but these were extenuating circumstances: the students of my Yoga for Healthy Backs class would start arriving in fifty-five minutes, Bella needed a bathroom break, and my head was about to explode. Besides, Michael was already mad at me. What did I have to lose?

I left Bandit with Michael, gave Bella her bio break, and still had time to stock the bathroom supply cabinet with the month's inventory of hand soap, toilet paper, paper towels, and facial tissue. When the clock rolled around to five forty-five, I greeted my students with a virtuous smile and a self-satisfied sigh. In one day, I'd helped a long-lost relative, managed the studio's inventory, given an old friend a new job, and proven to the world once and for all that I was an incompetent babysitter. Some days, life was good.

I checked in the final student, locked the front door, and joined the fourteen yogis already seated in the practice space. I asked them to lie on their backs with their knees bent and their feet flat on the floor—a comfortable position for most back pain sufferers—and rang the Tibetan chimes three times.

"Take a moment to check in with your bodies. Start by noticing any areas of tightness or discomfort. Imagine a heat lamp warming those areas, melting away all muscle tension."

After a few minutes, I asked my students to change how they breathed in order to strengthen their core. "With each inhale, allow your belly to relax and your low back to rock gently away from the earth. With each exhale, contract your abdominal muscles, as if you were closing the zipper on a pair of too-tight jeans. You should feel your low back flatten toward the floor." This exercise strengthened the deepest core muscles that stabilized the lumbar spine and pelvis.

I'd taught Yoga for Healthy Backs often enough that I could do it practically without thinking. Normally, I would have kept my mind focused anyway, as if I were teaching the class for the first time. Tonight, I allowed my mind to wander.

Over two hours had passed since Dale left for the courthouse, and I hadn't received a single voicemail message. Was he at the jail gathering intel from Dharma or in a bar tossing back cold ones with his lawyer buddies?

The heavy-set man in front of me twitched and started to snore. The students around him giggled and fidgeted. Time to get them all moving. I guided them in Apanasana—Knees-to-Chest Pose. "Place your palms on your kneecaps, with your fingers pointing toward your toes." This deceptively simple yet powerful pose warmed up the muscles of the lumbar spine. "On inhale, rock your knees away until your arms are straight. Notice how your lower back gently arches away from the floor. On exhale ... " My voice continued speaking on autopilot. My mind wandered to suspects, means, motive, and opportunity. What did I already know?

Frustratingly little, and yet more than I thought.

I mentally outlined what I'd observed the morning of DogMa's fundraiser.

First odd factoid: Dharma and her buddies at HEAT had traveled over seven hundred miles from Sacramento to Seattle to protest a well-regarded animal shelter. That act by itself seemed unusual. Was there something I didn't know about DogMa that had made it a target, or had the day's protest merely been a pretense for something else?

I moved the class to their stomachs and guided them through several repetitions of Cobra Pose to strengthen their backs. "Place your palms on the floor under your shoulders and ... "

Come to think of it, Sally and Maggie had seemed upset, but not exactly floored, to learn that HEAT was going to protest the event. When Maggie saw the picket line, she'd said, "I can't believe she's actually going through with this." Dharma and Goth Girl were both mysteriously missing at that time. Was Raven the "she" Maggie referred to? And if so, how did they know each other?

A student to my right lay on his belly with his forehead resting on his forearms. The face of the young woman next to him was turning bright pink. Perhaps I should give the class a break. "When you finish your next repetition, press your hips back to your heels and let your forehead rest on the floor in Child's Pose. Imagine that you can breathe warmth into your low back muscles."

Warmth. The fire. Raven had said to Dharma that someone was going to burn. Could she have known about the impending arson? Setting a dumpster on fire wasn't the same as drowning someone, but it was still an act of violence. Hanging out with violent criminals was a good way to wind up dead.

I brought the class to standing for several repetitions of Uttanasana, or Head-to-Knees Pose, a posture I'd specifically adapted to safely stretch the lower back. "On inhale, raise your arms over your head. On exhale, bend your knees and fold forward, bringing your fingertips toward the earth." A man near the back of the room ogled the bent-over bottom of the woman in front of him, then quickly averted his gaze and smiled sheepishly at his wife.

Which reminded me of love triangles, like the one between Raven, Eduardo, and Dharma. What was going on there, anyway? On the surface, Eduardo and Raven weren't all that surprising a couple. Physically, they were a good match: both in their thirties, both attractive, both interested in the same social causes. Dharma, though beautiful, was old enough to be Eduardo's mother, yet she seemed genuinely surprised to learn that he was having an affair with Raven. Did Raven have some hold over Eduardo that Dharma wasn't aware of?

By the time I led the class in a long, luxurious Savasana, the only conclusion I'd reached was that while I had lots of questions—mainly for Dharma—I had no answers, and I wasn't likely to get any in the near future. Dale would string me up by my toenails if Dharma and I discussed the case in front of the guards again. I'd have to make a list of questions and hope Dale and his oh-so-convenient attorney-client privilege could find the answers.

I rang the chimes three times and brought the class back to sitting. After a brief Q&A session and a discussion of the upcoming week's home yoga practice, I wandered to the lobby with my students and unlocked the front door.

A vibrating, growling, foaming monster-beast lurked on the other side.

His name was Michael.

He held a wiggling Jack Russell terrier in his outstretched hands. "Take. Him. Before. I. Strangle. Him."

He thrust Bandit into my hands, spun his back to me, and stomped away, muttering phrases about broken treat jars, gutted dog beds, and soon-to-be fricasseed terriers. Somehow I doubted that Bandit was about to become the new Pete's Pets store mascot.

I smiled at the four students still putting on their shoes in the lobby. "Anyone up for a few hours of dog-sitting duty? He's a sweet little guy."

Bandit added a wiggle and a growl to the conversation. Two sympathetic smiles, one "no way," and an "I'm outta here" later, Bandit and I were completely alone. I locked the door and peered down at the little beast.

"What am I supposed to do with you now?" Putting him in the car with Bella was a non-starter. I wasn't sure which one of them would win the inevitable scuffle for dominance, but I didn't want to find out the hard way. Tying him to my desk again was equally unattractive. I considered releasing him to the wild, but Seattle might never recover. I checked voicemail instead. Dale had left a message.

"Sorry, Miss Kate. I'm going to be later than I thought. I managed to get a meeting with your momma and her assigned attorney." I stiffened at his use of the M-word. "I'll be back to pick up Bandit as soon as I can."

In other words, I might be stuck with the little fur-demon all night. Fortunately, there was one room in the studio that might actually be Bandit-proof. I felt a little guilty locking him in the bathroom by himself, but only a little. Not nearly guilty enough to change my mind.

"Try sharpening your teeth on porcelain, you little beast."

I marched through the yoga studio and into the lobby, then closed the door separating them. Bandit's scratches and ear-piercing yelps were much less aggravating when heard through several layers of soundproofed sheetrock.

I straightened the retail area, emptied the garbage cans, and vacuumed the lobby. By the time I unplugged the vacuum, Bandit's barking had finally stopped. Hopefully he'd relax and nap until Dale arrived to reclaim him.

I tiptoed through the yoga room and reorganized the mats, blankets, straps, bolsters, and blocks that my students had haphazardly tossed back on the shelves. Once I finished that multiple-times-daily job, I grabbed the dust mop and started sweeping the yoga space.

I heard a thud and the sound of muffled scuffling from inside the bathroom. Bandit must not be sleeping after all.

Wait a minute…

If Bandit wasn't sleeping and wasn't barking, what, pray tell, was he doing? I quietly swept my way to the bathroom and pressed my ear against the door. At first I didn't hear much of anything, other than Jack Russell toenails clicking across linoleum. Then I heard the distinct sound of ripping paper.

Paper? Where could he have gotten paper? I shrugged. He must be getting his jollies unwinding the toilet paper roll. Annoying, but how much damage could he do with a single role of—

The realization hit me like a stack of solid bamboo yoga blocks.

The supply cabinet!

I tossed the dust mop to the side and threw open the door. The supply cabinet's door hung open and half off its hinges. Fifty rolls of toilet paper and four eight-packs of paper towels had been shredded to make a bathroom-sized dog nest. The fifth eight-pack of Bounty swam in the toilet where, as advertised, it soaked up significantly more than its weight in water. Toilet paper wrapped around Bandit's head and under his collar.

Facial tissue was obviously next on Bandit's hit list. He was currently making confetti out of box number four.

Then he spied his escape route.

Bandit bolted, unwinding three hundred linear feet of bathroom tissue behind him. He made a quick victory lap around the yoga room before jumping on my newly straightened shelves, where he knocked down the basket of yoga straps, grabbed one between his pointy little teeth, and taunted me with it.

I should have known where this was going, but in my defense, I'd just survived a toilet-paper tornado. How could I possibly be expected to think clearly? I grabbed onto one end of the strap; Bandit gripped the other. He tugged and he growled and he whipped his head back and forth as he tried to get purchase on the slick hardwood floor. I tugged and I growled and contemplated canine homicide.

"Bandit, let go!"

I was so caught up in the turmoil that I didn't hear Michael's key turn in the lock or the tinkle of the front door's bell as it opened. I didn't realize that I had company until Dale's voice boomed across the room.

"Kate! What on earth is wrong with you? You shouldn't rile Bandit up like that!"

Two things happened at once. Bandit dropped the strap and I gave it one final tug. Bandit flew to Dale's side, where he skidded to a stop in a perfect sit-stay. I flew through the air and landed on my rear in a not-so-perfect Staff Pose. When I looked up, Dale's whiskers trembled with righteous indignation. Michael chewed on his lower lip and tried not to laugh.

"I'm surprised at you, Kate," Dale scolded. "I thought you and Bella had worked with a dog trainer. Didn't she warn you about playing tug with a high-strung dog like Bandit? It will take me all night to get him calmed down."

I would have argued with Dale, but what was the point? I was just grateful that he'd actually come back to retrieve the little demon.

"I'm sorry, Dale. I'm not used to this little guy's energy. Bella's a lot more laid-back. Maybe next time you should leave him with Tiffany." Michael held up his palms and took several steps back. "In her apartment," I added quickly.

I dusted the shreds of toilet paper off my pants and prayed that Dale wouldn't ask to use the bathroom. He'd probably accuse me of trying to suffocate his dog in recycled single-ply. After all, there wasn't enough water left in the toilet to drown the little bugger.

"Let's go talk in the lobby," I suggested.

Dale and Michael sat on the bench. I remained standing and tried not to rub my bruised tailbone.

"Were you able to talk to Dharma?"

"For a little while, yes." I could have sworn that Dale blushed behind his beard. "She's quite the woman, your mother. Did you know she spent several years in Uganda helping to protect endangered mountain gorillas?"

I didn't correct his use of the M-word. "What did she say?"

"Sorry, Kate. I can't tell you that. Dharma's and my conversation is bound by attorney-client privilege."

"She agreed to let you represent her?"

Dale's expression turned serious. "Yes, and I've got my work cut out for me."

"What you mean?"

"The DA has a good case, and your mom, well, she's not exactly acting in her own best interests. First, she blabbed to you in front of the guards, and now she's hiding something from me. I can't help her if I don't have all of the information."

Michael smirked. "Get used to it, Dale. Secrecy runs in the family."

I didn't respond to his jibe. To be truthful, I welcomed it. Teasing was Michael's way of letting me know he wasn't mad anymore.

"What's Dharma hiding?"

"Well, Miss Kate, if I knew that, we wouldn't have a problem, now would we?"

I gave Dale a droll look. "Come on. You have to tell me more than that."

"Honestly, there's nothing to tell, except my suspicions. I've been in this business a long time. I can tell when a client is holding back, and Dharma's doing it in spades. The question is, what is she hiding and why? Something's weird about her involvement with HEAT, that's for sure. She gets cagey when I ask about the organization, and I don't buy her story of how she ended up with them. Going from protecting mountain gorillas to picketing dog owners? There's a story there, and it's not the one she's giving me." He raked his fingers across his beard. "I'll do what I can, but ... " His words trailed off.

I had a very bad feeling about his use of the word "but."

He reached into his pocket and removed a black plastic card. "I was able to get this, though. Dharma asked me to give it to you."

I knew the answer, but I asked anyway.

"What is it?"

"Dharma's room key." He handed me the card and a note with the motel's name. "It's on Aurora Avenue, not far from here. Dharma was staying in room 231. She said you agreed to pick up her belongings." Dale looked serious. "I hate to say it, but unless something changes, you may be keeping them for her for a very long time."

ELEVEN

AFTER DALE LEFT TO go back to his hotel, Michael and I spent the rest of the evening putting my supply cabinet door back on its hinges and filling four garbage bags with Bandit's shredded debris. Shortly after ten, we finally arrived home and cuddled together on the couch. Bella slurped down her dinner while Michael drank a Guinness and I sipped my second glass of wine.

Michael absently stroked my hair. "Kate, promise me one thing."

"What's that?"

"If anything ever happens to Dale, swear to me that we won't adopt Bandit."

I snuggled in deeper and smiled. "Deal."

I wanted that moment to last forever. Wrapped up in Michael's arms. Warm. Contented. Safe. But I knew that our temporary harmony would crumble under the weight of the next secret, and in my life, there would always be a next secret. Michael and I both deserved a relationship that was solid. A relationship we could count on.

I drained the last drops of oaky Chardonnay and took a deep, bolstering breath.

"We need to talk."

Michael's body stiffened, but I forced myself to continue. "The last couple of days have been tough on us. I know that, and I know you want more."

He didn't contradict me.

I pushed several piles of junk mail aside, set my glass on the end table, and turned to face him.

"We keep fighting about the same issue over and over again. I love you. I will always love you. But I'm not perfect. Frankly, being in a relationship with me will sometimes be lonely. I know I promised not to shut you out, but this whole mess with Dharma made me realize that's a promise I can't keep.

Michael opened his mouth to disagree, but I cut him off.

"Please, Michael, hear me out." My throat ached, but I kept talking. "Growing up as the only child of a single-parent cop wasn't easy. Every time I said goodbye to Dad, I knew it might be the last. I learned to be independent. I had to, to survive." I poured another half-glass of wine and took a large swallow. "Heck, maybe that's just an excuse. Maybe self-reliance is simply part of my karma, left over from a prior life."

"You don't think you can learn to depend on someone else? To depend on me?"

"I already depend on you, more than you know. And it terrifies me." I took his hands. "I'm growing, Michael. I know you see that, but I don't think your expectations of me are realistic. How can I promise not to hide things from you when most of the time I hide them from myself?"

Michael's chin trembled. "What are you saying, Kate? Do you want to break up?"

I teasingly nudged his arm. "You should be so lucky. I'm afraid, my dear, that you're stuck with me."

He looked confused. "Then what is this about?"

I gestured around the living room at his junk. "Neither of us is perfect. If this relationship is going to work, we have to learn to accept each other—good, bad, and messy. Keeping things inside is my messy." I shrugged. "I can't be the only one who changes."

Michael didn't reply and I wasn't sure how to continue, so I slapped the couch cushion next to me. Bella jumped up, turned a quick circle, then lay down with her head resting in my lap. "Telling you about Dharma was hard for me, Michael, and you reacted by scolding me because I'd told Rene first. I'm doing my best to open up to you. When I do, you can't jump all over me for not having done it sooner."

Several infinite seconds of silence passed before Michael replied. "Okay."

I smiled and took another deep swig from my glass. "Good. I need one more promise from you."

"What's that?"

"You need to support my decisions, even when you think I'm making a mistake."

Michael's eyes grew wary. "What mistake are you making now?"

I answered by avoiding the question. "I know you worry about me. We almost broke up when I tried to solve George's murder. You even wanted me to stay out of Monica's murder investigation, and I was trying to prove my own innocence that time. We're about to start the whole process again."

Michael remained quiet.

"Believe me, I don't seek out violence, but it obviously follows me. I don't know why, but there must be a reason." I averted my eyes. "Maybe I deserve it somehow."

"Kate, that's crazy. How could you possibly deserve it?"

"I don't know, but I'm beginning to think there's a reason. The universe has certainly been kicking me in the ass lately. Maybe there's some weird life lesson I'm supposed to learn. Maybe helping bring killers to justice is the universe's way of making me atone."

"Atone for what?"

I couldn't tell him. My nagging guilt about Orcas was one of the secrets I still kept hidden inside.

I closed my eyes and consciously released a long, slow breath. "My point is, Dharma is in trouble, and I have to help her."

"You did. You got Dale to represent her."

"Yes, but you heard him tonight. Even he thinks Dharma's case looks bad." I brushed my fingertips down Bella's muzzle. She sighed and relaxed her weight into my lap. "I'll be the first to admit, for a cop's daughter, I haven't been the most effective sleuth so far. Dad didn't share much of that part of his life with me. But I'm learning, and I'm going to do what I can to help solve Raven's murder. I know you won't approve, but I hope you won't try to stop me. I don't want to hide from you anymore."

I held my body completely still, hoping Michael wasn't about to explode.

He stared down at the floor for several long moments before he looked up and met my eyes. "You're right, Kate. I hate it when you put yourself in danger."

"Who said anything about putting myself in—"

Michael held up his hands, clearly asking me not to argue. "Harassing murder suspects can't be safe, Kate, and you know it." His lips turned downward. "But I won't try to stop you."

"Thank you."

"Don't thank me. I'm simply being pragmatic. Trying to stop you wouldn't do any good, anyway. I'm better off helping. What have you learned so far?"

"Not much, honestly."

I outlined what I knew about Dharma's past, Eduardo and Raven's affair, and my suspicions about Maggie and her prior knowledge of HEAT.

"I thought Maggie acted funny on Saturday, too," Michael replied. "I looked up HEAT online, and from what I could find, they've never protested an animal rescue before this weekend. There has to be a reason they started with DogMa."

"You've been researching?"

"I'm the one who set up this whole fiasco with DogMa, remember? If something hinky is going on with Maggie or her organization, I need to know about it. Besides, you're not the only one in this room with a healthy sense of curiosity."

I smiled.

"Like I said, though, I didn't find much. Maggie opened DogMa a little over three years ago. She must have had private funding of some sort, because she opened with space for almost a hundred animals. She didn't apply for 501c3 status until over a year later. I should have done more research before I decided to back them in such a big way, but I liked Maggie, and DogMa is well regarded. The only criticism of them is that they don't take hard-to-place animals."

"They wouldn't take Bella, that's for sure. They were one of the first places I called after George died." I looked down guiltily at my furry best friend. "Sorry, sweetie. That was before I realized you and I were meant for each other."

"You didn't want to hear it at the time," Michael replied, "but they were right to refuse her. Bella wouldn't have survived in a shelter environment. 'No-kill' and 'hard-to-place' don't generally go well together. DogMa's goal is to get animals into new homes as quickly as possible. Remember, every animal Maggie places in a new home frees up space at her shelter for another."

I frowned. He was right, but that was little comfort to special-needs animals like Bella.

"If the answers were easy, Kate, every pet would have a home."

"So, what *did* you find about HEAT?" I asked after a moment.

"Well, they don't have tax-exempt status with the IRS, so they don't qualify as a nonprofit, at least not yet. They started showing up online about two years ago. Historically, their actions have seemed reasonable enough. Protesting inhumane farming practices, going after companies that use animal testing, promoting veganism, that sort of thing. Attacking a reputable shelter, especially one in a different state, isn't like them."

"Where does that leave us?"

"I think we should start by questioning Maggie. Luckily, I have the perfect excuse to pay her a visit."

"What's that?"

"Her favorite subject. Donations."

———

Michael was off work the next morning, so he stayed home with Bella and promised to set up a meeting with Maggie, ostensibly so we could drop off some last-minute donations. We opted to keep our ulterior motives to ourselves.

In the meantime, I was on Dharma's errand duty. I drove down Aurora Avenue North to an area that housed a collection of dingy, pay-per-hour type motels. I pulled into the parking lot of Dharma's motel at ten, which left sixty minutes for my search-and-retrieve mission before the eleven o'clock check-out time.

At one time, the motel's exterior had probably been inviting, with weatherproof vinyl siding, flower-filled window boxes, and the requisite soda and snack room. Today, the beige plastic siding was covered with cobwebs, the ice machine sported a handwritten *Out of Order* sign, and the flower pots were filled with desiccated brown ivy.

I tapped on the door to Dharma's room, waited a few seconds, then slid the key card into the slot and slowly pushed open the door.

"Hello? Anybody here?"

Flattened blue carpet, a sixties-style threadbare bedspread, and the unappetizing scent of disinfectant-laced mildew greeted me.

I opened the curtains for light and blocked the door open for ventilation. I grabbed Dharma's empty suitcase, tossed it on the bed, and wandered around the tiny room, looking for items to fill it. There wasn't much. The black shirt with the HEAT insignia that Dharma had worn Saturday morning lay crumpled on the floor next to the television. Several blouses and two pairs of jeans hung in the closet. A makeup case, hairbrush, and assorted toiletries were scattered around the bathroom counter. Thus far, I couldn't see what Dharma was so concerned about. I hadn't found anything that couldn't easily be replaced with ten minutes and a hundred-dollar gift card to Fred Meyer.

The nightstand was empty except for some cheap motel stationery, so I moved on to the dresser. I opened the top drawer and scooped out several pairs of clean socks, a bra, three pairs of white cotton underwear, and a light blue sleep shirt.

The wooden box Dharma had mentioned occupied the bottom drawer. It was old, likely antique, and about ten inches long and six inches wide. Yellow daisies decorated the top; intricate carvings were etched on its sides. A tiny padlock was latched closed at the front. I gently shook the box left and right. The items inside made a muffled sound.

Papers, maybe? Something wrapped in cloth?

With my luck, it's Dharma's cocaine stash.

I held it up to my nose and sniffed at the edge. Nothing but the scent of old cedar.

I looked around for a key, but I couldn't find one. I was about to try gently prying it open when a voice startled me from behind.

"What are you doing here?"

Goth Girl stood in the doorway wearing a long-sleeved black T-shirt and black jeans, just as she had on Saturday. Up close, she looked younger than I'd originally thought, perhaps as young as sixteen. The pale foundation covering her skin hid a proliferation of old acne scars. Her nails had been bitten to the quick, and a yellow stain between her second and third fingers hinted at a nicotine addiction.

I almost couldn't believe that this was the same girl I'd seen at the fun walk. When she'd released Blackie, she'd seemed bold, frustrated. Angry, even. Today, she looked vulnerable somehow. As if the dyed hair, makeup, and multiple piercings were shields—armor she wore to keep the world from seeing her true self.

I held Dharma's box to my chest and tried to look nonthreatening. "My name is Kate. Dharma is my … Dharma is a friend of mine. She asked me to pick up her belongings."

Goth Girl looked uneasy, like a feral kitten hoping for handouts but afraid of a trap. She took a single step toward me, then hesitated and took two steps back. "Is she okay? Everyone's talking trash about her, saying that she killed Raven. But she was always good to me."

"I don't think Dharma killed anyone, do you?"

Goth Girl shook her head, almost imperceptibly.

I should have been wary. Goth Girl was, after all, one of my suspects. She might be a murderer. Logically, I knew I should be careful, but at that moment, my biggest fear was that she would bolt.

"You say Dharma was good to you. You might be able to help her." I smiled, hoping to encourage her. "Why don't you come inside and talk to me."

Goth Girl glanced furtively behind her. "I can't talk to you. Eduardo won't like it."

"Why not? Eduardo is Dharma's friend too." I sat down and patted the space on the bed next to me. "Please come in and sit down."

She took two cautious steps into the room. "Aren't you that woman from the yoga studio? Eduardo said you and Dharma are related somehow."

"Yes, I'm her daughter."

Goth Girl shifted her weight back and forth and worried the edge of her thumb nail. "Raven said I should never talk to strangers alone. It isn't safe."

Eduardo, and now Raven? This might be the first teenager on earth that actually paid attention to her elders. Still, their counsel made sense, for both of us.

"That's smart advice. Tell you what—let's go to the lobby. There will be other people there, so we won't be alone. I think they might have coffee."

I took her silence to mean assent. "Let me grab Dharma's stuff."

I carefully wrapped Dharma's wooden box with a shirt, placed it inside her suitcase, padded it with the rest of her clothes, and started to close the zipper.

The door slammed shut behind me. When I whipped back around, Goth Girl was gone.

TWELVE

LESS THAN TWO HOURS after my failed interrogation of Goth Girl, Michael and I drove across the Ballard Bridge en route to our meeting with Maggie.

"I know I promised not to second-guess you, Kate, but really? Talking to a murder suspect in a deserted motel room? Alone? Are you trying to get killed?"

Michael spit out his questions in rapid-fire succession, leaving no opportunity for me to sneak in an answer. I sat back and observed him instead. He looked cute, in a wavy-haired Elmer Fudd kind of way. His hands gripped the steering wheel precisely at ten and two o'clock, as if by mastering the car he could somehow manage his out-of-control girlfriend.

Good luck with that.

"I know, Michael. Inviting her into the room was reckless. But in my defense, she confronted me, not vice versa. Honestly, I think she was more afraid of me than I was of her."

"That's what hikers say about rattlesnakes right before they strike."

He had a point.

"She didn't strike, Michael. She bolted, before I got a single useful piece of information out of her."

"At least now we know that HEAT is still in Seattle."

"Some of them, anyway. They're probably all staying at that same motel." I paused. "I wonder why they haven't gone back to California. Does that seem odd to you?"

"Not really. The police might have asked them to stick around, or they may have other business in Seattle. For all we know, there's some animal rights convention in town this week."

"I tried to get the guy at the front desk to give me their room numbers, but he wouldn't talk to me, not even after I offered him twenty bucks. He said if I wanted him to snitch on his guests, I'd either need a court order or a heck of a lot more money."

"Have you tried calling John O'Connell?"

"Yes, but he won't tell me anything. I barely conned him into helping me get on Dharma's visitors list. He said that he'd rather lock me up with her than help me get mixed up in another murder investigation."

I drummed my fingers on the dashboard. "I really want to interview Dharma's friends. Do you think I should go back to the motel? I could dress up as a maid and knock on doors."

Michael's grumbled answer contained words never written in *The Bhagavad Gita*. I changed the subject.

"Why are we going to Queen Anne, anyway? I thought we'd meet Maggie at the shelter. I would have enjoyed seeing it."

Michael shrugged. "Honestly, there's not much to see. The main building has offices, a clinic area, and a large training room. The one next door houses the animals."

"That's the part I'd enjoy visiting."

"No you wouldn't. Not unless you like spending time in a crowded space filled with desperate-looking animals."

"Desperate-looking? I thought DogMa was supposed to be good."

"It's a shelter, Kate. They do the best they can, but it's not a home. Maggie's facility is state-of-the-art and well maintained, but like most shelters, it's also understaffed and overcrowded. The animals who end up there are frightened and confused, and they have no idea why they've been separated from their human families. Maggie uses trainers and volunteer dog walkers to enrich the animals' lives as much as she can, but it's still not perfect. The kindest thing she can do is get the animals she rescues into new homes as quickly as possible."

He reached over and took my hand. "Very few abandoned pets are as lucky as Bella, Kate. Some of them truly suffer, especially emotionally, even in the best of shelters. If I spent too much time at DogMa, Bella would have a whole slew of new siblings."

I grimaced. Bringing *one* other dog into Bella's territory would be a disaster. "Just what I need. Another murder."

"Of me or the dog?"

"Don't test me, funny man." I winked to let him know I was kidding.

Michael grinned. "Maggie said that the shelter will be closed for a couple of days, but I'm sure she'd be happy to give you a tour when she gets back."

"Closed? Is someone taking care of the animals?"

"I assume so, but we can ask when we see her."

"How'd you convince her to meet with us on her day off?"

"I told her I'd received several large cash donations for DogMa, and that I wasn't comfortable keeping them in the store. She gave me this Queen Anne address and said we could come by any time today."

"Is she going to believe you? I mean, do you have enough money to give her?"

"My customers are very generous, and I've been harassing them about the DogMa fundraiser for weeks. Even with the fire, Maggie took in over fifty thousand dollars at the event. I've collected almost three thousand more at the store."

I leaned over and kissed his cheek. "Have I ever told you that you're wonderful?"

Michael smiled. "Once or twice, but I never get tired of hearing it."

We drove up to the Queen Anne mansion a few minutes later.

Or rather, drove by it.

Every parking spot in a five-block radius was taken. We finally squeezed into a not-quite-legal spot near a fire hydrant and took our chances with a ticket.

"It's a good thing Rene was able to watch Bella again today. We'd never have found a spot in the shade."

Michael locked his Explorer and we started the five-block hike to the top of Queen Anne Hill and the front gate of the huge Victorian mansion. I paused at the entrance and stared, gape-mouthed.

"Wow."

Not super eloquent, I'll admit, but appropriate. Even for Queen Anne, the house and its grounds were impressive. Seattle's Queen Anne neighborhood was named after the architectural style of its early homes, most of which were custom-built mansions designed for the city's social elite. At the time of its construction in the early 1900s, this house must have been one of the finest. Its precisely trimmed evergreen hedges lined the yard's front border and provided privacy from the street; the southern-facing windows opened to a gorgeous cityscape view.

Michael gestured to a crowd of uncomfortable-looking people congregated behind the living room's sheer curtains. "No wonder we couldn't find parking."

"Did Maggie say she was at a party?"

"Nope. She just asked me to meet her here." He rang the bell.

A woman I didn't recognize answered the door. Her breath—which smelled like a mixture of bourbon and breath mints—arrived a second before she did. She wore a form-fitting black dress, black pumps, and a solemn expression.

Michael spoke first. "Hi, we're friends of Maggie's. Is she here?"

"Thank you for coming. I'm Ginny." She gestured with a highball glass for us to come inside. "Maggie is with her grandmother right now, but she should be able to see you shortly."

We followed her into a large foyer lit by a three-tiered chandelier. She pointed toward a long, dark hallway. "Put your coats in the first bedroom on the left. Food is in the living room to the right. Alcohol is at the wet bar. Believe me, you'll need it."

She closed the door behind us, rested her fingertips on the wall for balance, and then teetered back to the crowd.

I looked at Michael and silently mouthed, "What is this?"

He shrugged his shoulders.

I could say this much—if this was a party, it was the creepiest one I'd ever attended. Somber-looking people whispered, gripped platters of food, and avoided eye contact. The energy of the space was stilted, as if the guests were anticipating something decidedly unpleasant, though I couldn't imagine what.

Michael and I put our coats in the bedroom and wandered to the living room. I glanced around the crowded space, trying to get my bearings. Ivory furniture and Oriental rugs precisely matched the room's eggshell-white walls. Every decoration, every detail seemed painstakingly positioned—as if super-glued to a specific location. In spite of the floor-to-ceiling views of downtown Seattle, I suddenly missed my messy, chaotic Ballard bungalow.

The room's temporary centerpiece was a gluttonous-looking buffet containing every edible species of the animal kingdom. Prime rib, peeled shrimp, chicken, salmon, a leg of lamb, even a large, pink bone-in ham. I always tried not to judge other people's food choices, but the sheer number of dead beasts on the table made my stomach churn a little. I ignored the smell of cooked flesh, picked up a plate, and filled it with a colorful collage of fruits, vegetables, breads, and desserts, hoping that holding something would make me feel less uncomfortable.

Michael glanced at me and surreptitiously covered his slice of prime rib with a pile of mixed salad greens.

"It's okay," I said.

He nodded sheepishly, then added four bright pink shrimp tails and a large chunk of salmon.

Of the concessions Michael and I had made when we moved in together, his biggest was agreeing that our shared kitchen—aside from Bella's special food preparation area—would be completely vegetarian. I knew that he still ate meat outside of our home, and it wouldn't have been fair for me to ask him to stop. But I still cringed internally whenever I saw the man of my dreams eat the food of my nightmares.

Then again, it wasn't much worse than watching Rene snarf down one of her jalapeño pineapple pregnancy concoctions.

I pointed to a relatively uncrowded area across the room. "I'll meet you over there."

I wandered to a display table covered with photographs.

What the ... ?

Over a dozen Ravens smiled back at me.

As in Raven, the murder victim.

The photographic display created a visual timeline of Raven's life. Brunette-haired baby, gap-toothed grade schooler, college graduate. A pedestal toward the back displayed an eleven-by-seventeen framed photo of Raven standing next to Ginny, the black-clad woman who'd greeted us at the door. From the creases surrounding the two women's eyes, I assumed the photo had been taken recently.

I took in the hushed room with new awareness. This wasn't a celebration; it was a send-off.

What was Maggie doing at Raven's wake?

I set down my plate and examined each photo, trying to get a better sense of who Raven had been. Young Raven seemed happy, light, and carefree. Over time, she'd transformed. Her clothes became darker; her eyes angrier. Until, in the final photo, her forced smile seemed like a paper doll's outfit, cut out and taped to an unhappy face.

Michael's expression, when he joined me, looked as confused as I felt.

"What is this?"

Maggie's voice sounded from behind us. "It's my grandmother's shrine to Raven. Displaying photographs of the dead is a family tradition." Her mouth hardened. "Grandma values nothing as much as tradition."

I gestured toward the large photo. "Is that Raven's mother?"

"Yes, that's my Aunt Ginny. Leave it to Grandma to make that one center stage. Raven always hated that picture."

"Wait a minute," Michael said. "You and Raven were related?"

"Yes. Raven is ... " Maggie closed her eyes and swallowed. "She *was* my cousin. Our fathers were brothers."

"Were?" I asked.

"They both passed away years ago." Maggie shrugged, almost resignedly. "Cancer."

"I'm sorry for your losses." I pointed at Raven's photo. "All of them."

My words came out automatically. They were, after all, what you were supposed to say at a funeral. But part of me wondered if

Raven's death had truly been a loss at all, at least to Maggie. She never mentioned knowing Raven at Green Lake on Saturday. Had she hidden their connection for a reason?

"Thanks for meeting me here," Maggie said. "I hated to inconvenience you two, but I couldn't leave today. Did you bring the donations?"

"Yes." Michael patted his pocket. "I have them right here."

Maggie glanced around the room. "Let's go into my grandfather's office. I'd rather not deal with money issues in front of the guests. It doesn't seem…" She paused, as if searching for the right word. "It doesn't seem respectful, I guess."

We followed Maggie down a hallway lined with stilted-looking family portraits to a dark-paneled office decorated with the mounted heads of dozens of animals: deer, antelope, bison—even a moose. An open display case of hunting rifles hung behind an imposing walnut desk. I stared into the blank glass eyes of a nine-foot-tall grizzly and shuddered.

Maggie noticed. "I know. It's pretty creepy, especially if you're an animal lover. Grandpa was an avid big-game hunter. I tried to talk Grandma into redecorating now that he's passed on, but she won't hear of it." She gazed around the space, as if fully taking it all in for the first time. "Frankly, she should skip redecorating and move, but she insists on staying. Aunt Ginny says Grandma won't leave this house until we wheel her cold, rigid body out on a stretcher." She smirked. "If I know Grandma, she won't even leave then. She'll have her head mounted and hung here in the office."

I winced before I could stop myself.

"Sorry, dead body jokes are inappropriate, especially today. You'd get it if you knew my grandmother, though. She can be a tough old bird sometimes." Maggie sat on a corner of the desk and turned to Michael. "You said you had some donations for me?"

He handed her an envelope. "You might want to put this in a safe. It's almost three thousand dollars. I hope to collect more over the next few days."

Maggie grabbed a silver letter opener off the desk, ripped open the envelope's seal, and ran her thumb across the tops of the bills.

"Thanks. We can use every penny."

Light tapping on the door interrupted our conversation. Sally opened it and peeked through.

"Sorry to bother you, Maggie, but the caterer needs to see you in the kitchen."

Maggie stood. "Sally, do you mind showing these two out?"

I nudged Michael's leg, silently asking him to follow my lead. "Is it okay if we stick around until you're done? Michael has a few other fundraising ideas he wants to run past you, and I'd like to give my condolences to your family."

Maggie shrugged. "Suit yourself. Sally will introduce you around." She left the room before Sally had a chance to reply.

Sally's jaw hardened, so subtly that I almost missed it. "Come on. Let's get out of here. I hate this room."

"Between the guns and the mounted animals, it's pretty imposing," Michael replied.

"The guns aren't the problem. They're a tool, like anything else. I carry a handgun for self-defense. But I'd never use it to kill an animal just so I could hang its head on my wall. It's barbaric."

Michael whispered in my ear as we followed Sally back to the living room. "What fundraising ideas do I have?"

I whispered back. "I don't know. It was the best excuse I could come up with on short notice. Suggest a yogathon or something."

Sally glanced back at us quizzically. I smiled and tried to distract her with conversation. "Did you know Raven well?"

"I used to. She helped get DogMa up and running. I lost track of her when she moved to Sacramento and started that vegan activist nonsense. Frankly, I was glad to see her go. I always thought she was unstable, but that's not surprising, considering that grandmother of hers."

"Raven helped start DogMa?" I frowned. Maggie's secrecy about Raven was even more suspicious than I'd originally thought. "If she was one of DogMa's founders, why was she protesting it?"

Sally didn't reply, at least not to my question. She waved at a woman across the room. "I see someone I need to talk to. Are you guys okay on your own?" She was halfway across the room before she finished the sentence.

"That was weird," Michael said.

"What about this situation *isn't* weird? I know you like Maggie, but I swear she's hiding something."

Michael's brow wrinkled. "I'm beginning to think you're right." He glanced around the crowded room. "We should talk to as many people as possible before Maggie comes back. Want to split up so we can cover more ground?"

"Good idea."

Michael headed back to the food table, ostensibly to talk to the people in line. I suspected he was really after another slice of prime rib.

I divided my time between unobtrusive eavesdropping and asking hopefully innocent-sounding questions.

I didn't learn much. Certainly nothing that would get Dharma out of the King County Jail.

The general consensus was that Raven had been pretty, intelligent, passionate, and troubled, but no one volunteered what those troubles might have been. When I asked about Maggie, everyone agreed that she and Raven had been close growing up, but then they quickly changed the subject.

I was about to find Michael to compare notes when I saw two fifty-something women—one bottled blonde, the other bottled red—huddled near the wet bar, whispering. I meandered next to them, poured a glass of Chablis, and pretended to read the label.

The blonde spoke first. "This whole display is shameful. Everyone acts like losing Raven is such a blow to her grandmother. They hadn't even spoken for almost a year."

"Can you imagine what Raven would have said about the food? Seeing all of that meat would have sent her right through the roof."

"It's the old bat's way of having the final word." The blonde nudged her friend and pointed at Maggie, who was setting out another huge platter of seafood. "Have you noticed the way Maggie's cozying up to her now? She's angling to get the money back."

"Why bother? Maggie will get it all when her grandmother croaks, anyway. How much longer can she live?"

"I thought the granddaughters were cut out of the will."

"Just Raven. It was her punishment for taking up with those California nut jobs." The redhead leaned in closer. "I heard she went back to that biker boyfriend of hers from high school."

The blonde's eyes widened. "The Mexican one?" She sniggered. "Ooh, I'll bet Grandma Dearest didn't like that one bit. She tolerates nothing but the purest white blossoms on *her* family tree. What was his name again?"

"Ned … Ed … Something like that."

The name popped out before I could stop it. "Eduardo?"

The redhead glared at me over the top of her glasses. "Yes, that might be it."

Both women gave me a scathing look and scurried away.

So much for any additional gossip I'd glean from that conversation. Still, the tidbits I'd overheard were intriguing. Obviously, I needed to learn more about Raven's inheritance. Now that she was dead, she could never be added back into her grandmother's will. An estate likely worth millions would be a great motive for murder. And what about Raven and Eduardo? They had a much longer history than Dharma had implied. Did Dharma deliberately hide it from me, or did she not know? More importantly, did something in that history cause Raven's death?

I needed to talk all of this over with Michael.

He wasn't in the living room, so I wandered down the hallway toward the office. No luck there, either. I was about to give the coat room a try when I heard angry whispering. I couldn't make out most of the words, but I would have sworn one of them was "Raven." I followed the sound to a partially closed door, edged up to the opening, and pretended to examine the photograph hanging on the wall beside it.

Ginny, Raven's mother, stood next to an antique armoire in what appeared to be a bedroom. She was speaking with an older woman who wore a dark wool pantsuit and a short strand of pearls. The woman's lips pressed into a thin, tight line.

The evil grandmother, I presumed.

"Get yourself together, Virginia, and lay off the alcohol. I will not tolerate any more drunken displays. Today is not about you. Raven was my granddaughter. I'm grieving, too. "

"My daughter was *murdered*."

"Which is tragic, but not unexpected. Raven was always wild, never levelheaded like Maggie." The old woman's blue eyes turned icy. "Frankly, I blame you and my son—God rest his soul. You both coddled her too much."

Ginny's mouth fell open. "Listen, you coldhearted prune. Raven's death isn't my fault, it's yours. If you hadn't cut off her trust fund

121

allowance when Herbert died, she would have been fine. She'd have stayed in Seattle and kept working with Maggie. Instead, she ran off to join those animal rights nut jobs."

"Herbert overindulged those girls. It was time someone put a stop to it."

"Fine. But why single out Raven? You broke that girl's heart."

The older woman's shoulders stiffened. "I treated my grand-daughters equally. I cut off both of their trust funds, and you know it."

"But you didn't *disinherit* Maggie."

"That's because Maggie actually *did* something with her trust fund money, even if it was setting up that idiotic pet warehouse. I gave Raven over a year to get her act together after I cut off her allowance. I would have put her back in the will as soon as she proved herself."

"Proved herself? Raven would never have been good enough for you."

"Don't be ridiculous. Raven was given every opportunity to succeed. I paid for her business degree and what did she do? She pissed her education away on drugs and sit-ins."

Ginny's voice trembled. "That's not fair. Raven never wanted that MBA. You bullied her into it, just like you bully the rest of us into doing anything you want."

"She snorted away her future because I sent her to college? Please. You can't possibly be that naïve."

"Raven hadn't touched cocaine in over five years, and you know it. She did the work. She got clean. She's not the only person in this family with addictions, but you don't care about that. You save all of your love for your precious Maggie."

"Virginia!" the old woman spat. "That is quite enough! Don't you *dare* try to tell me that I didn't love Raven. *I* bailed her out of jail. *I* hired the attorneys that got her off with probation. *I* paid for her rehab. Raven made her choices, and they were poor ones. Spending my money on drugs, anti-meat lobbyists, and spray-painting fur coats? It was humiliating." The grandmother's jaw clenched. "Maggie may be impulsive, but she would never shame me and this family. Not the way Raven did."

Tears streamed down Ginny's face. "Maggie's no angel when it comes to your precious money either, and Raven was going to prove it. She finally had the evidence. But that crazy woman killed her before she had the chance."

She leaned in close to the older woman's face. "I hate you, you know. We all do. And for the last time, I go by *Ginny*!" She ran out of the room, dashed past me, and disappeared down the hallway.

The older woman glared at the door—or more accurately at me, standing behind it—and shook her head. "So many histrionics. Exactly like her daughter."

She glanced to my left. "Maggie, I'm going to rest now. See if you can calm down Virginia. I no longer have the patience." She paused before closing the door between us. "And for heaven's sake, lock up the alcohol."

When I turned around, Michael, Maggie, and Sally stood behind me, gaping like a silent Three Stooges.

Maggie spoke first. "I'm sorry you had to witness that. My Aunt Ginny can be a little hysterical when she's drunk."

"No problem," Michael replied. "We get it. This is a tough day."

Maggie turned to Sally. "Would you mind putting away the alcohol while I talk to Kate and Michael?" She looked at her watch. "After that, you'd better check to make sure that the animals have been taken care of. The volunteers can be flaky."

Sally's mouth fell open. "Seriously? Today is my day off. I'm supposed to be with my own family, but instead I've been stuck here with yours. And now you expect me to take care of the animals, too? For once, could you please do your part?"

"This is my cousin's memorial. My place is here with my family." Maggie's expression hardened. "When Victor dies, I promise that you'll get the whole day off, too. Now go."

Sally's face blanched, then flashed bright red. "You've become as awful as that old hag. Tell me, Maggie, is all that money worth losing your soul?" She turned to Michael and me. "Enjoy the rest of your time with the Addams family. These ghouls are all yours." She pushed past Maggie and stormed down the hallway.

Maggie reached for her. "Sally, I'm sorry. Wait."

Her words echoed off Sally's back. Ten seconds later, the front door slammed solidly behind her.

"What was that all about?" Michael asked.

Maggie stared at the door, as if willing Sally to walk back through it. "The most recent battle in Sally's and my ongoing war. As usual, I think we both lost." She looked back at Michael. "She's right, you know. Not about me pulling my own weight. I work practically twenty-four/seven on fundraising, and I honestly can't leave here today. But I *am* turning into a ghoul. Mocking Sally's sick husband was completely out of line. I don't know what's gotten into me."

"You've had a death in the family. Cut yourself a little slack."

"Thanks, but Sally's and my conflict started long before today. Sometimes I wish I'd never started that damned rescue."

Michael frowned. "What do you mean?"

"Building a shelter was supposed to be fun. I had an amazing vision for DogMa. It was going to be an example for no-kill shelters everywhere. I hired Raven to manage the business and Sally to take care of animal welfare and adoptions. I was in charge of fundraising and publicity." She shook her head. "None one of us knew what we were getting ourselves into, but it worked, for a while anyway."

"What happened?" I asked.

She shrugged. "The money disappeared. My grandfather died and my grandmother cut off Raven's and my trust funds. I certainly wasn't happy, but Raven had a complete meltdown. She abandoned her work at DogMa and took off for California to found HEAT. Without the trust fund money, I had to drum up donations—fast—so Sally was forced to take on the bulk of Raven's work." Maggie sighed. "As if that wasn't bad enough, Sally's husband had a stroke two months later. Sally kids herself, but he won't ever recover. Dying would be a blessing."

I didn't know what to say, so I remained silent. Maggie continued.

"We're under so much pressure it's a wonder we both haven't imploded. I hoped that Saturday's fundraiser would make a difference, and it did. But our bills have skyrocketed in the past year. Most of that money is already spoken for."

She closed her eyes and pinched the bridge of her nose. "I'm sorry. I don't know why I'm unloading all of this on you. Apparently my aunt isn't the only one who's had too much alcohol today." She turned toward Michael. "I appreciate everything you've done for us. I hope you don't hold Sally's and my tiff against DogMa."

Michael smiled. "Of course not."

I felt bad for pressing, but my priority had to be Dharma. "I understand why Sally is frustrated, but that doesn't explain Raven."

Maggie's expression stiffened. "What you mean?"

"Raven helped start DogMa, right?"

Maggie didn't reply.

"So why was she picketing Saturday's event?"

Maggie stared at the ground for several long seconds. "This is really family business, but I guess I owe you an explanation. My grandmother didn't react well when Raven took off. She was certain that Raven had started using cocaine again." She shrugged. "Heck, she was probably right. Either way, she cut Raven out of the will and left everything to me. Raven convinced herself that her disinheritance was my fault—my idea, even. I told her to be patient. That Grandma would eventually change her mind. She didn't believe me. She said Grandma always let me get away with murder."

I winced at her poor choice of words.

Maggie blanched. "You know what I mean."

"Why didn't you tell me about any of this?" Michael asked. "If Raven was planning to organize a protest on Saturday, shouldn't I have known?"

"I was as surprised as anyone. She'd made some threats, but I never thought she'd actually go through with them."

I gestured toward the closed bedroom door. "From what I overheard, picketing wasn't all Raven had planned."

Maggie looked suddenly wary. "What do you mean?"

"According to your aunt, Raven had something on you. Something that would get her back into your grandmother's good graces. Any idea what that might have been?"

Her shoulders stiffened. "My aunt is grieving. And drunk. And frankly, a little delusional. As far as I know, Raven did exactly what she intended to do this past weekend: cause a scene, embarrass me, and leave."

Maggie was hiding something. She knew it. I knew it. From the look on Michael's face, he knew it too. These two cousins had karma: past actions that were now bearing fruit. In Raven's case, karma might have been a killer.

Michael spoke in a low, stern tone. The tone Dad always used when he knew I was lying. "Maggie, where were you on Saturday night?"

Maggie's eyes grew wide. "Where was I? You think I had something to do with Raven's death?" She took several steps back. "Look, I loved my cousin, but she hung out with a bunch of crazies. Half of them are on drugs. And before you accuse someone, you should at least pick up a newspaper. The police already arrested the loony old cougar who drowned Raven."

I felt my face flush. True, I didn't think Dharma deserved to win Mother of the Year, but "loony old cougar"?

My mouth opened before my brain could stop it. "I don't know, Maggie. Seems like you had more reason to harm Raven than my mother did."

Maggie gaped at me, mouth open in a hollow O. "Your *mother*?" She whipped her head back and forth between Michael and me. "Who are you two, really? Have you been conspiring with Raven all along?"

Michael answered by repeating his question. "Maggie, where were you on Saturday night?"

She pointed a shaking finger toward the door. "Get out of this house. Both of you."

"We'll leave," I promised. "But first answer the question."

Her eyes flashed with stubborn indignation. "I said leave. Now."

I would have pressed her again, but a ratcheting sound startled me silent.

Maggie looked up and screamed. "Aunt Ginny, no!"

Michael grabbed my arm and yanked me behind him.

Raven's mother stood five feet away, leveling a hunting rifle against her shoulder. It pointed at Michael's chest. A small crowd of shocked-looking people filled in behind her.

"You have a hell of a lot of nerve coming here today. I believe Maggie asked you to leave."

She gestured with her head toward the door. "If I were you, I'd get moving."

THIRTEEN

My hands were still shaking when Michael parked the Explorer in front of Pete's Pets a half hour later. He turned off the ignition and faced me.

"Way to go incognito back there, Kate."

"I know, I really stepped in it, didn't I? I can't believe Raven's mother pointed a shotgun at us in front of all of those people."

"At least it wasn't loaded."

"Or so the grandmother said. Did you see the look on her face when she snatched that rifle from Ginny? I don't trust any of those people."

The right side of Michael's mouth lifted in a lopsided grin. "You know, for a minute there I thought your head was going be the next one mounted on that big game wall. Maggie certainly won't be giving you a tour of DogMa anytime soon."

"She wasn't all that happy with you, either. I doubt she'll have much to say to either of us from here on out." I shook my head. "What on earth possessed me to call Dharma my mother?"

"Maybe you're starting to think of her that way."

I shuddered.

"It wouldn't be such a bad thing, you know."

"No way. I just got caught up in the moment. Like I told Rene, Dharma might as well have been an egg donor. I'm helping her because ... I paused. "Well, because it's the right thing to do." My denial sounded flat, even to my own ears.

I changed the subject before Michael could dig any deeper. "Do you think Maggie killed Raven?"

Michael thought for a moment. "She's hiding something, but I'm not sure it's murder. Maggie never struck me as the violent type. Besides, it sounds like Raven had more of a motive to murder Maggie than vice versa. After all, Maggie was the one inheriting the money."

"Maybe." Something tugged at my mind, but I couldn't place it. I felt like a child staring at a puzzle a little too advanced for her grade. Something didn't quite fit, but darned if I could figure out what it was.

"What if money's not the motive?" I asked.

"It might not be. What are you thinking?"

"I keep coming back to the question of *why*."

"Why kill Raven?"

"No. Why protest DogMa? It couldn't have been easy. Raven had to convince almost two dozen people to travel over seven hundred miles to protest an organization that she founded."

"Yes, to get even with Maggie."

"Maybe, but Raven was written out of the will over a year ago. What made her come after DogMa now?"

"If what you overheard Ginny say is true, Raven had dug up some sort of dirt on Maggie."

"You know Maggie better than I do. Any thoughts on what that might be?"

Michael shook his head. "None."

"What do you know about her background before DogMa?"

Michael frowned, as if thinking. "Nothing, now that you mention it. I wonder what I'd find if I scoured the Internet?" He drummed the Explorer's steering wheel with his fingertips. "Tell you what. I'll do some digging around online tonight. It would be easier if I knew what I was searching for, but I can look."

"If you get a chance, try calling Sally, too."

"What for?"

"I'll bet she knows all of Maggie's skeletons, and she trusts you. She might be willing to spill."

"It's worth a try." He looked at his watch. "For now, I need to get to work. Tiffany was supposed to go on lunch break two hours ago."

I gave Michael a long kiss goodbye in front of Pete's Pets, smiled and waved pointedly at a grumpy-looking Tiffany, and told Michael I'd meet him for dinner at PhinneyWood Pizza at six. Date night plans set, we parted company to spend the afternoon managing our separate businesses.

Rene was watching Bella and I wasn't scheduled to teach the rest of the day, so I had the entire afternoon to do paperwork without any dog-related interruptions. First up was writing a blog article about yoga practices that could reduce belly fat. Then I'd send the studio's long overdue newsletter. After that, I'd start planning the summer series and workshop schedules. Perhaps filling my mind with creative distractions would entice my subconscious to do some work of its own. Like figure out how to get more information on Raven, her organization, and her dysfunctional family.

I glanced at my watch: 2:20 p.m. The Power Yoga class would end in ten minutes. I'd never get any work done in the flurry of post-class activity. Besides, my nerves were still shot from staring down the hollow end of a double-barreled shotgun. Time for some liquid fortification.

A quick stop at Mocha Mia secured my drug of choice, a triple soy macchiato. I commandeered my favorite table by the window, sipped from the *Zombies Are People Too* mug the barista had chosen for me, and stared across the street at my studio. A discouragingly small number of students filtered out the front entrance. Hopefully today's class size wasn't an omen for the future.

I waited another fifteen minutes, then drained the dregs from my cup and left for my blissfully empty studio.

Or so I thought.

When I opened the door, I saw Chai, the Power Yoga instructor, sitting at the front desk looking overwhelmed. A crowd of students huddled around her.

This couldn't possibly be good.

All eight women turned toward me in unison.

"Kate, thank goodness you're here. It's injured. You need to do something."

At the word "injured," my stomach dropped to my toes. Yoga—especially the gentle style I taught—was relatively safe, but no physical activity was completely risk-free. A yoga teacher protected her students by designing an intelligent sequence, choosing poses appropriate for the level of the class, and adapting the form of the poses to each individual student.

Likewise, a yoga studio owner protected her business by hiring qualified instructors and purchasing an ironclad liability insurance policy. In the three years Serenity Yoga had been open, I'd never had reason to call my insurance adjuster. I had a feeling that today might be my day. Visions of heart attacks, ambulances, herniated cervical discs, and legal depositions danced through my head. They were doing the hustle.

I slipped—pardon the pun—automatically into damage-control mode. Thought number one: calling a student "it" wasn't the best choice of words, given the circumstances. Thought number two: if a student was hurt, why was everyone hanging around the front desk instead of attending to her? I put on my responsible, take-charge business owner facade and said, "Don't panic. I'll get the first aid kit. Who got hurt, and where is she? Have you called an ambulance?"

Chai gaped at me like I'd just suggested she teach outdoor nude yoga in Iceland.

"An ambulance? For a pigeon?"

Now I was the one confused.

"A pigeon?"

"Yes, the gray pigeon. You know, from the back doorway. Something's wrong with it, and we don't know what to do. He's on the ground by the bottom stair and, from the mess, he's been there awhile. He barely moves when we walk by, and he doesn't fly at all." She picked up the phone. "Should we call building maintenance?"

I took the phone out of her hand and placed it firmly back on the receiver. "Absolutely not." If Alicia's maintenance manager got his hands on the bird, things wouldn't end well for Mister Feathers.

"Well, we can't leave him there. The Kids' Yoga class starts in an hour. We can't let a bunch of five-year-olds find a hurt bird—or worse, a dead bird—on our doorstep. What if one of them touches it?"

Ugh.

Part of me wanted to give in and let the instructor call the maintenance manager. Part of me wanted to ignore the issue and hope that it would somehow magically resolve on its own. Part of me wanted to find a stray alley cat, release it in the stairwell, and let nature take its course. After all, the animal was "just" a pigeon, and one I'd been trying to get rid of at that.

But I couldn't.

I had witnessed way too much death in the past year. I couldn't stand another. Not today. Not on my watch.

"I'll go take a look. He's probably already gone."

I slipped off my shoes and walked through the yoga room, praying that the bird had miraculously recovered. When I cracked open the back door, the gunmetal gray pigeon that had happily roosted above my entrance two days before huddled, looking helpless, on the ground next to the stairs. I quietly closed the door and went back to the desk.

Chai took one look at my face and said, "We have to do something, Kate. He might be suffering."

She was right, of course. Fortunately, I had an idea.

"Go keep an eye on him and make sure no one disturbs him. If maintenance comes, tell them I'm handling it."

Having delegated responsibility for the injured animal squarely onto my shoulders, the students all happily filtered out the front door.

I rummaged around in my purse until I found the flyer that Judith from Precious Life Wildlife Center had given me on Saturday, then picked up the phone and called the number. Judith briskly talked me through a few bird-catching pointers.

"It sounds like he can't fly. If you approach him slowly, he'll likely stay put. Lay a blanket or towel over him to keep him calm, place him in a dark, covered box with plenty of air holes, and bring him to me. I'll help him if I can." She gave me a single warning. "Whatever you do, don't chase him." She recited the address for her center and promised to be ready for Mister Feathers when I arrived.

I armed myself with the essentials and did a pre-fight-or-flight check.

Closable cardboard box with air holes punched along the side. Check.

Towels to line said box and place over injured bird. Check.

Goggles and leather gloves in case injured bird is diseased or decides to attack his would-be rescuer. Hmm ... that was a problem. Sunglasses and rubber dishwashing gloves would have to do. Check.

I slipped my shoes back on, cracked open the door, and quietly eased outside.

Chai didn't look hopeful. "He hasn't moved since you left. Do you need help getting him in the box?"

"No. Go ahead and stay at the front desk. I can handle this."

Famous last words.

Of stupid people.

The small, frail-looking bird still huddled in the corner, feathers ruffled, head down. He looked up warily at my approach.

"Easy there, guy. No one's going to hurt you."

I set the box on the ground, secured my sunglasses, snapped a yellow glove onto each hand, and unfolded the towel. I slowly edged up to the bird and lowered my body into a Full Squat about a foot away from him. I spoke in a low, soft yoga voice.

"Hey there, beautiful. Nice and easy now ... "

I leaned forward, shifted my weight to the balls of my feet, and reached out my arms to drop the towel safely over the bird.

Mister Feathers exploded.

He flapped; he squawked; he jumped; he ran. He spewed feathers in every direction. I let out a loud shriek, instinctively covered my face, and jerked backward, falling squarely on my sitz bones in the day's pile of wet bird droppings.

Well, didn't this give Pigeon Pose a whole new meaning?

I let loose a stream of invectives that should never be uttered within a thousand yards of a yoga studio, ineffectually dabbed at my rear with the towel, and reassessed my options.

Judith's warning taunted me: *Whatever you do, don't chase him.*

Did she have a better idea?

I chased that damned bird around the underground parking lot three times, cursing myself for not insisting that the others help me. I dodged between cars; I crawled underneath them. I begged. I pleaded. I muttered at least twelve dozen pigeon-related expletives.

After fifteen minutes of feathered hide-and-seek, I cornered the animal—literally—between the electrical room and the far end of the garage. Mister Feathers either gave up or was too exhausted to continue the chase, because this time he allowed me to gently lay the towel on top of him. I scooped him up, placed him in the box, secured the lid, and victoriously set it on the passenger seat of my car.

I marched back into the studio to call Judith and let her know we were on our way. Chai gaped at me from behind the desk.

"Kate, your pants. Is that … ?"

"Don't ask."

She tried, unsuccessfully, not to snicker.

I locked myself in the bathroom and cleaned up as best I could. I didn't know how long I'd be wrapped up in the pigeon fiasco, so I wrote a note for the Kids' Yoga teacher telling her I'd be out that afternoon and then left a message on Michael's cell phone asking him to pick up Bella and give me a rain check for dinner. Within five minutes of setting the pigeon-containing box in my Honda, I'd pulled out of the parking garage and headed south to Renton and the animal sanctuary.

Now that I had a moment to find some perspective, I had to admit that the situation could have been worse. Bella could have been in the car with me. She would have taken about twenty-five seconds to devour the entire passenger-seat box and its contents. Then I would have had a dead bird on my conscience. Even worse, I would have needed to guess how much medicine a hundred-pound German shepherd with EPI needed to digest a raw pigeon.

I turned off the radio so the DJ's voice wouldn't frighten the already-traumatized animal. It was awfully quiet in that box. No bumps, no scratches, no coos—nothing. I lightly placed my hand on the box's lid, hoping to sense movement. More nothing.

Please don't let him be dead, I silently prayed.

Thirty long, silent minutes later, I turned right on a gravel road and passed a peeling sign that read *Precious Life Wildlife Center*. A few seconds after that, I pulled up next to an old, beat-up station wagon, turned off the ignition, and frowned.

Could this really be it?

I don't know what I was expecting. A sanitized-looking cement building with a neon-lit emergency entrance? A zoo-like fenced pasture filled with happily grazing deer? Maybe a farm, complete with several outbuildings, each providing sanctuary for a specific kind of creature?

I certainly hadn't expected a small, poorly maintained, single-story house. A handwritten sign was taped near the open garage door: *Bring animals in through the garage. Do not knock before entering.*

Call me crazy, but this place looked less like an animal hospital and more like somebody's home. And a pretty darned dumpy home at that. I glanced left and right as I walked through the dusty garage. It was crowded, not with cars, but with an assortment of dog crates, dirty and clean towels, large sacks of animal food, and clear plastic bags filled with wooden shavings. I lifted my hand to knock on the door, but remembered the sign and stopped. I slowly pushed it open instead.

The room on the other side had likely once been a large family room. Now it was an animal holding facility. A waist-high metal exam table was set up to the right. Cages filled with owls, blue jays, pigeons, crows—even a chicken—were stacked on shelves lining one side of the room. The other side held dog crates containing a raccoon, three rabbits, a possum, and several bald-tailed rats. The animals watched from their cages with bright, interested eyes.

I glanced through a baby-gate-blocked doorway near the exam table. It led to a kitchen and an open living room, complete with couch, end tables, television set, and a worn leather recliner. I strongly suspected that the rehab center and Judith's home were one and the same. Talk about taking your work home with you.

"Hello, is anyone here?" I whispered the words into the empty space so as not to disturb the animals.

Judith appeared, opened the baby gate, and walked through, drying her hands on a dish towel. She reached toward me, palms up. "I'm ready. Where's the bird?"

"I left him out in the car." I swallowed. "Umm … he hasn't moved in a while. I think he might be dead."

She frowned. "It's possible, depending on how badly he was hurt. But they often settle down in the dark. Get him in here and let me take a look at him."

I removed the box from the passenger seat and reverently carried it into the house. Judith set it on a desk near the door, opened it, and pulled out a limp-looking pigeon. She cradled the bird in her arms, softly stroked the tiny feathers along the back of his neck, and murmured a lullaby. The bird turned toward her voice.

"He's alive, but he's scared as tarnation. What'd you do, chase him?"

I exercised my right to remain silent.

Judith *tsk tskd* and whispered under her breath, "Why don't these fools ever listen to me?" She carried Mister Feathers to the exam table. "Let's see what we've got going on here. I'll need you to help me."

After she laid a clean towel on the stainless steel table, she placed the bird on top of it and examined him with brisk yet gentle fingers. I couldn't explain it, but the pigeon seemed to relax underneath the spell of her whispered assurances. "It's okay, baby," she said. "Mommy will take care of you."

She leaned over the table, brought her face close to the bird, and gently palpated his wings. "Neither of his wings are broken. That's good." She checked the feathers along his neck and back. Then she deftly flipped him onto his back and continued her gentle but thorough inspection. After several minutes, she stood up straight, looked at me, and shrugged.

"I'm sorry, I can't find any injuries."

I smiled, feeling unaccountably relieved. "You mean he's okay?"

Her gaze met mine, unflinching. "I don't think so."

Tears threatened my eyes. I reached forward and touched Judith's wrist, taking care not to startle the bird. "Please. Don't give up. Keep looking."

Judith began her head-to-tail-feathers examination again. After what felt like three pigeons' lifetimes, she gestured to me. "Hand me that bottle of rubbing alcohol." She wet a cotton ball and used it to part the feathers on his chest. "Ah, here it is, hidden. I almost missed it." She pointed to an angry-looking red puncture on his breast. "Looks like a hawk got him. See that bruising? The bleeding was internal, into his chest cavity. That's why he can't fly, and that's why the wound was so hard to find. He's lucky he got away."

She gestured for me to come to her side of the table. "Hold him for a minute and don't let him move. Be firm now, but gentle." The bird's heart beat rapidly under my hands, but he seemed significantly calmer than he had been in the parking garage.

"He doesn't seem frightened. Is he in shock?"

Judith looked at me, deadpan. "Nope. He knows I'm trying to help. I'm not acting like some crazy fool chasing him all over the countryside."

I would have assured her that the bird's and my game of hide-and-seek had taken place in an enclosed parking garage, not the country-side, but somehow I didn't think it would win me any brownie points.

Judith rifled through a stack of medications and pulled out two bottles and a syringe.

"What's that?"

"Antibiotics and pain medication. This poor little thing will need both. You did the right thing bringing him here."

I hated to ask, but I needed to know. "Do you think he'll make it?"

"That's up to him and God."

"Does he stand a chance?"

"Of course he does. I've saved birds so mangled that their wings were barely attached. It all depends on whether he makes it through the next couple of days. When my husband gets home tonight and can help, we'll put him under anesthesia, give him some fluids, and clean out the wound. We might put in a couple of stitches. If I were a betting woman, I'd say he'll be all healed up and ready for you to take home before you know it."

"Home? You mean you expect him to live with me?"

"No, of course not. He's a wild bird. But you should release him back where you found him."

I visualized the never-ending supply of bird droppings outside my back door. I hoped Mister Feathers would forgive me if I chose a nice, shady spot in Greenwood Park instead.

Judith put him into a small cage underneath a heat lamp.

"Time to leave him be now. He needs to rest. Come with me and I'll buy you a cup of coffee."

I hated to leave the pigeon, but I suspected she was right. The best thing I could do for him now was to leave him alone. I followed Judith toward the kitchen.

"Do you take cream or—"

A loud squawk interrupted her sentence.

"Oh no you don't!" she yelled. She moved faster and with greater agility than I would have thought possible for a woman of her age and apparent condition. She dove in front of me and snatched a red-tailed hawk off the edge of a rabbit pen.

"That's it, Mr. Hawking. No more freedom for you. If you're feeling good enough to hunt, you need to hang out in your cage."

She carried the bird like a feathered football to the other side of the room and secured him inside a large dog crate. "Looks like this one will be ready for release any time now." She patted the top of the crate. "Until then, it's cage time for you, mister. I've got enough trouble without my patients hunting each other." She continued walking toward the kitchen. Come on now, let's get that coffee."

I followed her through the baby gate and into the kitchen. She pulled two chipped cups off a dish drying rack, filled them with what smelled like coffee-flavored battery acid, and handed one to me. I stared at it uneasily, wondering which would be more hazardous to my health: drinking the foul-looking brew or insulting Judith by abstaining.

Judith's eyes flashed with humor. "Cheers." She took a big swig from her cup.

I took a sip from mine and suppressed a gag.

It tasted worse than it smelled. So bad, in fact, that I would have sworn that my hair follicles shuddered. I ignored the annoying sensation the first time, even the second. By the third, I realized the tickling I felt wasn't caused by the coffee. I reached up to brush what I assumed was an errant feather off my scalp.

My hand collided with something.

Something large.

Something large with a sharp, pointed beak.

"Holy crap!"

I whipped toward the cabinet behind me and came face to face with a monster with the biggest, roundest eyes I'd ever seen.

I screamed.

The monster screamed back.

Judith doubled over and laughed so hard I thought she might wet herself. "Oh my golly, I'm sorry."

Funny, she didn't *look* sorry. In fact, she looked positively giddy.

She wiped the tears from her eyes. "I know I shouldn't laugh, but it's so darned funny. He loves to hide up there and surprise visitors. I should have warned you, but I hate to ruin his fun." She bowed and chivalrously swept her arm toward the pterodactyl-sized bird. "Kate, meet Spook. He's my resident barred owl."

I had a feeling I knew how the bird got his name.

Spook continued to stare, unblinking. He walked to the edge of the cabinet top, bobbed his head toward Judith, and made a hooting noise.

Judith shook her finger. "Not now. You've already had your lunch." She smiled at me. "Go ahead, you can pet him."

I hesitantly reached out my hand and touched Spook's soft feathers. "You let him wander around loose in here?"

"Why not? It's his home."

I looked across the room, toward the windows. "Aren't you afraid he'll fly away?"

She shrugged. "He can't. When he came to me a few years ago, his wing was so mangled that it couldn't be saved. I had to amputate." She pointed across the room. "Same with his buddy over there, only he's a couple of years older." I followed her fingers. A second owl, bigger than the first, perched on the back of the recliner. "These two can't fly, so they'd never survive in the wild. They live here with me."

"They're happy as house pets?"

Judith waved toward the birds. "What do you think?"

They certainly seemed happy to me.

"But I have to correct you. These fellows are not house pets. They are wild birds living in captivity for *educational purposes*." She made finger quotes around the final two words. "Like I told you before, when it comes to the law, verbiage is important. I take those owls to visit grade schools at least twice a year. I even donate their owl pellets." She pointed to a glass jar filled with what looked like small, foil-wrapped baked potatoes.

I picked one up and examined it curiously. "Owl pellets? What are they? Eggs?"

"They're a digestive byproduct." I gave her a blank look. "They're basically the parts of prey that an owl can't digest. Science classes use them for dissection. It teaches kids about the cycle of life."

It suddenly occurred to me that I might well be fingering "pellets" that came out of the wrong end of an owl. I quickly dropped the foil-covered ball back into the jar and wiped my hands on my already-soiled pants.

"I don't understand, Judith. From what you told me at Green Lake, I thought you couldn't keep wild birds or you'd lose your license."

Judith paused as if considering her words carefully. "I said I couldn't keep wild birds as *pets*. And as I just said, these two are not *pets*."

"Oh, right. Educational purposes." I was still confused.

"I'll admit," Judith continued, "it's a gray area of the law, and I work pretty close to the edge sometimes. I try not to break the rules, but I've been known to bend them on occasion." She held up her index finger. "Not that I'll ever admit that in public."

She took another long swig of her coffee and set the mug on the counter. "Birds like these, well, most places would euthanize. But the way I figure it, animals aren't all that much different from humans.

We each get one chance at life. The decision to take that life away should be considered very carefully." She shrugged. "Or at least that's what this old lady thinks."

"Couldn't they go to a zoo or something?"

"Depends on the animal. Sometimes yes. Most times, no."

"Do you keep all the animals you help? If they can't be returned to the wild, I mean?"

"Heavens no, child. I'd be shut down for sure. I only keep a few very special ones, like Spook here. Besides, domestication doesn't work for all wildlife. Some could never get used to being around people. Pigeons, ducks, this owl here—for them, it's pretty easy. All I have to do is figure out how to get around the legal bureaucrats. Birds like kingfishers would be miserable. In their case, if they can't be returned to the wild, euthanasia is the only humane option. So far, I've been lucky with Spook and his buddy. The state looks the other way as long as no one complains and I don't take government funding."

"Government funding?"

"Yes, most rehab centers—most animal shelters, for that matter— operate using grants. But those come with mighty big strings attached."

"Like what?"

Judith took my mug and set it next to hers on the counter. "Follow me." She continued her monologue as we walked. "You think I *want* to work out of my garage like some hoarding hobo? I can't afford anything else. I've practically bankrupted my husband and me."

She pointed at the varied inhabitants of the dog crates, glass enclosures, and cages. "See all these animals? Your pigeon, that squirrel, that rat, those baby bunnies? If I followed the restrictions of the government bureaucrats, not one of them would be alive. To them, those fellows are all nuisance animals—not worth saving. If I took their precious money, no matter how little, I'd have to euthanize every one of them, whether they could be saved or not."

She scowled. "So I do my best to drum up donations, and my seventy-eight-year-old husband works a day job to pay for the rest. I decided a long time ago that those navy-suited numbskulls could take their government grants and shove them up their white skinny behinds. I will not euthanize a healthy animal without a danged good reason."

Judith crossed her arms. "And that's what I told that protester who got herself killed, too. Comin' around here threatening to close me down." She mumbled under her breath. "Over my dead body."

My skin prickled. Over Judith's dead body, or someone else's?

"Wait a minute," I said. "Raven was here?"

Judith swiped her hand through the air as if shooing away an invisible horsefly. "Whatever her name was. The one in the paper. She showed up here Saturday afternoon after the fun walk, dragging along that pale-skinned vampire girl."

"How did she know where to find you? The address on your pamphlet is a PO Box."

"You're right. I don't publish my address. That's how I keep the crazies away. That no-good PETA wannabe tricked me. She called here claiming that she found an injured possum. I gave the lying sack of owl pellets my address and told her to bring him on by." Judith wrinkled her lips. "She and little Miss Vampira barged into my house, took one look at my owls, and started hollering that I was abusing them. She said she was going to make sure they were put down for their own good."

Spook hooted loudly from the kitchen, as if he understood and was offended by the statement. "She could have caused me some real trouble," Judith went on. "If someone else hadn't killed her, I might've done it myself." She pointed with her thumb to the corner.

"I picked up that broom over there and swatted her with it. I told her to get the heck off my property before I rang her scrawny neck."

I took a step back, horrified.

Judith laughed. "Oh honey, wipe that look off your face. I'm seventy-five. I say what I think. Keeping crap like that in—that's what gives you cancer. I already told you. I don't kill anyone unless they're suffering. Not even if they deserve it."

She held up her swollen-jointed hands and rotated them back and forth. "Besides, look at these claws. You think they're capable of strangling someone?"

Strangling, no. But holding someone—especially someone already weakened by a blow to the head—under water?

Maybe.

After all, she'd moved deceptively fast when cornering that hawk.

I wanted to ask her a thousand more questions. Like *Exactly how much trouble could Raven have caused for you?* Maybe *How far would you go to protect these animals?* Oh, and this one for sure: *Where were you on Saturday night, anyway?*

I idly considered transporting her to the King County Jail for a nice cozy chat with Officer Chuckles, but I didn't get the chance. A car pulled into the driveway, and few seconds later, an older, equally stooped-over man walked through the front door.

"Hey sweetie. You done spending my day's earnings yet?"

Judith gave the elderly gentleman a peck on the cheek. "Not yet. We've got pigeon surgery to do." She turned to me. "Kate, it's been nice talking to you, but it's time for you to go now so we can get to helping that bird of yours. Give me a call in a couple of days, and I'll let you know how he's doing."

She ushered me out the door and clicked the deadbolt solidly between us.

FOURTEEN

I battled I-5 and Mariners game-day traffic for over sixty minutes on the drive home. Sixty minutes in which I struggled to reconcile my conflicting feelings about Judith. I liked Judith. I didn't want her to be the killer. But I had to admit: if Bella's life were at stake, I might take extreme measures. Drowning the threat in Bella's favorite swimming hole wouldn't be my first option, but who knew what I'd be capable of, given sufficient provocation? Bella had risked her life to save mine in the past. Did I owe her any less?

Michael's Explorer wasn't parked in the driveway when I arrived home at six-thirty. Hopefully he'd gotten my message and was off cavorting with Bella somewhere, not grumpily waiting for me at PhinneyWood Pizza. I popped open the trunk and grabbed Dharma's suitcase. It seemed like a hundred years had passed since I'd visited her motel room that morning. I trudged to the kitchen door, cursed the construction workers for trampling my tulips, and inserted the key in the lock. It turned easily.

Too easily.

Those blasted contractors! They'd left the house unlocked—again. I whispered contractor-related expletives under my breath and pressed the door open.

To a disaster.

Michael had truly outdone himself.

Debris littered every square inch of the kitchen, and only part of it was the contractors' doing. Our one remaining cabinet hung open, and the towels normally stored inside were tossed in a pile on the floor. Clean and dirty dishes lived in unsegregated harmony all over the countertops, and a half-eaten apple lay on the floor next to the garbage can. My sacred Bella food-preparation area was covered with sawdust, power tools, and scattered dog food, and my special tried-and-true measuring cups were strewn across the floor. A five-pound bag of flour lay open and on its side next to the sink. Michael must have been planning to cook something, though what, how, and why, without benefit of a working oven, was a mystery to me.

I pressed through the plastic covering the doorway. The living room hadn't fared much better. Throw pillows and couch cushions decorated the floor. The storage boxes for the displaced items from the kitchen, bathroom, and office were empty, their contents piled haphazardly next to them. How one man could do so much damage in a single day was truly beyond comprehension.

I set Dharma's suitcase on the floor and took several deep breaths, trying to calm myself. I didn't want to lose my temper anymore. I wanted to learn how to control it. I *needed* to learn how to control it. I took a deep breath and prepared to practice Pratipaksa Bhavanam, a meditation sometimes referred to as "replacing with the opposites."

In other words, I would try to replace my current impulse to wring Michael's neck with something …

Well, something less violent.

That was the best I could hope for in this particular moment.

I rearranged the couch cushions, sat down, closed my eyes, and imagined that I was the sweet and understanding girlfriend I wanted to be. In my mind's eye, perfect, fictional Kate greeted Michael at the door, not with frustration, but with love and acceptance.

As I'd been taught, I utilized multiple senses to make the visualization as vibrant and detailed as possible. I imagined my breath becoming long, slow, and rhythmic. Tension oozed from my muscles like butter melting on a hot August afternoon. I inhaled Michael's clean, soapy scent and felt my face melt into a smile. I tasted his moist, salty kiss. In my mind, I reached my arms up over Michael shoulders and . . .

Wrapped my fingers around his throat.

No matter how often my mind played out the scenario, it always ended the same. With me shaking Michael until his head almost popped off. Somehow I didn't think this was what the ancient teachers had in mind.

I gave up and poured myself a glass of Merlot.

I loved the man, truly I did. I wanted to spend the rest of my life with him. But his slovenliness was rapidly becoming the stuff of legends. The only way Michael's and my cohabitation would end in anything other than violence was if this home renovation project got finished, and soon. Then I could reclaim my bathroom and ban Michael from ever stepping foot inside it. I needed one peaceful place where I could retreat from the wreckage.

I heard the back door open, followed by a sharp bark and the telltale sound of Bella's claws scrambling against linoleum. Michael's voice echoed from the kitchen.

"Bella, stop!"

Bella crashed through the plastic into the living room, dragging her leash behind her. The wiry hair along her spine stood on end like a porcupine's quills. She charged up to the first empty box, let out a single, high-pitched bark, and attacked, sinking her teeth into the cardboard and ripping out a large chunk. First box destroyed, she moved on to the next.

And the next.

What had gotten into her?

These weren't the first boxes that my overly territorial German shepherd had destroyed. Bella attacked every package delivered by her nemesis, the brown-suited psycho killer who drove the UPS truck. But until today, her box-biting behavior hadn't included items already inside the house.

"Bella!" I admonished. "What is wrong with you? Stop that!"

Bella whipped toward my voice and gave me a look that clearly said, *Don't worry, I'm on it.* She gave three quick air-sniffs and roared up the stairs to the master bedroom.

Michael pushed through the plastic carrying a large, steaming pizza box. The delicious aromas of garlic, hot cheese, and tomatoes wafted around him.

"What on earth happened here?"

I opened my mouth to scold him, but before I could utter a single reprimand, I got a good look at his face. Michael's expression wasn't guilty; it was horrified.

I gestured at the upended boxes surrounding me. "Wait a minute. You mean you didn't do this?"

Michael's eyes widened; his lips turned down. He held the pizza box close to his chest. "Of course I didn't do this. Jeez, Kate, I'm not *that* messy. We've been burglarized."

I took in the room with new eyes. He was right, of course, but how was I supposed to know? When you shared your home with a living poltergeist, it was hard to tell the difference sometimes.

Michael set down the pizza box, picked up an umbrella, and gripped the handle in his fists like a baseball bat. I swore I could smell the testosterone oozing from his pores. "Kate," he ordered, "go outside. Lock yourself in your car where it's safe and call the police. I'll make sure the house is clear."

I pointed to the umbrella. "What are you going to do if you find someone? Poke him in the eye? Threaten to open it and curse him with seven years of bad luck?"

Michael didn't answer. He was too busy stomping around the room, looking for someone to bludgeon. I briefly considered handing him a box he could bite, but Bella had already destroyed most of them. I tried reasoning with him instead.

"I'm not hiding in the car. Believe me, Michael, whoever broke in here is long gone. Otherwise, Bella would already have cornered him somewhere."

As if on cue, Bella trotted back down the stairs, muscles rigid, tail pointing straight up on high alert. She pranced on her toes and grumbled under her breath, as if offended that she'd been cheated out of her first bite of burglar.

Michael's grumble wasn't much sweeter. "Fine then, but keep Bella close and call the police."

I grabbed Bella's leash and the two of us followed Michael around the house to assess the damage. The upstairs and what was left of my office were all similarly trashed.

"What were they looking for?" I said to no one in particular.

Michael and Bella both answered by growling unintelligibly.

I locked Bella in the bathroom when the police officer arrived a half-hour later. She serenaded him by snarling, barking, and scratching at the door. He alternated between taking notes and glancing apprehensively over his shoulder.

"Is she always that aggressive?"

Bella answered by sniffing under the door, clearly trying to memorize the officer's scent so she could hunt him down later.

"Sorry, she's a little worked up," I said. "She takes her guard-dog job pretty seriously, but she's not as ferocious as she seems." I flashed him a tepid smile. "She's never actually eaten anyone."

The officer didn't look amused. "I don't want to be the first. Make sure no one opens that door until I'm in my car." He scooted farther away from the bathroom. "Better yet, give me five minutes to get out of the neighborhood." He shuddered, then glanced down at his notepad. "Back to the burglary. You said the workmen have left the door open before?"

"Several times, even after I called and read them the riot act," I replied. "They promised that they would be more careful."

The officer tapped his pen against a notepad. "If the door was left open, you were an easy target. It was likely kids, looking for drug money or playing a prank. You're sure nothing was taken?"

"I don't think so. At least, nothing I can see so far. We don't have much to steal, but I'm surprised they didn't take my computer."

"Unless it's a laptop, they usually don't. Kids take electronics that are portable and easy to sell—things they can hock for quick cash."

"Well, if they were looking for money, they came to the wrong place. We've given all of ours to irresponsible construction workers."

"I'll file a report, but honestly, unless something easily identifiable is taken, break-ins like this are almost never solved." The officer stood up. "Let me know if you find anything missing, and from now on, lock your door." He glanced toward the bathroom. Bella was still snarling inside it, doing her best impersonation of a rabid wolverine. "Taping a photo of that dog to the front of the door wouldn't hurt, either."

Thirty minutes later, Michael and I sat on our reassembled couch, eating cold pizza. Bella ignored the gruel in her bowl and lay at Michael's feet, begging for morsels. He tossed her a piece of crust.

"Stop feeding her pizza," I snapped. "She hasn't eaten her food, and it has her medicine in it. She doesn't have enough enzymes in her system to digest all that crust."

Michael frowned. "You act like I don't already know that. I gave her one bite." He made eye contact with Bella and pointed at her food bowl. "No more treats until you eat your dinner."

Bella—who understood a remarkable amount of English—stood up, padded to her bowl, and began slurping down her premedicated food.

"See," Michael said. "There's a method to my madness."

"You're right. I'm sorry for snapping at you. I'm just tired." I sighed. "What a day."

I poured another glass of Merlot, took a sip, then added the rest of the bottle. "Hey, did you get a chance to call Sally?"

"Yes, but Maggie got to her first. She wouldn't talk to me. Evidently you and I are no longer welcome to visit DogMa or speak to any of their employees."

"I'm sorry, Michael." I took another deep drink of coppery-tasting tranquilizer.

"Isn't that your third glass of wine?"

"Maybe." He was counting now?

He looked at the half-eaten slice of pizza on my plate.

"You're not eating?"

"Sorry, I'm not feeling very well." I touched my belly. "I'm a little nauseated, probably from all of the stress. Dharma, the wake, the pigeon ... not to mention the break-in. Food doesn't sound all that appealing."

Michael set his plate down and turned to face me. "It's not just today, Kate. You haven't been eating for weeks, long before Dharma came onto the scene. I know you wanted to lose some weight, so I haven't said anything, but I'm starting to get worried. You've been acting like Rene did on Orcas, right before she told us she was ... " His face turned white. He snatched the wine glass from my hands.

"Kate ... you're not ... you know ... preg—"

I recoiled as if I'd been scalded. "No! Lord no! Of course not!" I scanned the room, searching for an uncluttered piece of wood to knock on. "Don't even joke about that!"

Michael's face sagged in an odd-looking combination of relief and disappointment. "Good, I guess." He stood and walked to the window. When he turned around, his eyes refused to meet mine. "Would having a baby with me really be all that terrible?"

I joined him at the window and took his hands. "Of course not, Michael. You'd be a great father. But not now. You know we're not ready." I gestured toward the ruins of the kitchen. "Can you honestly imagine bringing another life into this fiasco?"

Michael's lips lifted, but the rest of his face remained worried. "No, probably not. But are kids completely out of the question for us? In the future, I mean."

I stalled for time by feeding Bella a bite of my pizza. A year ago, I would have responded instinctively. The mere mention of children would have sent me bolting out the door, even of my own house. But a year ago, I didn't know Michael.

"No, Michael, children are definitely not out of the question, but I'm not ready yet."

The color returned to his face. "Honestly, neither am I. But maybe in a year or two ..." He looked back toward the construction zone. "Do you think we should expand the remodel to add on an extra bedroom, just in case?"

The phone rang, interrupting Michael's thoughts. Proof positive that there actually *was* a benevolent being out there who loved me. Whoever he was, I owed him one.

I answered the phone, then handed it to Michael. "It's your sister."

"Hey Shan, what's up?" Michael froze. His complexion turned gray. "How serious is it?"

I set down my wine glass. "Michael, what's wrong?"

He held up his hand and turned his back to me, clearly asking me to give him a minute. I moved to the couch, huddled next to Bella, and drew comfort by stroking her warm, soft fur. Whatever Michael was discussing with his sister, it was serious.

After a few minutes, he slowly placed the phone back on the receiver. When he turned toward me, his eyes were wet.

"My dad was in a car accident. They're airlifting him to Portland for surgery right now. It doesn't look good."

FIFTEEN

"Michael, go. Your family needs you. If your dad dies and you're not there, you'll never forgive yourself." Unfortunately, my words weren't hyperbole. I spoke from experience.

Michael's eyes shifted from me, to the door, and back again. "I can't go, Kate. I can't leave you here alone. You're tracking a killer and someone broke into our home. It's not safe." He grabbed my hand. "Come to Portland with me."

"I wish I could, but I need to stay in Seattle. If I miss Dharma's visiting hours on Thursday, they won't let me see her again until next week."

"So? Let Dale talk to her. He can fill you in."

"I need to speak with Dharma personally. Dale's great at his job, but I'm the closest thing she's got to a friend right now. I can't let her think I abandoned her." I flashed Michael an insincere smile. "I'll be fine. What happened here today wasn't even a break-in. It was a walk-in, most likely committed by some kids who thought it would be fun to trash a house. All because an idiotic construction worker never learned how to lock a door."

"Maybe, but what if we're wrong?"

"You heard the police officer. Burglars almost never hit the same house a second time. I'm safer now than I ever was." I laid my palm on Bella's back. "Besides, I won't be alone. I'll have Bella."

Michael looked unconvinced.

I grabbed his keys off of the end table and tossed them to him. "Seriously. Go. Portland is only three hours away. If I need anything, I'll call."

It took some convincing, but I eventually prevailed. Michael threw a few items into an overnight bag and headed off for Portland twenty minutes later. Bella pawed at the door and whined, as if asking him to return, or at the very least come back and invite her to go along. I rubbed the soft spot behind her ears.

"Sorry, babe, it's just you and me, like old times." I knelt in front of her and touched my nose to hers. "We girls will be fine on our own, won't we?" Bella replied by covering my face in wet, warm German shepherd kisses.

To be honest, I selfishly wanted Michael to walk back through the door, too. The house felt achingly empty without him, especially considering he'd been gone less than five minutes. What a difference a few months had made. Before Michael moved in, I'd relished the sacred girls' nights I spent home alone with Bella. Now being here without Michael simply felt lonely. I didn't look forward to sleeping next to his cold, empty side of the bed.

I considered draining my wine glass, but somehow being alone and drunk seemed more desolate than being alone and sober. I picked up my still-full glass and poured the liquid down the guest bathroom sink.

I looked at my watch. Nine o'clock. It was too early for bed, and I wouldn't sleep well until Michael gave me an update on his family, anyway. I paced around the house, looking for something that would focus my fractured attention. Bella followed close behind, unwilling to lose sight of her one remaining human.

I started by calling Dale. The news wasn't good. As expected, Dharma had been denied bail and Dale hadn't unearthed any new evidence in her favor. Even worse, he planned to go back to Orcas on Friday and continue working the case from there. He warned me that with the current evidence, pushing for a speedy trial would not be in Dharma's best interests. Unless something changed dramatically, she'd spend the next year in jail, waiting for her case to go to trial. I didn't want to think about how long she'd be stuck there if she was found guilty.

I filled Dale in on everything Michael and I had learned that day about Raven, Maggie, and HEAT. He, in return, shared a list of topics I wasn't allowed to discuss when I visited Dharma at the jail. The list was significantly longer than I'd expected: I couldn't ask her about her fight with Raven, her involvement with HEAT, what she'd done the night of the murder, or anything else that could potentially implicate her in a crime.

Way to hamstring a girl, Dale.

I was, however, allowed to ask Dharma about her past *before* she met Raven, as long as nothing in that past would incriminate her. Our meeting wouldn't tell me much about the murder, but I might learn a little about myself.

I hung up the phone feeling even more restless. Bella was busy scrounging the floor for microscopic pizza crumbs, so I decided to clean up the mess in the kitchen.

It was a valiant effort.

All ten minutes of it.

I gave up halfway through refolding the towels. Each item I put away made me feel further away from Michael.

If we were going to be apart, I might as well take advantage of the alone time.

I poured a bath, lowered my body into the hot, lavender-scented water, and leaned my head against an inflatable pillow. Instead of relaxing me, the steaming water had exactly the opposite effect. I felt trapped, hot, stymied. The bubbles seemed to mock me with an iridescent sneer. *This is the best you can do, Girl Detective?*

So much for that idea.

I drained the tub, put on Michael's bathrobe, and called Rene. Her phone went straight to voicemail.

Bella rested her head on her paws and let out a heavy sigh.

"You're one to complain. Got any better ideas?"

She sat up and cocked her head to the side, as if considering our options. Then she groaned and flopped on her side.

"That's it? That's the best you've got?" I continued speaking out loud to fill the echoing quiet. "Rene always comes up with creative ways to get us in trouble. What would she do?"

Four words bubbled up from my subconscious.

Snoop through Dharma's suitcase.

Of course Rene would encourage me to snoop. She was genetically incapable of exercising good manners. In this case, however, she might be right. I hadn't taken time to thoroughly look through Dharma's belongings at the motel. What if I'd missed an important clue?

I patted the side of my leg. "Come on, Bella, we're going downstairs."

Guilt tickled the base of my sternum. I couldn't cite a specific verse, but I was pretty sure that *The Yoga Sutras* frowned on rifling through someone else's possessions.

Not that I planned to let that stop me.

Looking for evidence to clear your mother of murder had to be some sort of exception, right? Besides, Dharma might not have *explicitly* given me permission to look through her belongings, but she didn't expressly forbid it, either. How could I know for sure that the suitcase didn't contain anything relevant unless I actually looked?

I pushed Michael's cardboard boxes to the side, laid the ratty blue suitcase on the sofa, and kneeled in front of it. First I ran my hands through the outside pockets. Empty. I opened the lid and removed the items I'd packed earlier, mentally reciting a running inventory. *Baby blue blouse, T-shirts, black tennis shoes, jeans, black pants, extra-large sleep shirt.* I set the clothing to the side and continued with the smaller items. *Socks and underwear, yellow flowered makeup bag, red plastic case*—I opened it up—*clear dental night guard.*

Bella sniffed the new plastic chew toy. "Leave it," I said absently.

I examined each piece of clothing in painstaking detail. I read every tag, felt along every seam, and turned every pocket inside out. I opened Dharma's makeup bag and sniffed every jar of organic cosmetics. I tried out her face cream. I felt inside the toes of her tennis shoes. There were no secret notes, no telltale receipts. Not even a stray stick of chewing gum. Nothing that shed light on the enigma who birthed me. Nothing, for that matter, that told me anything about the crime for which she was incarcerated.

Twenty minutes later, a single item remained—the one I'd been dying to examine all day. I pulled out the antique wooden box and traced my fingers across the faded daisies that decorated its top. Compared to the items I'd already examined, this old wooden box felt precious. If the lock was any indication, it contained items that weren't simply *important* to Dharma, but also deeply private.

Bummer.

No matter how much I wanted to know what lay inside the tiny treasure chest, I couldn't justify breaking into it. I placed the box back in the suitcase and started carefully refolding Dharma's clothes.

Then again . . .

Didn't most spiritual belief systems—yoga included—posit that there were no true accidents? Didn't the teachings tell us that life gave us experiences—both good and bad—so that we could grow from them? The universe had clearly sent me Dharma's box. The universe trusted me with it. The universe *wanted* me to open it.

Or at least that's the lie I told myself.

I dropped the blouse I was folding and picked the box up again. The lock on the front was tiny, more a symbol of security than an actual deterrent. I could easily pick it, if I wanted to.

And man, did I want to.

Sorry, Dharma. But you had to have known that I would be curious.

I carried the box into the not-yet-dismantled part of the office, tossed Bella one of Dale's goat-shaped dog cookies, and rifled through the top desk drawer until I found Michael's set of tiny computer screwdrivers. I pulled out the tiniest, poked the end into the keyhole, and moved it around until I heard a soft click.

I slipped the miniature padlock out of the loop, closed my eyes, and took a deep breath.

"What you think, Puppy Girl. Should I do it?"

I took Bella's silence to mean yes.

I must have suspected what I would find inside, but I could never have anticipated its impact. My throat ached; my eyes burned. For a moment, I thought my heart might stop beating.

Dharma's box contained dozens of items, most of which were related to me. Photographs, drawings, cards, printouts, letters. Some of the objects were shockingly familiar. Others seemed like mementos from the life of a completely different Kate, raised in an alternate universe. On the very top was an old, fading picture of Dharma, my father, and a brown-haired toddler that had to be me. Assembled in date order underneath it was an assortment of items ranging from crayon drawings I'd created as a child to poems I'd written as a teenager.

Behind that were printouts of several articles that had obviously been scavenged from the Internet: Dad's obituary, a puff piece about the grand opening of Serenity Yoga, even that god-awful *Dollars for Change* article written about Bella's and my escapades last year.

The very bottom of the box contained over a dozen rubber-banded-together letters, each addressed to Dharma in my father's handwriting. The mailing addresses varied—from India, to Africa, to Central America, to Peru. Many of the letters had been forwarded multiple times.

Dad had written the first when I was four. I had few memories of that year, but I could feel the pride in his words:

Kate is turning into an animal nut like you. She made me plant extra lettuce so the snails wouldn't go hungry. She gathers the blasted things from the neighbors and transports them to our yard. Needless to say, we don't have much of a garden this year.

I smiled. I still planted extra lettuce for the snails each spring.

Every day, I see more of you in Kate's eyes. Stubborn, willful, sweet, and sensitive. I have a feeling she'll grow up to be a lot like you. The first few months were hard, but she's happier now. More stable. The nightmares are lessening.

I stopped reading and shuddered. The nightmares. I'd almost forgotten about the nightmares.

Most people called the visions I'd experienced as a child lucid dreams. I called them torture. Horrible episodes in which I knew I was dreaming but couldn't wake myself up. I understood that the images tormenting me weren't real, but somehow that made them even more terrifying.

I picked up the letter and read to the end.

Daisy, I'm sorry for hurting you. Our arrangement might not seem fair, but after what happened, Kate's well-being has to be my priority. Thank you for honoring my decision. I will always love you.

His decision? Decision about what? Their marriage? Their divorce? Me?

I folded the page and placed it back in the envelope, feeling surprisingly ambivalent. I longed to read the rest of Dad's letters, but I dreaded it, too. Each handwritten paper promised to teach me not only about my mother, but also about myself. Each contained information that might explain why Dharma left me. Each held within it the potential to break my heart.

Bella whined, clearly sensing my discomfort.

"It's okay, girl."

Was it?

I wouldn't know until I finished perusing the rest of the letters. I opened the box of ostrich tendons Michael had special-ordered for Bella and pulled out the biggest one I could find. It might be a long night.

"Come on, girl. Let's go settle in the living room."

Bella pranced behind me and nudged my hand.

I removed Dharma's suitcase from the sofa, sat down, and patted the space next to me. "Bella, up!"

She jumped on the couch, turned a quick circle, and flopped down beside me.

I didn't normally encourage Bella to eat on the furniture, but tonight's circumstances were special. I curled my feet underneath her warm belly and relaxed into the rhythm of her delighted chewing.

I thumbed through the rest of the letters, trying to get a sense of their energy. All I felt was my own trepidation, at least until I pulled out the final envelope.

Then I felt dread.

The unopened envelope was addressed to me. And it was from Dharma. Her name was written above the return address.

A thick red slash bisected the envelope's front. The words *No longer at this address* were written above it in Dad's unmistakable handwriting.

Liar.

Dad had lived at this address my entire childhood, until he died and I inherited the house from him. The returned letter was his version of a no-contact order. One that Dharma had obviously obeyed.

I set the sealed envelope aside to read last and tackled the rest of Dad's letters in chronological order. With each abbreviated story, I cycled through multiple emotions: surprise, grief, remorse, loss, nostalgia. Ninety minutes and a thousand unanswered questions later, I curled up on the couch and fell into a troubled sleep.

———

I rode the elevator upstairs to the King County Jail's visiting room, weighted down by a deep sense of dread. The disconsolate people around me all faced outward, slumping toward the elevator's walls like the gray-brown petals of a dying daisy.

One by one, they turned to face me.

And laughed.

The cruelly guffawing faces of Dharma and my father, Eduardo and Goth Girl, Maggie and Sally, Dale and Judith all swirled around me, as if I were trapped in the center of a derisive, carnival-like merry-go-round. The elevator door opened and I looked down at my suddenly bare feet. Officer Chuckles pointed at my blood-burgundy toenails and ordered in a deep, booming voice, "Shoes must be worn at all times."

I opened my mouth to explain that being barefoot wasn't my fault—that my shoes had mysteriously disappeared—but my world dissolved into darkness. I wasn't blind, but I couldn't see, either. My eyelids refused to open. The stench of disinfected hopelessness burned my sinuses. I tried to pry my eyelids open with my fingers, but they were too heavy. I stumbled out of the elevator and thrust my hands forward, searching for walls, a doorway, anything.

I bumped into stranger after mocking stranger until I found a cold cement wall. I leaned my back against it, covered my face with my arms, and sank to the floor.

My own disembodied voice echoed across the emptiness. *Kate, you're dreaming.*

I knew that already, but the insight was useless. I still couldn't stop it: my first lucid nightmare in well over a decade.

You're dreaming. You have to wake up.

"I can't," I sobbed.

Yes, you can.

I crawled sideways until I found a corner in which I could cower. A place where nothing could attack me from behind.

Wake yourself up.

It had never worked before, but I had to try.

"Wake up!" I yelled. "Wake up!"

I shouted the words over and over and over again, but they didn't penetrate my consciousness. I tried pinching myself, but I couldn't feel it. I jumped up and down. I counted backwards from one hundred to one. Nothing worked.

The walls behind me dissolved and I heard footsteps. It was happening again, exactly like it had when I was child. Someone was coming. Coming for me.

"Wake up!" I sobbed.

My disembodied voice spoke again.

You don't have to do this alone anymore. You have Bella. Ask her to help you.

It was worth a try. Bella had saved me before.

Dream-me stood up, tensed every muscle, and bellowed in a voice louder than I'd ever used in real life. "Bella!"

My still-asleep form moaned. It was working!

"Bella!" I yelled again.

A cold, wet nose nudged my face and jolted me awake. I sat bolt upright, wrapped my arms around my dog, and sobbed into her warm fur. "It's okay, girl. It's okay. It was only a dream." I said the words to soothe myself much more than her.

I took several deep, long breaths and tried to slow down my pounding heart. "Good job, Bella. Gooooood girl."

Bella whined and licked my face. I hugged her back and covered her muzzle in kisses.

No doubt about it. Reading Dharma's letter right before falling asleep hadn't been such a great idea.

At least this time my dream's symbolism was obvious.

What was it that I couldn't open my eyes to see?

I didn't understand everything I'd read before falling asleep. Frankly, I wasn't sure I wanted to. But now that I'd opened Dharma's Box, so to speak, that which had escaped could not be put back. My subconscious was obviously telling me something that I didn't want to hear. Only one question remained: was it about Dharma or about me?

I placed my feet flat on the floor. Whatever it was, I wouldn't be sleeping the rest of the night. I stood up, gave Bella a well-deserved chew toy, and moved to the office. It was time to learn more about this stranger who called herself my mother.

I might not have Michael's genius computer skills, but even I could type a few words into a search engine.

I started by trying to answer Dale's question: What was Dharma hiding about her involvement with HEAT?

HEAT didn't have much of a website, but they had a reasonable blog. The first entry had been posted two years ago and highlighted the squalid conditions of factory chicken farms. Raven and four other women—all wearing the orange-flamed black T-shirts I'd seen on Saturday—were pictured.

Subsequent blog posts were inconsistent: sometimes once a month, other times more frequent. They covered a variety of animal rights issues, ranging from primate research at a state-run university to the slaughter of wolves in the Rocky Mountains. All pretty horrifying, but unfortunately not all that surprising.

As time went on, the number of black-clad people in the photographs grew. From four or five individuals to the two dozen people we'd seen at Green Lake on Saturday. Eduardo and Goth Girl started showing up in pictures starting nine months ago; Dharma, a few weeks later. I didn't see any references to DogMa or the supposed slavery of pet ownership.

I continued scanning the web. HEAT was mentioned in several articles, primarily ones written by Raven or other members of her organization. Nothing struck me as out of the ordinary. HEAT appeared to be making more of a ripple than a splash in the animal rights world.

The cursor blinked at me accusingly.

Come on, Kate. Stop procrastinating. You know what you're really looking for. What have you refused to see?

Dharma.

I knew nothing about Dharma. At least nothing I hadn't created and embellished in my childhood imagination. As a child, I'd convinced myself that she was out in the Congo or someplace equally exotic, trying to do good for the world. For all I knew, she was really a Sacramento-based ax murderer.

It was time to find out.

I typed in every permutation of Dharma's first and last names: Dharma, Daisy, Davidson, and Carmichael. I tried adding Sacramento and the phrase "animal activist." I got plenty of hits, none of them useful. Not even a relevant Facebook page or Twitter profile. I leaned back and drummed my fingers on the desktop.

Think, Kate.

Everyone left an online trail, no matter how hard they tried not to. I simply had to figure out how to unearth it. I didn't know much about Dharma, but surely I had some relevant piece of information.

I closed my eyes and replayed our visit at the King County Jail. Dharma had talked about her cellmate. She complained about the food. She compared her current cell to the one she'd been incarcerated in while visiting Juarez.

My eyes flew open.

Dharma had been arrested in Mexico.

It was a start.

I typed in the words "animal activist," "arrest," and "Juarez." The search engine returned several pages of hits, including an article published almost a year ago in an El Paso, Texas, newspaper. The article profiled a group of animal rights activists that had been jailed for six weeks in Juarez after protesting the city's mass euthanasia of street dogs. It included a photo of the protesters.

I squinted my eyes and leaned closer to the screen. Dharma was pictured in the second row.

Eduardo stood next to her.

Dharma and Eduardo were together in Texas? Before HEAT? I kept searching.

I added the name "Eduardo" to my search terms, but I didn't find anything relevant, so I went back to the El Paso news site and scanned for articles written around the same time period. A headline two weeks after the Juarez article made my mouth go dry.

Homeless Woman Dies in Fourth Suspected Arson

Police in El Paso are investigating the death of a homeless woman who died last night of apparent smoke inhalation. Investigators believe the woman had been sleeping in an abandoned building on Sugartree Avenue when the structure caught fire. The blaze initially started in a dumpster, but quickly spread to the adjacent structure. The fatal fire is the fourth suspected dumpster arson this summer. Thus far, no suspects have been identified.

A string of dumpster fires? Like the fire at Green Lake?

I continued scanning the paper's archives. The suspicious fires stopped after the homeless woman's death. After a few weeks, articles about the investigation became intermittent. After a few months, they disappeared. No arrests were mentioned. I assumed that meant the police never caught the arsonist.

Dream or no dream, I suddenly wished that I'd kept my eyes closed.

I turned away from the screen and stared at the wall, as if the newly installed sheetrock would provide a clean slate on which I could create a different, more palatable, answer.

Dumpster fires weren't all that rare, but they weren't common, either, and I doubted that serial arsonists kicked the habit any more often than serial killers did. If the fires stopped, it was for one of four reasons: the arsonist died, he got caught, he became better at hiding his crimes, or he moved to another jurisdiction.

Like California. With the occasional road trip to Seattle.

My stomach churned. Eduardo was marching with HEAT when the Green Lake fire broke out, but Dharma wasn't. She could easily have started it.

Could Dharma have set the fires in El Paso, too? She certainly had means and opportunity. As for motive, I hadn't rubbed match sticks with many firebugs—at least not that I knew of—but wasn't fire-starting a compulsion for pyromaniacs?

I stood up and started pacing. This was all supposition, of course, and Dharma as a pyromaniac seemed like a stretch. Still, if *I* had figured out that she was living in El Paso at the time of the fires, Raven might have, too. And even if Dharma hadn't set the fatal fire, she or Eduardo might know who did. That would make them accessories after the fact. Either way, I realized, the homeless woman's death might be a secret worth killing for.

I sat back down at the computer and resumed typing, determined that the next time I confronted Dharma, I would be armed with irrefutable information. Dharma would never fool me again.

Or so I thought.

SIXTEEN

MICHAEL CALLED AT EIGHT the next morning. His father had survived surgery but was still in critical condition. His doctors said that if he made it through the next forty-eight hours, he would likely survive.

If.

I didn't tell Michael about my late-night Internet discoveries. I certainly didn't tell him what I'd read in Dad's letters. In my defense, I wasn't hiding information for my own benefit this time. In fact, I wanted—even needed—to talk it all through, and the person I most wanted to talk with was Michael. But he was already under enough stress. Adding mine might tip him past the breaking point. I'd have to wait and share my burden with Rene after Prenatal Yoga.

In the meantime I fed Bella, loaded her into the car, and drove to Serenity Yoga.

I parked Bella's mobile home in the covered garage and filled her water dish. Today's projected high wouldn't hit sixty, and the garage would be several degrees colder. Still, I cracked the windows an inch and partially opened the sunroof. I finished our normal routine by giving her a few chest scratches.

"I'll come get you for a walk after I meet with Alicia."

Bella ignored me. She was officially on duty, guarding the garage against evil intruders. I took off her leash, tossed it on the passenger seat, and headed for the studio. By the time I entered, Alicia was already in the yoga room, seated on her mat in Lotus Pose.

I slipped off my shoes and set them on the shelf outside the practice space. "Sorry to keep you waiting. I'm running a little late this morning."

"No problem at all. I was getting in a little pre-class meditation. The morning instructor let me in before she left."

Alicia and I made small talk as I turned on a Deva Premal CD and lit the candles at the front of the room—my personal pre-class rituals. I consciously avoided talking about Dharma, my connection to yet another murder, and my late-night research project. Although Alicia was my friend, I wasn't ready to share what I'd learned with anyone other than family. And family, in my world, meant Michael, Bella, and Rene. I didn't even plan to loop in Dale until I understood how all of the disparate pieces fit together.

"Hey, is the rumor true?" Alicia asked. "Did you really save that stupid pigeon?"

I smiled. "I did, indeed."

"Unbelievable. Our one chance to actually get rid of that flying waste generator and you decide to play Florence Nightingale."

"Count your blessings," I replied. "At least I'm not gathering the neighborhood snails for a lettuce party."

Alicia looked confused.

"It's an inside joke. But that reminds me: I need to call Judith and see how Mr. Feathers is doing."

"Now you named him?"

I shrugged. "I'm a sucker for animals. Don't worry. If he survives, I'm not bringing him back to the garage. I'll let him loose over at the park."

I sat on my meditation rug and rang the Tibetan chimes.

After almost two years of private work, Alicia and I had established a pattern. Rather than ask her what she wanted at the beginning of each session, I created a plan for each week based on where we had left off the week before.

Today's theme was balance: balance poses, balanced energy, balanced breathing. I started with some simple kneeling poses to warm Alicia's muscles and deepen her breath. Then I led her through a flow that included Downward Dog, Upward Dog, Plank, and Side Plank. By the time she held the final Side Plank, Alicia's face was dotted with sweat. Her arm muscles quivered.

I continued with a standing Warrior I, II, and III flow that I rarely taught but knew Alicia adored, then brought the energy back down with a few seated postures. We ended with a breath practice designed to help rebuild her breath capacity, which was still compromised from the cancer treatments.

What felt like five—but was actually over sixty—minutes later, I rang the chimes again to bring our session to a close.

We ended with our normal "Namaste."

"See you on Saturday?" Alicia asked.

"Deal." I didn't need to write it down. Wednesdays and Saturdays with Alicia were an indelible part of my weekly routine.

I walked her to the front door and grabbed my keys.

"Hey, are you going to walk Bella?" she asked. "I'd like to say hi to her."

We reversed course and headed out the back exit to the parking garage. Alicia walked up the three steps to garage level and froze.

"Oh, geez, Kate. I'm so sorry."

I followed her gaze to my car.

The doors of my Honda stood open. What was left of the passenger-side window lay scattered all over the ground. The trunk was cracked open as well.

I didn't care about any of it.

I tore across the lot toward my car, so focused on reaching my destination that I was only vaguely aware of Alicia running behind me. A single question taunted me.

Where is Bella?

My mind whirled with scenarios, motives, fears, and outcomes in that ten-second race to my trashed automobile. What would a car prowler expect to find in my beater Honda that was worth confronting a hundred-pound German shepherd over?

Could he have been after Bella herself? It seemed unlikely. Dogs were stolen every day, but they usually disappeared while tied up outside coffee shops and grocery stores, not while on guard duty inside locked cars. And most of the animals pictured on lost dog posters weren't nearly as intimidating as Bella. Still, the shattered window and open doors could only mean one thing: Bella was gone.

Bright red splotches stained the broken glass littering the cement floor. My stomach lurched.

Blood.

I ran faster.

Please, God. Please don't let her be hurt. Please don't let her be—

"Kate, be careful." Alicia's words barely reached my consciousness. They certainly didn't slow down my actions. I threw the passenger door open wider and peered inside.

My throat convulsed.

Oh thank God.

Bella huddled on the floorboard behind the driver's seat, ears flattened against her head. The driver's seat was folded forward, as if someone had tried to crawl back there with her. Broken glass covered every square inch of her normal resting spot.

"You okay, sweetie?"

She uncertainly placed her front feet onto the seat cushion, preparing to climb through the littered glass toward me. I held up my hand, palm forward.

"Bella, freeze."

She froze.

But for how long?

One wrong move and she could end up with sliced-open pads, glass embedded in her skin, or worse.

Alicia's shoes crunched through the glass behind me. I motioned for her to edge closer.

"Alicia, hold your hand up like this." I showed her the hand gesture for Bella's "freeze" command. "I'm going over to the driver's side. Don't let her move."

"How am I supposed to stop her?"

"Keep telling her to stay. Sound like you mean it."

Alicia spit out the command "stay" like a drill sergeant, over and over again. Bella looked confused, but she didn't move.

I ran over to the driver's-side door, wrapped my jacket around my left hand for protection, and grabbed Bella's collar with my right. I brushed away as much of the glass from the area as I could see.

"The leash is on the passenger seat, Alicia. Can you hand it to me?"

Alicia handed me the leash, still brusquely repeating the "stay" mantra every two seconds.

I clipped on Bella's leash.

"Thanks, Alicia, that's enough."

I pushed the driver's seat as far forward as it would go and looked at Bella. "Okay, girl. Slow."

As trained, Bella moved toward me slowly, one tentative foot at a time. After I coaxed her to safety several feet away from the car, I carefully examined her feet, legs, belly, and back, inch by painstaking inch. Miraculously, I couldn't find any cuts.

"Is she okay?" Alicia's voice startled me.

"She seems fine," I said. "The blood must have come from the prowler. I hope he bleeds to death."

"Kate!"

I didn't mean it, of course, but in spite of Alicia's stern admonishment, I didn't take the words back. Yoga principles of nonviolence be damned. Anyone who messed with Bella had better be ready to feel the full wrath of Kate.

I hugged Bella to hide the angry tears forming in my eyes. "What kind of person would break into my car with Bella inside it? She could have been hurt. Frankly, she could have hurt the car prowlers, too. Were they crazy?"

"I don't know, but whoever they are, they messed with the wrong landlord." Alicia pointed at the garage's security cameras. "Follow me. We're going to kick some car-prowler ass."

———

Alicia asked the maintenance manager to sweep up the glass and cover my car window with plastic. She and I huddled in front of the computer monitor in the apartment complex office, examining the past hour's security footage. Bella explored the rest of the office, checking out her new territory. She finally lay down between us.

"I still can't believe someone was stupid enough to break into your car with Bella inside. What did they think she would do? Say hello?"

Bella responded to the familiar command by standing up and offering Alicia her paw.

Alicia ignored her and continued fast-forwarding through the footage.

"I'm surprised no one saw or heard anything," I said.

"The garage is empty this time of day. Most of the residents work weekdays." She pointed at the screen. "I think these are our prowlers."

We watched the grainy video as two ski-masked individuals—a female in jeans and a male dressed in black—moved into camera range. The male carried a knapsack. The female tried both car door handles in a futile attempt to open them. Bella watched with interest, but she didn't bark.

Alicia frowned. "Is Bella always that laid-back?"

"No," I replied. "Not at all. Bella is very territorial." I drummed my fingers on the desktop. "This doesn't make any sense. For some reason, she doesn't see them as a threat."

The female turned toward the male, said something, and shrugged.

"Do you have sound?" I asked.

Alicia shook her head no.

We silently watched as the scene continued to unfold. I didn't need sound to know the two strangers were arguing, or at least the agitated-looking female was. The male seemed to be largely ignoring her. He reached into his bag and pulled out a metal tire iron. As he leaned forward, I noticed his shirt—or, more specifically, the logo embroidered on the front of it.

"Pause that for a second, would you?" I pointed to the screen. "What does that look like to you?"

Alicia squinted her eyes. "I don't know. Fire, maybe?"

"That's what I think, too."

"What does it mean?"

"These people are from HEAT." Not-so-nonviolent thoughts raced through my mind. "I think that jackass is trying to free my dog."

Alicia started the video again.

The man raised the tire iron, but the woman stepped in front of him, blocking him from my car window. She must have said something that got his attention, because he nodded and lowered his arms. She jogged to the opposite side of the car.

Wait a minute...

I leaned closer to the screen, frowning. I recognized that wiggle. Come to think of it, I recognized the fit of those tight jeans, too.

Alicia must have sensed my tension. "Kate, what is it? Do you know them?"

The growl in my voice sounded more threatening than Bella's. "Keep playing the tape."

Everything that followed seemed to happen simultaneously. The female slipped something that looked suspiciously like a heart-shaped dog cookie through the crack in the driver's-side window. Pointy German shepherd teeth reached up from the back seat and snatched it from her fingers. The man raised the tire iron over his shoulder and swung.

I knew what was about to happen, but I still couldn't watch. I turned away and involuntarily squeezed my eyes shut. When I glanced back at the video, broken glass littered the garage floor. Blood dripped from the man's fingers.

Alicia shook her head. "Some animal rights activists. Don't they know how dangerous that was for Bella?"

The man reached through the now-broken window and unlocked the doors. The female opened the door on her side, grabbed Bella, and pulled.

Bella didn't move.

I reached down and scratched Bella's neck. "Good girl." The man moved to the driver's side of my car, reached underneath the steering wheel, and popped open the trunk. Then he shoved his friend to the side, grabbed Bella's collar, and yanked. Hard.

Bella finally reacted.

She roared out of the car, landed on the man's chest, and knocked him to the ground.

The man did the most stupid thing he could do, given the circumstances.

He ran.

Bella ran faster. She grabbed onto the prowler's pant leg, gripped the loose cloth, and jerked her head violently back and forth. I prayed her teeth only ripped denim. Seattle had the toughest dangerous dog laws in the nation; a damaging bite might not end well for Bella, justified or not.

The woman grabbed Bella's collar and dragged her off the man. He scooped his bag off the ground and scrambled out of camera range. He must have kept running, because a few seconds later Bella went into a perfect sit and nudged the woman's hand, as if expecting a treat.

When Alicia turned toward me, she wore a confused expression. I'm pretty sure mine was homicidal.

"I don't get it," she said.

My lips pressed into a tight line. "I think I do." And if I was right, someone was going to die.

If she was lucky.

The female led Bella back to my car, pulled off her mask, and glanced up at the camera. She leaned in close to Bella's face and gave her the palms-up hand signal for the command "stay." I would have sworn she was crying. Not that I gave a damn.

Alicia slowly turned toward me, wearing the same shocked expression I would have worn in her circumstances. I kept my eyes glued to the video.

On screen, Bella watched the female walk out of camera range, then crawled into the back seat and sat on the floorboard, right where I'd found her.

Some prisoner.

Alicia broke the silence. "Do you want me to call the police?"

"Not yet. First I need to call Michael and find out if he has someone else who can manage Pete's Pets while he's out of town. Then you should probably call 911 and report a murder. I'm about to strangle Tiffany."

SEVENTEEN

By the time I got back to the studio, Michael had left three messages on my machine. Evidently, Tiffany had already contacted him, and for some unfathomable reason he was taking her side.

By the final message, his voice sounded frantic. "Kate, I know you're furious, but don't do anything rash. Call me before you get the police involved. We'll figure out some way to fix this. Remember, we were both young and stupid once, too."

Speak for yourself, traitor.

I took several long, cleansing breaths and tried to calm myself, to no avail. I picked up the phone to return Michael's message, but quickly set it back down again. Calling Michael right now would result in nothing but trouble. I was balanced on an emotional tightrope above two dark abysses: on my right side, fury at Tiffany; on my left, disappointment in Michael. The best I could manage was to ease down the wire one tenuous step at a time.

The first of those steps was calling Rene. I knew I'd see her in my afternoon prenatal class, but I needed her help before then. I asked if she could come by early and lend me her car for a few days. She said yes to both, though since she had a twelve-thirty doctor appointment she couldn't come as early as I'd hoped. But she promised to drive straight from her doctor's office to Serenity Yoga. That way we could get Bella out of the studio before the other prenatal students started arriving.

Which meant that I had to keep Bella safe until around two o'clock.

My lovely, traumatized girl was currently on guard duty, watching the front entrance so she could chase away evil yoga student intruders. I checked the afternoon's class schedule. Yoga for Men started at noon.

Fabulous.

In the past twenty-four hours, Bella had lived through a home invasion, a car prowl, and an attempted dognapping. Her adrenaline and cortisol levels had to be through the roof, which would make her even more reactive than normal. On a good day, Bella often didn't like men, particularly if they had facial hair. Having her in the studio with a bunch of male strangers—especially today—would be inviting disaster. Classes would have to be cancelled until Bella left the building.

I put up the *Closed* sign and started making phone calls.

By the time I finished notifying students thirty minutes later, Michael had left two more messages. I couldn't put off talking to him any longer, but I needed to steady my emotions first.

I took a deep breath. Then I counted to ten. Then I mentally chanted Om Santi, the Sanskrit mantra for peace. In spite of it all, my hands were still shaking when I dialed his cell number.

He didn't even say hello.

"Kate, Tiffany is an idiot. She screwed up and she knows it, but we can handle it. We don't need to call the police."

"Yes, she's an idiot. I've always known it, but now I have proof—on video. That little blonde bimbo could have seriously hurt Bella

181

today." I frowned. "Speaking of which, what kind of dog owner are you? You don't even ask about Bella?"

Michael's voice softened. "Bella's okay, right? Tiffany told me that she hid near the car to make sure Bella was safe until you found her."

I pulled out the desk chair and sat down with a heavy thud.

"Yes, Bella's fine, but she could have easily been cut. And whether Little Miss Boob Job played hide-and-seek or not, she's still a criminal. She broke into my car. She might have broken into our home."

A mechanical voice said the words "code blue" in the background—the same ominous words that echoed around me the night my father died.

Ease up, Kate.

I closed my eyes and consciously relaxed my grip on the handset. If Michael was still at the hospital, he was dealing with issues much more serious than a broken car window. No need to make it worse.

I eased the irritation out of my voice. "How's your father?"

"He's still in ICU, but he's doing better. Mom and Shannon are with him now. Look, about Tiffany. She told me what happened with your car, or at least her version of it. She said that she didn't break the window, and she claims that she doesn't know anything about what happened to our house." Michael paused, as if first registering my earlier words. "Wait a minute. Did you watch the video?"

"Yes, and you should have seen—"

"Slow down for a second and hear me out. That tape may verify what Tiffany told me. She said she was with Dharma's friend Eduardo, and that *he* smashed your window. She claims she tried to stop him."

"Eduardo. I knew it was someone from HEAT, but I wasn't sure who. Now I know who's next on my hit list."

Michael ignored my editorial comment and kept talking. "Eduardo told Tiffany that Bella was being abused and that he was going

182

to take her somewhere safe. He said that he needed Tiffany's help to get her out of the car—that Bella would be less traumatized if she left with someone she knew."

I took the phone away from my ear and gaped at the receiver. Bella? Abused?

I was angry before. Now I was livid. "That little bleached-blonde tramp is conning you, Michael." I stood up and paced, stomping to the end of the phone cord and back again. "Tiffany knows we would never hurt Bella."

Michael's reply sounded frustrated. With me. "Of course Tiffany knows we wouldn't hurt Bella. That wasn't the point. From her perspective, this little escapade was never about Bella."

"Look, Michael, I know you had a long night, but seriously. How sleep-deprived are you? That doesn't make any sense."

"Don't you get it? Tiffany wanted to score points with a cute guy." Michael took a deep breath. "Think about it, Kate. You lock your car doors. Always. And you never leave the windows open far enough that someone could reach in. Tiffany knows that. She thought Eduardo would try your doors, see they were locked, and walk away. She had no idea he was going to break a window."

"How did this Eduardo guy know Bella was in my car, anyway? Tiffany must have told him."

"I asked her the same thing. Tiffany says Eduardo came by the store to see her. He drove into the parking garage before he noticed the *Permit Parking Only* sign. When he pulled next to your car to turn around, he saw Bella."

I stopped pacing and wrapped the phone cord around my index finger. Michael kept talking.

"He showed up at the store, all worked up about seeing an 'abused' German shepherd. Tiffany told him the dog was yours and that you kept her in your car regularly. It was all a game to her, Kate. She knows Bella is perfectly safe in the garage. She was scamming him, hoping to get a date. She had no idea how it was going to turn out."

I ignored Michael's lame justifications, pulled out a pad of paper, and started making a to-do list.

1. Send flowers to Michael's father.
2. Call insurance company.
3. Slaughter Tiffany.

I crossed out the first two and circled the third.

Michael's voice continued pleading with me through the phone line. "Kate, at least tell me this: does Tiffany's story match what you saw on the videotape?"

It did, of course, but I didn't care. I added a doodle of Satan and wrote Tiffany's name underneath it. "You should see the damage that little tramp and her friend did to my car. She can't whine to you because she got caught and ask for a 'get out of trouble free' card."

Michael sighed. "She's not going to get off free, Kate. We'll make her work off the damage. Hon, she feels terrible. That's why she confessed. She kept an eye on Bella until you and Alicia showed up, but as soon as she knew Bella was safe, she called and told me what happened."

"If she feels so awful, why didn't she call me herself? Or better yet, come get me."

"She's scared of you, Kate." He paused. "Hell, *I'm* a little scared of you sometimes. And you have to admit, you're part of the problem. You egg Tiffany on every chance you get."

I set my pen on top of the pad and pushed them both away. "Why are you so worried about this, anyway? If I turn her in, she'll get a slap on the wrist. It might do her good to put in a few hours of community service."

Michael didn't reply. For several long moments, the only sounds that came through the phone line were the tinny announcements of the hospital's PA system.

"Michael, answer me. Why are you taking Tiffany's side?"

When Michael finally spoke, his voice sounded hesitant. "Promise me that you won't get all judgmental."

"What are you talking about? I'm a yoga teacher. I'm very open-minded."

"Uh huh."

Was that sarcasm?

Michael exhaled a resigned sigh. "Okay, Kate, but you can't tell anyone. Promise?"

I shook my head. "I'll keep an open mind, but other than that, no promises. Out with it."

"Tiffany has a record."

"A record?"

"Nothing major, just stupid kid stuff. Drugs, shoplifting, that sort of thing. She was a juvenile for her first two arrests, but she was nineteen the last time. She spent six months in jail."

I closed my eyes and pinched the bridge of my nose. "When did you learn about this?"

"She told me when she applied for the job. She'd been clean for eight months, and she was almost done with probation. She needed work, and no one would hire her."

"So you did?"

"Sometimes people are worth second chances, Kate. You, of all people, should know that."

I knew what he was referring to, of course. Michael had given *me* more than one chance, too. He had a good heart. It was one of the many things that I loved about him. It was also his greatest weakness.

"Tiffany will go to jail again if we get the police involved. It might ruin her future." I imagined him lacing his fingers together in the Begging-Boyfriend Mudra. "Please, Kate. We can find another way to teach her a lesson. You can make her clean the yoga studio for a decade, if you want."

I shuddered. "Tiffany breaks into my car, and then I have to hang out with her in the yoga studio? Why am *I* the one getting punished?"

"This is an opportunity to do something good." Michael's voice carried a grin. He was winning the argument, and he knew it. "Tiffany isn't as bright as you are, and she's easily influenced, especially by men. Eduardo took advantage of her, and frankly, your attitude toward her didn't help. The rivalry between you two isn't all her fault. You know that."

Michael's points were all valid, unfortunately. "What about Eduardo? He gets off free, too?"

"I don't know yet, Kate. I haven't worked out all of the details." I heard someone speak in the background. Michael's voice grew softer. "I'll be right there." He came back on the line. "The doctors are about to go in and see Dad. I should be there. Hopefully I'll be back in Seattle in a couple of days. Can you hold off on getting Tiffany into trouble until then?"

I would have countered that Tiffany had gotten *herself* into trouble, but I didn't think it would make any difference.

"You trust Tiffany's story?" I asked.

"I do. Tiffany doesn't know it, but I watched her like a hawk for the first six months after I hired her. I even installed a nanny cam. I went over the money every night. She's never been off by a penny. She's made some mistakes, but she's a good kid."

I'd already lost the argument, and I knew it. Truth be told, I didn't want to spend my afternoon filing police reports anyway. I still had to figure out what I was going to do about Dharma. I closed my eyes and shook my head.

"I suppose you think Tiffany should move in with us, too?"

I swore I could hear Michael wink. "Only if you don't behave yourself."

I crumpled up my Demon Tiffany doodle and tossed it in the recycle bin. "All right, you win. I'll wait until you come back. But Tiffany had better stay out of my way until then. I might coldcock her before I can stop myself."

"Thank you, Kate. You're doing the right thing."

I hoped, for everyone's sake, that he wasn't mistaken.

———

I had my car towed to a body shop, then spent the next sixty minutes entering new students into the database. As promised, Rene arrived with Sam's car over an hour before Prenatal Yoga. She parked the red Camaro in my now-glass-free parking spot.

"Are you sure Sam is okay with me driving his car?"

"I didn't ask him."

If Rene didn't ask, it was for only one reason: she knew the answer would be a resounding no.

"Rene…"

"What? You think I want dog hair caked all over the back seat of my Prius? Besides, Sam installed an ultra-high-tech security system in this baby. I'm pretty sure that if anyone even looks at it cross-eyed, they'll be teleported straight to a jail cell. If the car prowler comes back here looking for trouble, he won't be able to touch it. Besides, I hate driving this car. I'm getting so big now that I can barely fit behind the steering wheel. The girls don't like to be squished."

A leering, middle-aged man turned away from his own car, looked solidly at Rene's breasts, and smirked.

Rene pointed at her stomach. "These girls, not the ones you're looking at, mister." She pointed to his ample beer belly. "And you wouldn't fit behind this steering wheel any better than I do." She turned her back to him and shook her head. "Men. They're all the same. I've got a belly the size of a small towing barge, and they still go all gaga over a couple of glorified baby bottles."

She tossed me the car keys. "The Camaro is all yours until your car is fixed. Or until Sam finds out that I loaned it to you, whichever comes first." She looked at the drooling fur-beast tugging at the end of my leash. "What do you want to do with Bella?"

It was a good question. I wasn't comfortable keeping Bella alone in the garage again, at least not until I talked to Tiffany. Who knew what Eduardo might try next? On the other hand, I couldn't leave her at my house without risking the lives of the construction workers. And with Bella's separation anxiety issues, she might panic if left alone at Rene's.

I called her vet, who came up with a compromise: give Bella a half-dose of the prescription happy-dog pills she took on the Fourth of July and lock her in a small room. There was no appropriate room at the studio, but Rene's soon-to-be nursery would work nicely. I hated to drug Bella, but I didn't have a good alternative. At least on medication, she wouldn't panic and hurt herself.

An hour later, after our quick trip to Rene's house, my friend and thirteen other pregnant women stretched out their bodies in Prenatal Yoga. The class was arranged in a wagon-wheel-like circle, with my meditation rug at the hub and the students' mats pointed diagonally out from the center.

Teaching yoga to expectant moms presented a variety of unusual challenges. The first of which was keeping them in the room. Pregnant women didn't usually have good bladder control, so from my position in the center of the circle, I often felt less like a yoga teacher and more like the center of a revolving door that led to the bathroom.

Then there was the room temperature. No Hot Yoga here. Even when I set the thermostat so low that my toenails turned blue, my expecting moms still complained that the room was oppressively warm. I'd resorted to wearing slipper socks twelve months a year.

But by far the biggest challenge was choosing and adapting the poses. Pregnant women weren't supposed to lie on their bellies after the first trimester; resting on their backs could be equally problematic; their feet and legs ached if they stood for too long. And after the second trimester, many of the women hated going to and from the floor, so once they got down, good luck getting them back up again. I had to creatively choose poses that honored those restrictions, mitigated pregnancy's negative effects on each expectant mom, and honored the needs of the baby growing within her. In spite of its challenges, I loved teaching the class. I wasn't ready for children myself, but I enjoyed helping future moms find peace and physical comfort.

The next pose on the docket for today's practice was Anantasana, a side-lying leg stretch also called Vishnu's Couch Pose.

"Okay ladies, lie on your left side and rest your head on your arm. Bend your right knee and loop your index finger around your right big toe."

A new student gave me an odd look, which didn't surprise me. I'd received this reaction before, though it wasn't warranted. The pose—even though it sounded challenging—was surprisingly accessible to most students, whether they were expecting or not. If I could get them to try it, that was.

I flashed what I hoped was an encouraging smile. "When you inhale, straighten your right leg and press your heel up to the sky."

The new student released her big toe, pushed herself to sitting, and grumbled, "You have *got* to be kidding me."

Rene, never one to miss a moment in the spotlight, yelled from the opposite side of the circle, "It's easy, watch!" She quickly grabbed her big toe and thrust her heel to the sky, forgetting that she needed to move slowly in order to remain balanced. Her body wobbled; her top leg teetered.

"Kate, help!"

I arrived too late.

Rene rolled onto her back and remained there, waving her hands and legs in the air like a stranded turtle. "I'm capsized!"

"Maybe we should try something else," I suggested. "Everybody, press yourself up to hands and knees, rest in Child's Pose for a few breaths, and then come to your feet."

Lots of groaning and a couple of assists later, all fourteen women were standing.

We did several poses designed to strengthen each mom-to-be's body for labor and delivery. Half Squats, Half Forward Bends, Goddess Pose, and a Warrior Pose variation that strengthened the upper back. Fifteen minutes later, I ended the class in a modified Savasana.

I asked the students to rest on their sides and helped them position several yoga props that would help them relax more comfortably. I gave each woman a neck pillow and two bolsters—one to place between her knees; the other to hug between her arms—and slid a folded blanket underneath several of the larger bellies. Finally, I fluffed up a blue cotton thunderbird blanket and draped it over each resting woman.

The setup took longer than the rest period itself, but it was worth it. All of the women, even the newcomer, left looking paradoxically relaxed and rejuvenated. I ushered the final student out of the door, looked at my watch, and turned to Rene, who had just returned from her fourth trip to the restroom.

"Bella's drugs should keep her calm for at least three more hours. Do you have time for a cup of coffee? I need a sounding board."

We wandered across the street to Mocha Mia, where Rene ordered a decaf triple grande extra chocolate mocha, two peanut butter cookies—one for each twin—and a large piece of cinnamon crumble apple pie a la mode. I ordered a tall, fully caffeinated coffee and stirred in two packets of Splenda. Calories had to be conserved somewhere, right? I tried not to take the *I'm not short, I'm concentrated awesome* coffee mug that the barista gave me personally.

We grabbed an open booth by the window. I pointed at the smorgasbord Rene had assembled on her side of the table. "Rene, I know the doctor wants you to gain weight, but I don't think this is what he had in mind. You're going to eat yourself right into gestational diabetes. Do you ever actually get any nutrition?"

"You're wrong. First, I had an awesome doctor's appointment today. My blood sugar is completely normal, and I've gained two pounds in the last week."

Two? I would have gained five pounds *looking* at all those desserts.

Second, this is a completely balanced meal," Renee continued. She pointed to each item individually. "The mocha and the ice cream cover the dairy group. The pie has fruit in the filling and complex carbohydrates in the crust. The cookies have peanut butter, which is an awesome source of protein. This might be the most nutritious meal I've eaten all week." She dug her fork deeply into the pie, shoveled half of the slice into her mouth, and started chewing. "Now, stop criticizing my third lunch and tell me what's going on."

I ignored the ice cream smearing Rene's chin and filled her in on my Internet research. I started by telling her about the El Paso fires and my theory about the connection they might have to Raven's death.

"So now you think Dharma is a pyromaniac?"

"I did at first, but I'm not so sure anymore. After I read the article about the El Paso fires, I spent the rest of the night reading about arsonists. The profiles I found online are biased because most arsonists never get caught. But when they do, ninety percent of them are male."

Rene frowned. "So? That means that out of a thousand arsonists, one hundred of them are women. And maybe female arsonists are better at hiding their crimes. It certainly doesn't leave Dharma out."

"There are other characteristics that don't fit."

"Like what?"

"Unless they're setting fire for money—like an insurance scam—arsonists also tend to be socially isolated and of below-normal IQ. Fire is their way of lashing out in anger. Many of them have OCD."

Rene grinned. "You know, that would explain a lot. I always wondered why you had so many neuroses. Now I know. You inherited them from Dharma."

I reached across the table and slugged her in the shoulder. "Knock it off, Funny Girl."

She ignored me and broke her first cookie in half. I kept talking.

"I haven't spent enough time with Dharma to know if she's neurotic, but she seems intelligent to me. I can't imagine Dad marrying someone with significantly lower than average IQ."

"It still doesn't count her out. Sam always says that stereotypes exist in order to prove themselves wrong. You haven't ruled out Eduardo, for that matter. Didn't you say he was in that Texas photo, too?"

"Yes, but he wasn't anywhere near the dumpsters when the fire started. I saw him with the rest of the protesters, on-leash, no less."

"He still might be responsible. I'm sure there are lots of ways to start fires remotely." Rene narrowed her eyebrows. "Why don't you tell all of this to the police? They'll know whether or not it's worth following up on."

"I can't. Not without implicating Dharma." I absently stirred my coffee. "Besides, now I have a whole new problem."

I pulled out Dharma's formerly unopened letter and slid it across the table. Rene unfolded the page, scanned it quickly from top to bottom, then began at the top again and read it more slowly.

Time seemed to crawl as I watched her face, attempting to gauge her reactions while controlling my own. I tried focusing on the bittersweet smell of Mocha Mia's molten chocolate lava cake, but I was wound up so tightly that not even dark chocolate could make me feel Zen. By the time Rene finished reading, the pressure inside me had risen so high, I felt like a blowfish about to explode.

Rene wore a blank expression. She carefully refolded the paper, placed it in the envelope, and handed it back to me. The silence between us felt deafening.

"Well?"

She looked down at the table and chewed on her lower lip. When she made eye contact again, she seemed to carefully consider her words.

"How much of this did you already know?"

"None of it."

Rene raised her eyebrows.

"I mean, I had to have known, but I either blocked it out or I forgot. I still don't remember."

"No wonder your father was so overprotective. Do you think this is why he became a cop?"

"I don't know. But the thought occurred to me last night, too. Whenever I asked him about joining the police force, his stock answer was that he was born to 'protect and serve.' Now I suspect there was more to it than that."

Rene opened her mouth, then closed it again. She picked up her mocha and took a long, slow sip. After what felt like a century, she set the mug on the table and squared her shoulders. "Kate, you're not going to like what I'm about to say. I know we've argued about it before, but do you honestly think seeing a counselor would be such a bad thing?"

"Rene, I don't need—"

She held up her hand. "Hear me out. That letter proves that you've suffered a past trauma, and anyone with half a brain can see that something's been going on with you lately. Over the past six months, I've watched my best friend wither away to a skeleton wearing someone else's clothes."

If the words had come from anyone else, I would have been offended, but Rene and I had always been unflinchingly honest with each other.

"Frankly," she said, "given what's inside that letter, I'm not surprised that you have relationship issues."

"Hey, I'm better now. Michael and I have been together almost a year. That's over six times my prior record." I flashed my most mischievous grin, hoping she'd take the hint and change the subject.

She didn't.

"In some ways, yes, you *are* doing better, but you still have issues, and something new is going on with you. Something that started on Orcas." Rene stared me straight in the eyes, clearly telling me that she would tolerate no deception. "Today of all days, Kate, be straight. Don't lie to me."

Instead of answering her, I picked up my mug. "I'm going to get a refill. You want anything?"

"This is exactly what I mean," Rene chastised. "Something is going on with you, and you won't talk to me. Fine. That's your choice. But then please go talk to someone else."

Fiery pinpricks of defensiveness tingled my skin. I wanted to snap at Rene. I wanted to tell her to mind her own business. I wanted to stomp out of Mocha Mia in a huff and avoid the whole conversation. But I couldn't. Rene was right, whether I wanted to admit it or not.

I stood up, walked to the refill carafe, and drowned my reaction in hot, bitter coffee. When I returned to the table, Rene was wearing the same don't-mess-with-me-anymore expression she had when I left.

"Okay," I said. "You're right. I *have* been struggling. But I'm not ready to tell you about it."

"Fine. Then you'll call a counselor?"

I sighed. "I'll think about it."

Rene wrinkled her forehead. "I said, don't lie to me."

"I'm not. I'll think about it. I promise."

The answer seemed to mollify her, at least momentarily.

"What did Michael have to say about all of this?"

"I haven't told him yet."

Rene shook her head, looking disappointed. "You're not being fair to him, Kate. He deserves to know."

I held up my hand. "Hold up there on the judgments, Girl Chick. I'm not hiding any of this from him. I'm giving him a few days to focus on his own family's problems. As soon as his father's health stabilizes, I'll tell Michael everything. Right now he's suffering enough."

"Are you going to ask Dharma about the letter when you see her tomorrow?"

I shrugged. "I haven't decided. Reading it has left me with tons of questions, but frankly I might not want to know the answers. Some wounds are best left scarred over."

Rene finished the last bite of pastry and drained the dregs of her mocha. "Well, whatever you decide, you shouldn't have to deal with all of this alone."

I grinned. "I'm not. I've got you."

"Damned straight you do." She stacked her now-empty plates, crumpled her napkin, and tossed it on top. When she looked up, her expression invited no argument. "Meet your new roommate. I'm staying at your place until Michael gets back. You'd better have cleaned since the last time I visited you two."

I involuntarily flinched. I loved Rene, but when she had that stubborn look in her eyes, the only logical defense was to retreat. I couldn't do that with her snoring on the bed next to me.

"Thanks Rene, but you would be miserable. My place is covered in construction dust and dog hair."

"Nice try, Kemosabe. I've got enough Benadryl on hand to dry me out through October, which is exactly how long I'm prepared to bunk at your place. You'll get rid of me when you start seeing a counselor or Michael comes back. Not one day sooner. Fair warning, I get dibs on the bathroom. When the girls tell me I've gotta go, I've gotta go."

She stood up and looped her bag over her shoulder. "Now drive me home so we can pick up Bella. I need to grab some clothes and pack a couple of snack bags. We're going on an adventure."

I narrowed my eyes. "An adventure?" Whatever she had in mind, I had a feeling I wouldn't like it.

"Kate, my friend, we girls are going on a stakeout."

EIGHTEEN

RENE REACHED INTO THE paper bag at her feet and pulled out a party-sized bag of nacho cheese tortilla chips and a container of cheap onion dip. She cracked open the plastic tub, filling the car's interior with the smell of powdered fake cheese and onion-contaminated mayonnaise. Bella pressed her nose between the Camaro's bucket seats, obviously hoping she'd soon share Rene's onion breath.

"Not on your life," I said to the drooling wildebeest. "You have enough trouble digesting real food." To Rene, I said, "Really? Less than two hours after gorging yourself at Mocha Mia?"

Rene dragged a burnt orange chip through the pale, oily-looking goo, popped it in her mouth, and chastised me between crunches. "Everyone knows you're supposed to bring food with you on a stake-out. Just wait. You'll be begging me for some of these chips when you're starving at midnight. "

I looked at my watch. Six o'clock. I had a twenty-dollar bill in my purse that said she'd never make it to six-thirty. Rene had the attention span of a terrier in a squirrel sanctuary. She'd be lucky to last fifteen minutes, which was the only reason I'd gone along with her harebrained idea in the first place.

"I can't believe I let you talk to me into this. Why, again, are we sitting outside the motel Dharma stayed in?"

"Isn't it obvious?" Rene ticked off each point on her fingertips. "One. We think Eduardo is staying here, and we know he's up to no good. He's for sure a car prowler. He might be an arsonist and a murderer. Two. You can't talk to the police about Eduardo without exposing Tiffany, and Michael asked you not to do that. Three. You can't get any intel on Eduardo from Dharma without potentially incriminating her, and Dale forbade that. Dale and Michael have left us no choice. We have to corner Eduardo and interrogate him ourselves."

I held up my hands. "Whoa, there. Back the truck up, Rene. I agreed to stake out Eduardo, not interrogate him. I'm not putting any of us, especially the twins, in that kind of danger. Even if Eduardo isn't the arsonist—and I don't think he is—he's still a criminal."

Rene sighed dramatically. "Who said anything about putting anyone in danger? We'll watch Eduardo and follow him. He's bound to go somewhere public eventually. We'll trap him there."

I shook my head. "Nope. No way. We're not trapping anyone."

Rene flicked her hand dismissively through the air. "Fine, then. Be that way. We'll tail him and see who he hangs out with. Maybe we can sniff out some leads that Dale can follow up on." She pointed to the still-begging shepherd in the back seat. "If Eduardo sees us and tries to get smart, we'll toss a couple of chips at him and let Bella chase down her dinner."

As plans went, it wasn't my favorite, but it wasn't completely out of the question, either. I had a feeling that Michael wouldn't approve of Rene's and my newest adventure, but luckily I wouldn't have to tell him about it until it was too late for him to stop us. Besides, I didn't know for sure that Eduardo was still in Seattle, much less staying at this motel. At the very least, a stakeout would entertain Rene until she lost interest and decided to go out for pizza.

"I still think we should have brought your Prius," I said. "Parking in front of the motel entrance in a red Camaro isn't exactly inconspicuous."

"I told you, no dog hair in my car. The sun won't set for two more hours, and this spot is the last one left in the shade. Do you want Bella and me to fry? Besides, this is practically camouflage. After seeing your junk mobile, Eduardo will never expect to find you in a hot sports car." Rene wiggled and scrunched up her face.

I gave her a droll look. "Now what?"

"Darn it, I have to pee again. One of these girls is always kicking my bladder."

I handed her the thermos. "Here, use this."

"Very funny." She squirmed again. "Sorry, Kate, I can't sit here anymore."

Which was precisely the cue I'd been waiting for. I put the key in the ignition. "No problem, I'll drive us home."

Rene reached over and pulled the key back out. "Not on your life." She pointed across the street to Mary Jane Mocha, one of the new combination espresso bar/marijuana clubs that had sprouted up when pot was legalized in Washington State. "I'll use their bathroom and pick up some pastries. I can't have any green brownies because of the girls, but you can. You could certainly use a little mellowing." She tossed the keys in her handbag. "I'll be back in ten minutes."

I grabbed her arm before she could open the car door. "I told you before, Rene, I don't do drugs. And I'm not about to start when I'm driving."

Rene shook off my hand and rolled her eyes. "I'm teasing, Miss Grumpy Pants. Geez, you really *do* need to mellow out. I'll bring you back a latte. Decaf."

She heaved her body out of the passenger seat and waddled across Aurora Avenue. She stopped next to the spiky green leaf painted on the café's entrance, smiled, and wiggled her fingers at me before disappearing inside the dark, dingy storefront.

"What you think, Bella? Will we ever see her again?" Bella pressed her nose against the passenger-side window and drooled, whether in concern over Rene's departure or anticipation of what she might bring back, I wasn't entirely sure. I covered both contingencies. "If you're worried about Rene, she'll be fine. But if you think I'm letting you have any green dog cookies, you are sorely mistaken."

Bella stretched her body across the entire length of the back seat, placed her head between her paws, and sighed. I rolled down the window two inches, covered up with my sweater, and briefly closed my eyes. As surveillance went, it wasn't exactly a Sam Spade moment, but if Eduardo showed up now, I'd be hosed anyway. I wasn't about to drive off chasing a suspect while Rene was patronizing a glorified drug dealer, newly legal or not. Especially since she had the car keys.

I must have dozed off for a moment, because a knock on the driver's-side window startled me awake. Bella roared and hurled herself at the window, leaving a slug trail of saliva dripping down the Camaro's interior.

Goth Girl smiled on the other side, not seeming frightened of Bella in the slightest. She motioned for me to roll the window down farther.

I grumbled at my self-appointed security guard. "Bella, leave it. She's okay." *At least I think she is.*

Bella seemed to believe me. She sat and stared at Goth Girl curiously.

I rolled the window down the rest of the way. "Geez! You scared me half to death!"

Goth Girl flashed a shy smile. "I saw you sitting out here and wanted to say 'nice car.' Sorry I took off the other day. Eduardo pulled into the parking lot, and I was afraid he'd get mad if he saw me talking to you."

That was the second time this tentative young woman had mentioned being afraid of Eduardo. Whatever magical hold Eduardo had over women, I was beginning to think it might be abusive. I tried to inconspicuously look for bruises or other signs of domestic violence, but Goth Girl's arms and legs were both covered—completely in black again. Come to think of it, they'd been covered the other two times I'd seen her as well.

Goth Girl reached her fingers through the opened window and allowed Bella to sniff them.

"Your dog is gorgeous. Can I say hi to her?"

My cover, if I'd ever had one, had obviously been blown, so I figured why not? Bella could always use more human friends, and Goth Girl seemed to like her. Bella's presence might make the young woman relax enough to answer a few questions. Like, *Do you know who killed Raven?* and *Can I give you a ride to a battered women's shelter?*

"I'll let Bella out of the car, but step back from the door until I make sure she's calm enough to approach. She's not always friendly."

I clipped on Bella's leash and opened the door. Bella hopped out beside me and wiggled toward Goth Girl, ears at half-mast, body lowered in an I-am-a-cute-and-friendly-dog position. She slowly swished her tail.

"Bella, say hello."

As taught, Bella went into a perfect sit and offered Goth Girl her paw.

The young woman's entire face lit up in a smile. She wrapped her fingers around Bella's paw and gave it a tentative shake. "She's so pretty." She briefly made eye contact, then looked back at the ground. "I know Raven said owning pets is slavery, but I like dogs." She blushed underneath her pale makeup. "I might get one of my own someday."

Just the conversation starter I was hoping for.

"Did you know Raven very well?" I asked.

She didn't get the chance to answer. A stern voice yelled from the sidewalk. "Marla! Who are you talking to?"

The young woman jumped and looked over her shoulder.

Eduardo strode across the parking lot, carrying what appeared to be an extra-large bag of pastries. Rene waddled beside him. He dropped the bag and charged toward us.

Uh oh.

Goth Girl cringed. "He's going to be mad."

Not nearly as mad as Bella.

Even on happy pills, Bella took one look at her would-be abductor and exploded. She lunged, she barked, she growled, she foamed. She yanked so hard on the leash that I fell to the ground behind her, but I held on.

Barely.

Eduardo staggered back, swearing. I grabbed Bella's collar with both hands, pulled myself to my feet, and glared at the cowering car prowler.

"Bella, sit."

Bella obeyed, but with obvious objections. Her upper lip lifted, exposing a mouth full of sparkling white, pants-ripping teeth. Her body leaned forward. A long line of drool oozed from her jaw. She leveled Eduardo a laser-like stare. Its meaning was obvious: *One false move and I'm taking you out.*

I glared at Eduardo, then gestured to the huge, snarling protector-dog with my eyes. "I believe you two have already met."

Eduardo ignored me and grabbed Goth Girl's arm. "Marla, stay away from that vicious dog."

Bella lunged toward him again and snapped at the air. He released the young woman and stumbled several steps back.

Goth Girl, whose name was evidently Marla, looked back and forth between the three of us, confused. "But Eduardo, Bella is nice! And this is that lady from the yoga studio. You know, the one that's related to Dharma."

Rene finally race-waddled her way up to us. She pointed at the porcupine-like guard hairs standing at high alert along Bella's spine. "What's got Bella so worked up?" She looked at Eduardo. "And why did you throw my scones on the ground?"

"Rene, what are you doing?" I asked.

She held the paper bag Eduardo had dropped in one hand and what appeared to be two iced lattes in the other. "I couldn't go into the marijuana café to use their bathroom without a state membership card, so I went next door and got scones and coffee for later. This nice man offered to carry them for me." She paused, suddenly clueing in on the scene unfolding before her. "Wait a minute. Are you Eduardo?"

Eduardo spoke in a growl almost as frightening as Bella's. "What in the hell is going on here?"

I opened my mouth to blather an explanation—any explanation—that would give us enough time to escape, but Rene beat me to it. She shoved the pastry bag in Eduardo's face and shouldered her way between us.

"I'll tell you what's going on, mister. We're here to talk about murder."

I'd figure out how to properly punish Rene later. In the meantime, the five of us—Eduardo, Goth Girl, Rene, Bella, and I—sat in uncomfortable silence at a rickety picnic table next to Mary Jane Mocha. Quasi-public location or not, I didn't share Rene's delusions of safety. If Eduardo attacked us, the patrons at the marijuana café would probably be too stoned to care, much less intervene. Still, the bakery's outdoor seating area was the closest public location I could think of that would allow Bella, and there was no way I was willing to hang out with a potential murderer without her.

So here we sat.

I'd conned Eduardo into talking to us by simultaneously assuring and threatening him. I assured him that the murder Rene referred to was going to be his if he didn't pay for my shattered car window. I threatened to turn him in to the police if he didn't tell me why he'd gone after my Honda in the first place.

Bella stared at Eduardo, never breaking eye contact, as if daring him to make a false move. Eduardo glared back at her from the opposite end of the table, well out of striking range.

"Keep that vicious animal tied up tight. It's obviously gone crazy from being cooped up in your car."

I didn't want to ask, but I had to know. "Did she bite you?"

"No, but you should have seen how it ripped up my pants. That thing ought to be wearing a muzzle."

I half expected Marla—aka Goth Girl—to stick up for Bella, but she seemed strangely withdrawn from the conversation. She cradled her knees to her chest and almost folded into herself, as if given the opportunity, she would completely disappear. She picked at her thumb nail and stared at the table, rocking back and forth.

I continued admonishing Eduardo. "I'm glad you weren't hurt, but it wouldn't have been Bella's fault if you had been. She had every right to defend herself and her property." I leaned forward. "There's no sense in lying about my car. Tiffany confessed, and I have both of you on tape." I pointed to the bandage on his forearm. "I even saw how you got that cut on your wrist. Now tell me, why did you target my car?"

Eduardo frowned. "I didn't. That pet store chick did. I met her on Saturday at Green Lake. She seemed interested in HEAT, so I decided to drop by the store and invite her to join us. I figured having a member with pet store experience would be helpful, PR-wise."

He absently scratched the side of his chin. "When I pulled into the garage, I saw your dog trapped in that dented old Honda. I mentioned it to the pet store chick—Tiffany, you say her name is?—and she told me she knew the dog and that its owner was a real bi—"

I gave him a dirty look.

"Fine. You're an angel. She asked me to help her rescue it." He pointed at Bella. "Keeping a dog—even that one—locked up in a car is shameful, dangerous, even. It could suffocate. If anyone should call the police, it's me."

"Nice try, buddy. The windows were partially open and there's no sun in that garage. It's downright chilly today, but even on warm days, Bella's cooler there than in my house."

"Still, keeping a dog locked up in a car all day? You're torturing her. It's no wonder she's so vicious."

Bella, the supposedly tortured one, lifted her lips at Eduardo and showed him her teeth.

"She's not locked in there for long. I take her for a walk every couple of hours. And she's not vicious. She's pissed at you for trying to kidnap her. Where were you planning to take her?"

"I told you, I don't know. It was the pet store chick's idea."

I leaned back and peered at Eduardo, trying to decipher whether or not he was telling the truth. The pettiest part of me wanted to believe that Tiffany was responsible—not just for my car damage, but for everything else bad in the world. War, famine, and pestilence included. And Eduardo's explanation made sense, if you were looking at Bella's situation from his warped perspective. Still, his story didn't jibe, not completely. It certainly didn't match up with the video.

Rene pointed at Eduardo's outfit. "You're one to talk about harming animals, sitting there all comfy cozy in your leather jacket and boots. Hypocritical lately?"

Goth Girl recovered the ability to speak. "They're not leather, they're *pleather*. It only looks like leather. Not one animal was harmed to make that jacket. Eduardo gave me one on my birthday. It's in our room."

"Shut up, Marla," Eduardo said.

My stomach lurched. "*Your* room? As in the room the two of you share?" I gaped at Eduardo, disgusted. "You certainly get around, buddy. Three women, all who knew each other, all at the same time? Frankly, I don't understand why *you* weren't the one murdered." I gestured with my thumb to Goth Girl. "This one doesn't even look eighteen."

Rene agreed. "You're handsome, I'll grant you that, but no one is *that* handsome. What do all of these women see in you?"

Goth Girl interrupted. "Wait a minute … you two think … *gross!* I'm not sleeping with Eduardo. He's my brother!"

Her brother?

The puzzle pieces finally all fell into place. Eduardo wasn't an abusive lover; he was an overbearing family member.

Rene's eyes darted back and forth between the two siblings. One tall, dark, apparently of Hispanic descent. The other petite and pale, about fifteen years his junior. "You two are brother and sister? But you don't look anything alike!" She placed her hands on her belly and stared at it with a dazed expression. "You mean the twins might not look related?"

Coming from anyone else, the question would have sounded absurd, especially given the circumstances. But to Rene, the insight was huge. It added a whole new layer of complication to the baby-accessorizing dilemma.

Eduardo sneered. "We're half siblings, you nitwit. Same mother, different fathers. I was conceived in Mom's drug-runner phase. Marla was born after she turned white supremacist. Our fathers were both real charmers."

The diversion was interesting, but not relevant. I cycled back to my damaged car.

"Here's the thing, Eduardo. Like I said before: your and Tiffany's little escapade was caught on video, and I watched it. Your story doesn't make sense. If the whole thing was Tiffany's doing, why did she try to stop you? And if you were breaking in to free Bella, why did you pop open the trunk?"

Eduardo's body language remained carefully neutral.

Marla's, however, did not. Her hands drummed a staccato rhythm against the table. Her feet tapped the ground. Only her eyes remained motionless, glued to the table's surface, as if her mind were trapped somewhere inside the dense rings of wood.

"You must have been planning to steal something," I continued, "but what? My car is a beater. Why target it out of all of the other, nicer ones in the lot?"

"I already told you, the whole thing was the pet store chick's idea. I didn't even know what kind of car you drove."

Marla finally looked up. When she spoke, her voice quavered.

"Yes you did. I showed it to you when she picked up Dharma's stuff."

My skin tingled. *Dharma's belongings.*

"That's it, isn't it?" I replied. "You weren't searching for something of *mine*, you wanted something of *Dharma's*. You're the one who broke into my house, too. How did you know where I lived? Did Dharma tell you about me?"

Eduardo's complexion paled.

"I don't get it, though," I continued. "I've been through every stitch of Dharma's clothing. I even snooped through her makeup. I read every letter. I didn't find a single thing that would matter to anyone other than me. What did you think Dharma had hidden in that motel room?"

Goth Girl's tapping grew louder, more frantic. Her whole body—even her lip piercing—trembled. Eduardo reached over and trapped her hands.

"Marla, honey, stop. Everything's going to be okay."

"No, it's not," she cried. She yanked her arm out of Eduardo's grasp, pulling up her shirt sleeve. For the first time, I saw what she kept hidden under those long sleeves: shiny pink scars along her forearm.

Burn marks.

My chest tightened. Rene had been right all along. The El Paso arsonist *was* a woman. Just not the one we suspected.

Marla pulled her sleeves down and hugged her arms tightly against her chest. I spoke to her softly, as if soothing an anxious student. "Marla, how did you get those scars?" She didn't reply. I turned and spoke to Eduardo. "Did you think Dharma had evidence linking Marla to the El Paso fires?"

Eduardo stood and pulled Marla to her feet. "Come on. We're leaving."

She refused to move. "No, Eduardo. Not this time." She looked down at the table. Her words were so soft, at first I thought I'd misheard them. "It was an accident."

Eduardo's voice cracked. "Stop talking, Marla, please."

She shook her head. "I can't hide anymore."

Tears wet Marla's cheeks, but her voice betrayed little emotion. "I never meant to hurt anyone; I only wanted to watch the fire. That building was empty. It was always empty. I tried to put the fire out when it started spreading, but I couldn't."

For the first time since Green Lake, Marla spoke without hesitation. "I set the fires. All of them, even this weekend." She looked at her brother. "I'm sorry, Eduardo. I thought I could stop, but I can't." She turned back to me. "After the homeless woman died, Eduardo took me to California so we could hide out with Raven. He even slept with her to make her stay quiet. All to protect me."

Eduardo looked like he was about to be sick.

"You didn't think I knew that? Everybody says I'm so dumb, but I'm not."

Eduardo wrapped his arms around Marla and squeezed her tightly against his chest. "I never thought you were stupid, honey. Never. You've just been hurt by too damned much evil. And it was my fault. I'm your big brother. I was supposed to protect you. It was my job to protect you." He gently rocked Marla back and forth, whispering into her hair over and over again. "I'm sorry. I'm so sorry…"

I sat there staring at them, frozen. If I were my father, I'd have pulled out the handcuffs and whisked them both off to jail. If I were Dale, I'd have advised them to stop talking before they apologized themselves into a lifetime in prison. If I were Buddha, I'd have assured them that this life and their suffering were simply illusions, destined to dissolve away like some horrible nightmare.

But I was just a yoga teacher. All I could do was sit there helplessly and try not to sob. Marla's story didn't just break my heart, it shattered it. She was so vulnerable. So young. And there was nothing I could do to help her. I knew I should call the police, but I couldn't make my hand reach for the phone. A crazy part of me wanted to leap over the table, grab Marla's hand, and whisk her away. Away from her mistakes, from her guilt, from her pain. Especially away from the results of the phone call I knew I had to make.

I looked at Rene, silently beseeching her to come up with a different solution. The look on her face told me what I already knew: there was none. When she pulled out her cell phone, the tears in her eyes matched my own.

Marla pushed back from Eduardo's embrace and gave him a wan smile. When she turned to face us, she had finally stopped trembling.

"When the police answer, tell them I want to confess to a murder."

———

Rene took Bella back to the motel so she wouldn't try to protect Marla from the police. Two uniformed officers took the frail-looking teenager away in handcuffs about twenty minutes later.

To be honest, I didn't know how to feel. I had ostensibly solved the mystery of an accidental death—and it was an accidental death, whether the courts eventually agreed with me or not—so I should have felt proud, or at least self-satisfied. What I actually felt was ambivalent. Part of me was devastated that Marla's life had been ruined at such a young age. Another part was hopeful. If Marla was ever going to heal, she would have to atone for her crimes. Maybe in prison, she would get the help she so obviously needed. Maybe afterward, she would learn how to restart her life. Eduardo might even begin one of his own.

Eduardo spoke with me before he left for the police station. "Dharma always had a wooden box with her. You're sure there wasn't anything in it about the fires? She could have collected all sorts of information. Newspaper clippings, recordings of conversations, diaries . . ."

I shook my head. "Not that I found."

He squeezed his eyes shut. When he opened them, they looked hollow. "The day she died, Raven told me that Dharma knew about our affair and that she was going to get revenge by telling the police about El Paso. Raven always said crap like that, so I didn't believe her. But then you came to the motel and collected Dharma's belongings. I assumed she had some sort of evidence, and that her lawyer was going to use it to cut a deal."

"A deal?"

He slowly shook his head. "Yes. I convinced myself that Dharma was going to throw Marla under the bus in exchange for a lighter sentence."

"Raven lied to you," I said. "She was trying to turn you and Dharma against each other."

"I should have known better. Dharma's not the vengeful type. But Raven didn't use to be, either. Dharma and I drove by your house when we first got into town, and I knew you worked at a yoga studio near the pet store. I thought it would be easy to steal the box back…" His voice trailed off.

When he spoke again, it was filled with regret. "Finding that evidence was the only reason I didn't get Marla out of town yesterday. And now you tell me that it doesn't exist?"

"I'm sorry. No."

"Once again, I've let Marla down. If we'd left town right after Raven's death, she'd be safe in California right now."

I didn't expect an honest answer, but I had to ask. "Did you hurt Raven?"

Eduardo looked down at his boots. "No."

"Do you know who did?"

He paused for several long seconds, but once he started speaking, he didn't stop.

211

"I have no idea. Dharma and I only moved to California because Raven claimed we could keep Marla safe there. I thought I could trust her. We'd been friends since we dated in high school. She promised that she would give us a home and provide Marla some structure. And she did, for a while. Then she became obsessed with destroying her cousin. I could tell she was unraveling, so I told her we were leaving. That's when our so-called home turned into a prison. She gave me a choice: stay with her—sleep with her—or she'd turn in my sister. What could I do? I stayed. I slept with her. All for nothing.

"A couple of weeks ago, she told me that she'd finally figured out how to get back at her family. That stupid pet protest was part of her plan. I tried to talk her out of it. We fought. A lot. The stress is probably why Marla started setting fires again." He shook his head. "Raven didn't give Marla and me a home—she sent us to hell."

He looked up and grimaced, as if finally remembering my presence.

"Like I said, I have no idea who killed Raven. But when you find out, be sure to thank them for me."

NINETEEN

A FEW HOURS LATER, Rene and I sat on my couch and took turns sharing our day's drama with Dale. Bella, much to her dismay, was locked in my bedroom, primarily for Bandit's safety. Bandit and Bella had met on Orcas Island last fall, and suffice it to say, the introduction hadn't gone well. Bandit was now taking full advantage of Bella's incarceration by gluing himself to the opposite side of the door, where he sniffed, scratched, and barked at full volume. At least neither of them was off shredding boxes somewhere. Or each other, for that matter.

Rene sipped from a wine glass filled with non-alcoholic Chardonnay soda. Dale and I shared a bottle of the real thing. Dale seemed uncharacteristically somber. He even turned off the fake southern charm for the evening. He waited for us to tell the entire story—from parking at the motel to watching the police lead Marla off in handcuffs—before asking his first question.

"Why didn't the police arrest her brother, too?"

I set my glass on the table. "On what charges? Marla claims he had nothing to do with the arsons. I suppose he might eventually get in trouble for helping cover up Marla's crimes, but that certainly wasn't the police officers' highest priority today."

"What about for burglarizing your house and breaking into your car?"

"I couldn't turn him in for the car without implicating Tiffany, and I promised Michael I wouldn't do that. And if I told the police he broke into my house, they'd wonder why, and they'd eventually find out that Dharma knew about Marla's arsons. The last thing she needs is an accessory charge." I shrugged. "So for now, Eduardo goes free."

"Fair enough." Dale absently scratched his beard. "My main goal, of course, is to get Dharma out of jail. Do you think this 'Goth Girl'—"

"Marla," I corrected.

"Do you think *Marla* could have killed Raven? She had motive."

"I don't know what to believe anymore. But honestly? I don't think so. I know she's legally responsible for the homeless woman's death in El Paso, but she doesn't seem like a murderer to me."

Rene agreed. "Even if Marla wanted to kill Raven, I don't think she had the confidence to do it, not with her bare hands."

"For what it's worth," Dale replied, "I think you're right. It sounds like the homeless woman's death was an accident. A tragic accident. Starting a fire near an abandoned building is one thing. Holding someone's head under water and watching them drown? That's completely different."

Bandit must have gotten bored with tormenting Bella, because he trotted down the stairs, skidded to a stop next to Dale's chair, and hopped up on his lap. Dale stroked his fur. "I probably shouldn't, but I feel kind of sorry for the kid."

"Me too." I had a feeling I already knew the answer, but I had to ask. "I know this isn't your responsibility, but..."

Dale shook his head. "Sorry, Kate. I know what you're about to ask, and the answer is no. Marla will be extradited to Texas. I'm not licensed to practice law there. Besides, I'm Dharma's attorney. Representing Marla would be a conflict of interest."

It took every fiber of my willpower not to beg.

Luckily, Rene did it for me. She leaned forward, placed her hand on Dale's knee, and flashed him her no-man-can-refuse-me smile. "Please, Dale? Isn't there anything you can do? She's too young—too vulnerable—to have her whole life ruined. You're a legal miracle worker. There must be something you can do."

Rene and I both stared at him in silence, refusing to break eye contact. After a moment, he sighed.

"Fine, ladies, you win. I'll make some phone calls. I can't take the case, but I'll make sure she gets good representation." He affected his fake southern drawl. "Those kinfolk of mine oughta to be good for something."

I smiled. "Thank you."

"Don't thank me until we see if there's actually something I can do." He leaned back in his chair and rubbed Bandit's ears. "Marla's situation may solve one mystery, though."

"What's that?"

"Your mother's caginess. She's been hiding something from the beginning, and I suspect it's the El Paso fires. Maybe now that the girl has confessed, Dharma will be more forthcoming."

"Why would Dharma endanger herself like that? For Eduardo? She could end up in prison for the rest of her life."

"Not for the man, for the girl." He frowned "You really don't know Dharma, do you? Marla is emotionally vulnerable, exactly the kind of person your mother would be driven to help. She's spent her life fighting for those who can't protect themselves."

Except me.

My expression must have betrayed my thoughts.

Dale hesitated before speaking. "Can I say something to you as a friend now, not as your mother's attorney?"

I nodded my head yes.

"Dharma could have easily helped herself by turning that girl in. Even if we didn't cut a deal, I could have used what she knew about Marla as leverage for bail. She didn't so much as ask me about it. You haven't seen her in a few days, but believe me, she's not doing well in jail. Keeping that girl's secret may have been foolish, but it was also selfless." He stared at me until I made eye contact. "Are you with me so far?"

"Yes."

"Good. Keep listening and try to keep an open mind. I know you and your mother have a history. She hasn't shared the specifics, but I suspect they're not good. It's not my business to broker forgiveness. Heck, I don't know if Dharma *wants* you to forgive her. But remember, there are two sides to every conflict. Maybe it's time you heard hers. Whatever you may think, your mother is a good woman."

I didn't know how to reply, so I didn't. I reached down, picked up my wine glass, and drained it. The wall clock's hollow ticking filled the room's silence for at least a century.

Rene finally spoke. "So where does all of this leave us? In terms of solving Raven's murder, I mean."

I shrugged. "Pretty much where we started. From what I can tell, Raven had more enemies than friends. We haven't eliminated any suspects, not for certain. Even Judith from the wildlife center was glad to see Raven dead. If I can't eliminate a seventy-five-year-old do-gooder from my list, who can I?"

"What's our next move?" Rene asked.

"Legally, I've got my work cut out for me unless something changes," Dale replied. "The DA has plenty of evidence to get an indictment, what with Dharma's public fights with Raven, her ID being at the scene, and her skin under Raven's fingernails. Heck, if I were on the jury, I'd vote to convict. The only thing that could make the DA's job easier would be Dharma's confession."

"Are the police looking at Raven's family?"

"I'm sure they've interviewed them. They always investigate family members, especially when money's involved. And that family had more conflict than a herd of goats with too many Billies. I'll be danged if I can tie any of it to the murder, though. Dharma suspects that the Seattle protest was a front for something else, but she doesn't know what, and I can't figure it out. Everything I've found on DogMa so far seems legit."

"Have you looked at their financials?" I asked. "The original conflict between Maggie and Raven was about money."

"Maggie's stonewalling me," Dale replied. "She won't let me anywhere near their records."

"Doesn't that seem suspicious to you?"

"Yes. But then again, I'm defending her cousin's alleged murderer. Relatives of the victim rarely go out of their way to help the defense." He set Bandit on the floor. "Do you think Michael could talk her into cooperating?"

"I doubt it, and I can't, either. Michael and I destroyed any goodwill with Maggie the day of Raven's memorial. If we try to get anywhere near Maggie or her shelter, she'll probably shoot us with one of her grandfather's hunting rifles."

Rene sat up straight. "I could do it."

I turned to face her. "You could do what?"

217

"Snoop around at DogMa. Nobody there knows me, and everyone trusts a pregnant woman. I could sign up as a volunteer. Once I got in, I could find some excuse to look in their files."

"Absolutely not," Dale and I replied in unison.

"I'm not about to put you in danger." I said.

"I'm not going to let you risk Dharma's case," Dale added. "Whatever we find, I need to do it legally. I may have to use it in court."

"Besides, Rene. You'd get caught in a heartbeat. You're about as stealthy right now as a brontosaurus."

Rene looked a little insulted—and a lot hurt. "You don't have to be mean about it, Kate. I'm trying to help."

"I know you are, sweetie." I felt bad for the comment. Rene and I teased each other relentlessly, but comparing her to a twenty-three ton dinosaur was insensitive, even for me. "Tell you what—why don't we take a drive out to Fido's Last Chance tomorrow morning? My friend Betty's been in the rescue world forever. She might have some ideas. Right now, it's late, I'm too exhausted to think straight, and I need to get some sleep before I see Dharma tomorrow."

Dale leaned forward and set his feet flat on the floor. "About that visit..." His voice sounded unusually stern. "Before I let you get anywhere near my client, we need to revisit the ground rules."

Dale proceeded to outline, in his most lawyerly tone, everything I never wanted to know about jailhouse visits, recording devices, and the creative ways prosecuting attorneys could use them. Every word Dharma and I said at the jail could be used against her in court, not only for Raven's murder, but any conspiracy charges that the state of Texas might bring against her for helping cover up Marla's crimes. By the time Dale finished laying out his newest restrictions, there wasn't much left that Dharma and I *could* talk about.

The list of forbidden topics now expanded well beyond Raven's murder and HEAT to *anything* having to do with Eduardo, Marla, the fires, blackmail, or Dharma's time in Texas, Mexico, or California. In other words, I couldn't ask Dharma anything at all that might help me solve the murder.

No doubt about it, I was frustrated. But I was also relieved. Dharma and I had a mere thirty minutes, and Dale had taken away all of my excuses to waste them. If I couldn't talk about Eduardo or Marla in my visit with Dharma tomorrow, I'd be forced to learn about an entirely different enigma.

Me.

After three decades of silence, the conversation was long overdue.

————————

The mantra seemed to echo within and around me.

May you have peace.

May your heart be open.

May you be healed, and may you be a source of healing for all beings.

I reached my arms up and imagined that I was bathed in a warm, healing light. This ancient Buddhist metta meditation was one of my favorites. In it, I offered peace, healing, love, and joy to everyone who touched my life: acquaintances, loved ones, even myself.

Today's practice seemed especially powerful. The vibrations of the repeated words permeated my cells, soothing my nervous system like soft caresses. My prickly defensiveness lost its hard edges. My emotional nerve endings finally stopped throbbing.

I started to nod off—always a risk in meditation. I should have been a good yogi and kept my mind focused and alert, but the sensation of floating was simply too delicious. I closed my eyes and allowed myself to drift asleep.

What felt like a second later, I heard a low, distant rumble. The floor began shaking. The walls started to tremble.

Earthquake!

My eyes flew open and I scrambled to find something to hide underneath—a table, a doorway, anything—but I was suddenly surrounded by darkness. Cracks formed in the earth around me. The warm light I'd relished turned burning white cold.

He was back. The demon who lurked in the shadows. The evil that haunted my nightmares.

But this time, my eyes were open. This time, I wasn't afraid.

The familiar voice penetrated my subconscious: *Kate, you're dreaming.*

"I know."

Normally, this was the point at which I panicked. But not tonight. Dharma's letter—vague as it was—gave me power.

This time, rather than run from the dream universe, I changed it. I halted the shaking. I brightened the light. I smoothed out the cracks in my metaphorical foundation. I touched my fingers to the edge of the darkness, but I chose not to go inside. Instead, I faced it and gave my demon a message.

"If you come again, I'll be ready."

Much to my surprise, I meant it.

For the first time ever, I woke myself up.

TWENTY

I SPENT THE REST of the night in deep, dreamless sleep. When I awoke the next morning, I felt more rested, more balanced, than I had in a very long time. I jumped out of bed at eight o'clock, called Betty, and arranged to bring Bella over for a visit later that morning. After I fed Rene the first of her two breakfasts, we hit the road to Maple Valley and the headquarters of Fido's Last Chance.

"What do you think Betty will be able to tell us, anyway?" Rene asked.

"Honestly, I don't know. But I talked to pretty much every rescue group in Seattle when I was trying to find a new home for Bella. I got the feeling that the rescue community is like a small town—everyone knows everyone else's business. Betty would definitely be in on all of the dirt."

Rene rubbed her hands together. "Oh goodie. She'll be our snitch!"

I turned right and pulled into the gravel driveway of Fido's Last Chance. "Please, Rene. Don't say that in front of Betty. She won't think it's funny."

"Un-effing-believable," Rene muttered under her breath.

"You say some pretty rude things sometimes, and—"

"I'm not talking about the snitch comment—I'd totally say that." She pointed to the building in front of us. "That!"

I smiled. Betty's dilapidated house and converted garage/dog kennel had given me pause the first time I'd visited, too. But I was beginning to realize that state-of-the-art facilities with bright shiny cages weren't the measure of a good rescue. What counted was how well the humans who ran the facility cared for their charges. Betty and Judith's rescues were both proof of that.

I opened the car door to the clamor of barking dogs. Hundreds of them, from the sounds of it. Betty once said that having ten dogs on site was her personal limit, but I had a feeling she'd made some exceptions.

Rene looked at me, aghast. "You were going to surrender Bella to this place?"

I cringed at the memory. Thinking about parting with my canine best friend seemed like an abomination. Something only a completely different woman—one I didn't like very much—would have considered doing. But in reality, I *was* different back then. Bella had changed me, in every way for the better.

"Believe me, this place is a lot better than it seems from the outside. Most of the dogs rescued by Fido's Last Chance live in foster homes. Betty takes in the animals that no one else will. I called over forty rescues trying to get help with Bella. They all said Bella was too expensive, too aggressive, or both. All except Betty. She's a tough old broad, but I like her. I think you will, too."

I clipped on Bella's leash. She must have remembered her prior visit, because in spite of the deafening barking that emanated from the converted garage, she pulled me directly to Betty's front door. Before I raised my hand to knock, Betty threw it open.

"Well there she is!"

Bella wiggled her way up to Betty, plopped her rear on the ground in a perfect sit, and offered her paw.

"My goodness, aren't you a fatty!"

I could only hope that Betty was referring to Bella. For a dog with EPI, being called "fatty" was a compliment. Bella had lost over twenty-five pounds in the month before her diagnosis. She had gained it all back since I'd adopted her, and then some.

"Kate," Betty said, "I'm impressed. Looks like you've got that EPI of hers under control. Bella looks fantastic." Then she frowned, as if noticing me for the first time. "You could stand to gain a couple of pounds, though."

The barking dogs drowned out my snarky response.

"What's that you say?" Betty asked.

"Sounds like you have more dogs than when I was here last time," I yelled over the din.

"Yep. Along with my three, I have nine fosters right now."

"I thought ten dogs total was your limit?"

"It is. At least it was. I got a call a little over a month ago about two ten-year-old shepherds. Littermates who grew up together. As always, the rest of my foster homes were already over capacity. One of the old girls is blind; the other has epilepsy. They had to go as a pair." She huffed. "Good luck finding a home for that combination. It was either me or, well, you know." She sighed. "I may as well face it—they're my dogs now."

"What happened to their owner?"

"Poor old guy got Alzheimer's. His family put him in assisted living, and no one wanted his dogs. Surprising how often that happens." She shook her head. "I can't take in every hardship case that comes along. I know that. But these old ladies deserved better."

She wagged her finger at me. "You make sure you have written plans for Bella, in case something happens to you. She depends on you as much as a child would."

"Bella will be fine. Her future is more secure than mine is." I wasn't exaggerating. Michael and I had each made provisions for Bella in our wills, and Rene had agreed to be her guardian if necessary. Bella would never be homeless again.

Rene waddled up the porch steps to join us. After I made the requisite introductions, Betty ushered us into a hallway filled with dust, dander, and twelve dogs' worth of shedding season. She led us to the closet she called an office, cleared a stack of papers off the visitors' chair for Rene, and dragged in a folding chair for me.

The room had seemed crowded when Bella and I met with Betty last year, but that was nothing compared to this. By the time Rene lowered her three-person body into the chair, I was convinced we would use up all of the room's oxygen.

I was about to ask Betty to turn on a fan when two things happened at once: I lowered my rear toward the folding chair, and Bella charged the filing cabinet, knocking the chair out from under me. I landed on the ground and exhaled a loud "oomph!" On the following inhale, I smelled the unmistakable scent of recently used cat litter, which made sense, since my nose was four inches away from a cat box.

Rene sneezed. "Oh no, there's a cat in here."

Betty frowned, obviously not impressed with Rene's powers of deduction. "What? You got something against cats?"

Rene lifted her elbow to her nose and sneezed again. "I'm allergic." Clear fluid dripped from her nose and her eyes. "Where is it?"

As Dad used to say, I'd give her three guesses and the first two didn't count. Bella danced, whined, sniffed, and pawed at the filing cabinet, reveling in feline-induced ecstasy. Diablo, Betty's huge orange tabby, flattened his ears and showed her his claws from the top of the cabinet.

Betty ignored Rene and watched the two animals. "You know, Bella was interested in Diablo the last time you were here, too. Have you considered getting her a kitten? The company might help with those separation anxiety issues."

"Oh lord," Rene said. "Please, Kate. Please don't do it. I can't get anywhere near a cat without—" She sneezed again. "Can someone please take that cat out of here before my head explodes?"

Betty gathered the huge feline in her arms and carried him out of the room. Bella stared longingly after them, as if already mourning the loss of her mid-morning snack. She eventually lay next to my chair, let out a low groan, and rested her head between her paws.

Rene pulled out a bottle of Benadryl and swallowed two tablets dry. Her eyes were so watery, I was afraid her eyelashes would drown.

"Are you going to be okay?" I asked.

"I'll survive now that the dander generator is out of the room. Hopefully the antihistamines will kick in soon.

Betty marched back in and sternly crossed her arms. "Okay, you two. Now that you've made me evict my cat from his very own room, why don't you tell me why you're really here."

"What do you mean?" I tried to look innocent. "I thought you'd like to see Bella."

"Uh huh. Right." Betty lifted her eyes to the ceiling. "Look, Kate, I'm delighted to see Bella, but you haven't darkened my doorway since you adopted her last year. You want something."

She was right, on multiple levels. I did have a hidden agenda, of course, but that was just part of it. I should have brought Bella by sooner—Betty's no-nonsense encouragement had saved Bella's life, and I owed her. A lot. Much more than dropping by simply because I needed another favor.

"I'm sorry, Betty. I should have visited months ago. But you're right. I do need something: information."

I told her everything I knew about Raven's murder, including the part about my mother being the number one suspect. When I finished, Betty's expression was somber.

"I heard about Raven getting killed."

"You knew her?"

"A little. We rescue folk tend to run in the same circles. I liked her. She was a little crazy sometimes, but she had spunk."

"I'm trying to learn more about DogMa. The director, Raven's cousin Maggie, is acting cagey with Dharma's lawyer. Frankly, we're getting desperate."

"I don't know how much help I'll be. What little I know about DogMa is based on gossip and innuendo."

"Anything might help at this point."

She leaned back and crossed her ankle over her knee. "DogMa's relatively new on the rescue scene. It was formed by the two cousins—Raven and Maggie—and a woman named Sally a couple of years ago. I always got the feeling that the cousins were in it more as a status symbol. You know, rich kid do-gooders? Sally, though, she's the real deal. She's dedicated her life to that rescue, even after her husband's stroke. Gotta admire that."

"Is it as good as it seems? DogMa, that is."

Betty's jaw tensed. "Honey, we're *all* good. Us legitimate rescues, anyway. We just don't all get the credit."

"What do you mean?"

"It's a sore spot for me. I got to feeling downright defensive about all of the positive press DogMa got when it first opened. Everyone made out like those trust fund babies were Robin Hood and the Three Musketeers all rolled into one." She frowned and made air quotes with her fingers. "'Troubled girls make good.' Give me a break. We all have baggage."

"Troubled?"

"Sniffing white powder, spending too much time in Vegas, that sort of thing."

"Both of them?" Raven's grandmother had complained about Raven's addictions, but she'd never mentioned Maggie. Did it run in the family?

"One of them, both of them—heck, I don't remember anymore. Whoever it was, they supposedly cleaned up their act and decided to give back." She said the last two words with obvious sarcasm. "Heck, if I had their money, I could make a *real* difference."

"They don't? Make a difference, that is?"

Betty waved her hand through the air. "Don't let me badmouth them. I'm harping on like a jealous old bat. The work they do is important. I just get sick of places like DogMa getting all the positive press because they're 'no-kill' and flashy. It's easy to call yourself no-kill if you have state-of-the-art facilities and limit yourself to animals that are easy to place. Try doing it when you have twelve special needs dogs in your house twenty-four/seven."

As if on cue, a dog started howling.

"I know, Millie, I'm coming," Betty yelled. "Millie's getting senile. Freaks out if I'm gone too long. Anyway, I don't disagree with DogMa's philosophy, in principle. The faster they get the easy-to-adopt animals placed in homes, the more money and space there is for challenging dogs like Bella. Still, you don't see people holding huge fundraisers for places like mine. We just expand our garages and empty our personal bank accounts."

Again, Betty was right. I'd have to talk to Michael about doing an event for Fido's Last Chance next year.

Rene interrupted. "Have you heard anything about DogMa having financial difficulties?"

"Nothing to speak of. I know they started going after public funding not long ago. Before that, they were private."

"Maggie says that their expenses have been skyrocketing."

Betty shrugged. "Anything's possible. Lord knows my costs certainly seem to get higher every year. But they don't take in animals that require significant veterinary care, and as far as I know, they aren't housing more animals than they used to. If they're having money problems, I suspect it's due to revenue, not expenses."

Unless Maggie's "expenses" include cocaine and gambling.

But I didn't say that out loud. "Do you know how I could get a look at their finances?"

"Sorry, Kate. That's way out of my league."

"Ask her about the bird lady," Rene prompted.

"Bird lady?" Betty looked at me.

"Have you ever heard of Precious Life Wildlife Center?"

Betty grinned. "You mean Judith? Now *that's* an old battle-ax I can appreciate. If I were into wild animals, she'd be my hero."

Her description of Judith matched my impressions: opinionated, stubborn, and not afraid to skirt the law when she needed to protect her animals.

"Do you think she'd be capable of murder?" I asked.

"Honey, most of us folks in animal rescue are a few crayons short of a full box. We have to be, in order to do this kind of work. But murder?" She shrugged. "I'd like to think not, but then again, I could never imagine abusing a dog, and people do that every day. Maybe I'm not the right person to ask."

As the conversation dwindled, Betty turned her attention to Rene. First she looked Rene up and down, clearly appraising her. Then she watched her interact with Bella. When the questioning started, I knew Betty was up to no good.

"You look like you're about to pop any day. That baby of yours overdue?"

Rene looked aghast. "I'll have you know that I'm very thin for my stage of pregnancy. I'm having twins."

"You got a husband?"

"Yes…"

Betty grabbed a clipboard and started writing. "When's your due date?"

"In three months."

"Well, that gives us plenty of time, then."

Uh oh.

Rene froze. "Time for what?"

Betty didn't answer. She pointed a thumb at Rene but spoke to me. "You like this one?"

"She's okay…"

She wrote my name next to the word *references*. "Bella seems to like her too," she observed.

I knew exactly where this was going.

"And she's allergic to cats, not dogs, right?"

Rene scrunched her perfectly plucked eyebrows. "Why are you talking about me like I'm not in the room?"

Betty's eyes locked onto Rene like a tabby targeting a field mouse. "Fine. I'll ask you, then. Did you have pets as a child?"

"No. My mom was a neat freak."

Betty leaned in closer. "That explains those terrible allergies of yours. You don't want your twins to suffer like that, do you?"

Rene scooted her chair back several inches. "No, but ... "

"Babies who grow up with animals are rarely allergic. And kids need to learn how to be responsible. Nothing teaches that better than a dog."

Rene crossed her arms defensively. "I have never owned a dog, and I'm plenty responsible. Who do you think looks after Kate?"

Betty smiled and made a check mark on the form. "Well, that's great, honey. Dog owners need to be responsible."

"D ... dog owners?"

"Yes. That's why Kate brought you here."

I shook my head. "It is no—"

Betty silenced me with *the look*. The same look Dad used to flash when I slipped out a swear word.

"As I was saying, that's why Kate brought you here, whether she realized it or not. I see it in how you relate to Bella. You're ready to adopt a pet."

Betty opened a folder and pulled out a photograph of a happy-looking brown lab. "And I have the perfect one. He's a sweet old tripod. He loves kids, and now that he's seven, he's not nearly as rambunctious as he used to be. He only needs insulin injections twice a day, and as long as you keep his blood sugar stable, he almost never pees in the house anymore."

Rene stood up so fast that she tipped over her chair. "Um ... I um ... "

Evil Kate wanted to sit back and enjoy the show, but Best Friend Kate couldn't. Rene had fallen in love with Bella, but she wasn't ready to own her own dog, at least not yet. Still, if Betty poked at her ego hard enough, lord only knew what might happen. I needed to give Rene an easy way out.

"Sorry, Betty, but you can't have Rene. She's mine. She's my only dog sitter, and Bella won't tolerate another dog. You'll have to find someone else."

Betty's look would have frozen a Popsicle. "I thought you were working on Bella's reactivity to other dogs."

"I am, and she's better. She tolerates other dogs now as long as they stay at a distance. Sometimes she'll sniff at them from the other side of a fence. But I don't see any Fido best friends in her near future—not even any three-legged ones."

Rene mouthed the words *Thank you*.

Betty harrumphed. "You win, for today. But keep working on it." She slowly wagged her index finger at Rene. "I've got plans for this one."

Rene waddled out of Betty's house so fast, she even beat Bella back to the car. When I climbed in beside her, she said two words: "Drive. Fast."

Most days, I knew Rene better than I knew myself. If she was this panicked, there could only be one reason—Betty was right. Rene secretly wanted a dog. And what Rene wanted, Rene got. Period.

I had six months, nine at the most, before it happened. Rene wouldn't do anything drastic until she and Sam had settled in with the twins, but after that, all bets were off.

I needed to start looking for a new puppy sitter.

TWENTY-ONE

I dropped Rene and Bella off at Rene's house and headed to the jail for my second supervised visit with Dharma. Rene had offered to go along for moral support, but I asked her to look after Bella instead. In a moment so uncharacteristic that I thought she'd misheard me, she agreed.

At first I was suspicious. I knew Rene didn't buy my poor lonely dog argument. After all, we could have taken Bella along and parked her in one of the underground garages. I eventually concluded that she was simply being a good friend. Neither of us knew how I would feel after speaking with Dharma about the letters, but I might well need a few hours of privacy.

We arranged to talk about next steps at dinner.

But first I had to walk through the door of the King County Jail.

I wrapped my fingers around the handle. The door seemed unaccountably heavy.

Come on, Kate. You can do this.

I closed my eyes, took a deep breath, pulled open the door—

And smacked face-first into Eduardo.

He thrust his hand into his pocket. For an insane, terrifying moment, I thought he was going to pull out a gun and shoot me. But if his sallow complexion and slumped posture were any indication, any rage he'd once felt toward me—or toward anyone else, for that matter—was long gone.

When he removed his hand, it held car keys.

"Did you see Marla?" I asked.

"No, her cell block doesn't have visitation until tomorrow. I wanted to talk to Dharma, but she's taken me off of her visitors list. Looks like I won't be able to see her before I leave town."

"Are you heading back to California?"

He shook his head. "No, Texas. Marla's being extradited, and I'm going back with her. I'd hoped to see Dharma one last time and tell her I'm sorry."

"Sorry? For what?"

He shrugged. "So many things. For getting her mixed up in my secrets. For cheating on her with Raven. For thinking she'd turn against Marla. For..." His voice trailed off. "For everything."

Did "everything" include letting Dharma go to prison for a murder he committed?

"If you're truly sorry, you should stick around for a while. You might be able to help with Dharma's defense."

He buried his hands in his pockets again. "I belong with my sister. I already told the police everything I know about Raven's death. If anything, my testimony hurts Dharma. After all, I was sleeping with both of them." He nudged the pavement with his boot. "Will you please tell Dharma that I'm sorry? I did love her, you know. She's a good woman."

I hesitated. Dale had been clear: Eduardo was part of Dharma's and my no-talk zone. But surely relaying "goodbye and I'm sorry" couldn't jeopardize her case, and she probably needed to hear it. I would have.

"Yes, I'll tell her."

"Thanks." He turned and walked away.

I stared after Eduardo's slumped form until long after he'd disappeared down the crowded sidewalk. The energy left in his wake felt sad, tragic even. My heart broke for him, and for his sister. But that didn't mean either of them was innocent. The last year had taught me one inescapable lesson: good people, when pushed to extremes, sometimes did horrible acts. My heart had broken for killers before.

A metal detector and a surprisingly unpleasant pat-down later, I entered the still-crowded, still-desolate visitors' waiting room. Officer Friendly's clone took my information and sent me upstairs, where I soon found myself ensconced in a different makeshift phone booth staring through the same Plexiglas wall. Dharma shuffled toward the corresponding booth on the other side. My throat convulsed.

Dale hadn't been exaggerating.

Dharma looked awful.

A large purple bruise covered her left cheek. The left side of her upper lip was red and swollen, and her eyes were underscored by dark gray smudges. She slowly lowered herself onto the stool and picked up the phone.

I pointed to her cheek. "Dharma, what happened?"

"Evidently Ms. Crazy Eyes likes bananas. Refusing to give her mine wasn't one of my smartest moments." She smiled, but there was no humor in it. "Hopefully I won't end up being her bitch."

"Don't say things like that."

"I'm being realistic, Kate. Dale says my case doesn't look good."

I wanted to argue with her, but I couldn't. Not without lying. I changed the subject instead. "I saw Eduardo on my way in."

Dharma glanced at the guard behind her. "Dale came by this morning and told me about last night." I assumed she was being deliberately vague. But if she'd seen Dale, she knew about my involvement in Marla's arrest. "He said not to talk with you about Eduardo. He even made me take him off of my visitors list."

"I know. I'm only relaying a message. Eduardo is headed back to Texas with Marla."

"So he's leaving, then."

"Yes."

She frowned. "And you're his Dear Dharma letter."

"He came to speak with you himself, but yes. He wants you to know that he's sorry."

Dharma removed her glasses and rubbed them against her shirt. When she put them back on, she sighed. "Funny thing is, I'm not. Sorry, that is. I liked Eduardo; I probably loved him. But he won't be a loss. Not like your father was."

That was my cue.

"Dharma, I need to talk with you about Dad."

"You know more about your father than I do."

"Evidently not. I didn't know about the letters."

Dharma's face sagged. "You read them?"

"Yes. All of them." I paused. "I need to know what happened between the two of you."

"What did your father tell you?"

I didn't answer her question. Truthfully, Dad had rarely spoken of his time with Dharma, and when he did, his portrayal of her was significantly less than flattering. Dale was right. It was time to hear her side of the story.

"I'd like to hear it from you."

As the clock's minute hand ticked inexorably forward, Dharma spoke. I remained silent and listened, allowing her story to unfold in its own way.

"Your dad and I met in college. He was a political science major, a Republican, no less. I was a soon-to-be-dropout animal rights activist, hell-bent on saving the world. We were a match made in, well, made in hell, actually. But that didn't stop us from falling in love. Or me from getting pregnant.

"I never wanted a child. The world was already overpopulated, and I had big plans. I couldn't exactly take an infant to South America with me." She looked at the floor. "But your father ... " She sighed.

"Your father wanted you more than anything else in the world. He convinced me that we could make it work." She shrugged. "So we got married." She said the last words matter-of-factly, as if marriage was the most logical choice in a string of unacceptable options.

"Don't get me wrong, Dharma, I'm glad you didn't. But a liberal, unmarried woman who didn't want a child? Why didn't you ... " I struggled with the words.

"Terminate the pregnancy?"

I nodded. "Or give the baby—me, I mean—up for adoption."

Dharma kept her expression neutral. "I considered both, actually. I made an appointment for the procedure, but I couldn't follow through. I simply couldn't do that to your father. He was so happy about having a child."

She looked down at her fingernails as if examining her cuticles were her most important priority. "I tried to be a good wife, but I was miserable. The stay-at-home-mom scene went against everything I believed in, everything I'd ever dreamed of. I started to resent both of you. When you were six months old, I told your father that I was leaving. That I couldn't stay tied down—not for him, not even for you." She shrugged. "He convinced me that we could still make it work. He agreed to stay in Seattle with you while I did my work in South America. I'm sure he hoped that I'd hate being separated and come running back home.

"He was wrong. The arrangement worked out great, for me, anyway. I'd leave for up to a year at a time, and when I was ready, I'd come back to Seattle for a month or two."

It didn't sound like my idea of the perfect marriage, but it still didn't explain everything. Military families often lived apart for a year or more at a time, and Dad didn't give up easily. If the commitment had been there, he would have found a way to make it work.

Dharma must have sensed my skepticism.

"Remember, Kate, this was before the Internet. The places I worked didn't have plumbing most of the time, much less telephones. Your dad and I wrote, but his letters often arrived months after he sent them. Most of the time he didn't know whether I was dead or alive. The marriage couldn't take it." She shrugged. "He finally gave me an ultimatum."

I held my breath, waiting for Dharma to finish. She remained silent.

"That's not the whole story, Dharma," I said. "In the letter you wrote to me, you apologized, but not for being an absentee mother." I hesitated. Once I said the words, there would be no going back. "You said you felt responsible for my abduction."

"Yes. I still do."

Every part of me resisted asking the next question. My jaw clenched; my mouth filled with cotton; my throat ached. But somehow, I spoke.

"Dharma, when was I abducted?"

Her face cycled through multiple emotions: confusion, surprise, anger, understanding. It landed on regret. "You don't remember."

"No. What happened to me?"

Dharma closed her eyes and turned away from the partition. For a moment, I thought she was going to hang up and walk away without answering.

When she turned back around, she spoke in a flat, almost affect-free tone.

"Your father always wanted the best for you. I hope you know that. I'm sure he had reasons for allowing you to repress those memories, but whatever they were, he was wrong. You deserve to know."

She took a deep breath, then slowly released it.

"I had this friend in South America. He was a little … crazy, actually. He convinced himself that you were his child."

My stomach did flip-flops. I had mentally prepared for all kinds of contingencies, but not this. What if Dad wasn't my biological father?

"Was I?" I asked.

Dharma shook her head emphatically. "No. Absolutely not. You were already two when I met James." Her cheeks turned pink. "We had an affair. The night I broke it off, he went nuts. The next morning, he disappeared. I heard he'd gone back to the States, but I had no idea what he was up to." She swallowed. "He kidnapped you from your preschool."

"How did he know where to find me?"

"You weren't a secret. I told him lots of things about my life in Seattle."

I'd hoped talking to Dharma would shake loose some memories, but no matter how much she told me, I got the same result. Nothing. "How did I get home?"

"The police caught him two weeks later trying to smuggle you across the Mexican border." Her voice cracked. "No one could find me to tell me what had happened. Your father went through that awful time all alone. I didn't learn about your abduction until three months later."

I wasn't sure I wanted to know the answer, but I had to ask. "That man, did he..."

Dharma didn't hesitate. "No. He didn't harm you, at least not physically. There was no evidence of assault or abuse of any kind. But when border patrol found you, you were hungry, dirty, and terrified." Her eyes filled with tears. "All because I took up with a crazy man and gave him enough information to find you."

I tried to think back, to remember anything about those two weeks, but I couldn't. My mind felt completely numb. My belly, on the other hand, churned with the same visceral nausea I felt whenever I saw Dale, Santa Clause, or anyone else with facial hair.

"Your friend. Did he have a beard?"

Dharma looked up, startled. "Yes. Then you *do* remember."

"No, but it explains a lot. You said you found out about my abduction three months later. What happened then?"

"I came back to the States. By the time I got back, your father had hired an attorney, filed for divorce, and charged me with child abandonment. He gave me an ultimatum: either come home and be a consistent part of your life, or stay completely out of it. He said there would be no more compromises." She shrugged. "I agreed to give him full custody without visitation. I didn't even try to contest it."

"Why would he do that—not allow you to see me? And why would you let him?"

"Your father blamed me for what happened to you. I did, too. I think we both convinced ourselves that we were doing what was best for you. For what it's worth, I regretted it. I considered begging him to let me come back a thousand times. I wrote you that letter the day you turned eighteen. The returned envelope was the last time I ever heard from your father."

She was silent for several long seconds.

"After that, I tried to put you out of my mind, at least until a few weeks ago. When Raven decided that we all had to come to Seattle, I did some research. I found your father's obituary and that article about your dog saving your life last summer. I hoped, now that your father was gone, that you might be willing to connect."

Dharma looked down at her lap. When she looked up again, her eyes were wet. "Kate, what happened to you, especially my part in it, has plagued me for almost three decades. That's why I couldn't tell anyone about Marla and the fires."

I held up my hand. "Dharma, stop. Don't talk about that."

"Please, I have to say this one thing. Marla's father . . . what that man did to her . . ." Her voice trailed off. "Eduardo got her out as soon as he could, but it wasn't soon enough. The damage had already been done."

The clock's minute hand moved relentlessly forward, a stark symbol of the new urgency I felt about Dharma's situation. I would have the rest of my life to reflect on today's revelations, but for now, we were almost out of time.

"Dharma, is there anything I can do for you?"

"Yes. Stay safe. Dale told me that you're planning to help him look into DogMa. Please don't."

The guard announced that our time was up. Dharma gripped the phone and spoke as fast as she could. "Raven may have been a good person once, but not when I knew her. The last few weeks of her life, she was obsessed with taking down that shelter. Someone there has to be involved with her death. They're dangerous."

The guard approached Dharma. She got out one final sentence before he forced her to hang up the phone.

"I'd rather rot in prison than let you get hurt again."

I sat in that make-believe phone booth for what felt like an eternity, long after the next group of depressed-looking visitors started filing into the room. Anxious, sour stomach acid gurgled up into my throat. Dharma needed to get out of that jail cell—and soon. She knew that. I knew that. Still, the only favor she asked of me today was to stop helping her. This paradoxically strong yet beaten-down woman was not the uncaring monster I'd created in my imagination. Not even close.

What should I do?

Dharma's entreaty left me with two choices: keep investigating Raven's death and potentially risk my own life, or sit back and let Dharma spend the rest of hers in prison.

What would a good daughter do?

Obey her mother, of course.

Luckily for Dharma, I'd never claimed to be good.

TWENTY-TWO

I CALLED MICHAEL'S CELL phone as soon as I got back to the studio, but the call rolled directly to voicemail. I left a brief message saying that my meeting with Dharma hadn't yielded any useful information—which was true as far as Raven's murder was concerned. As for the revelations about my childhood, that bombshell was best dropped in person.

I taught my four-thirty Yoga for Core Strength class on autopilot. Rather than focus on my students, I obsessively reviewed everything I'd learned in my meeting with Dharma and anguished over everything I hadn't.

Suffice it to say, the class wasn't my best effort. I'm not sure what words came out of my mouth during that sixty-minute disaster, but my students seemed anything but blissful at its end. I'd barely finished ringing the chimes to indicate class was over when they popped up like Eggos, gathered their belongings, and scurried out of the studio.

"See you next week!" I yelled to their rapidly retreating behinds.

The teacher sitting behind the desk smiled knowingly. "One of *those* classes, huh?"

"The worst."

She pointed at the bench in the waiting area. "Your friend's here."

Rene was sitting quietly between the schefflera tree and the ficus. Her face looked swollen and puffy—much worse than when I'd dropped her off at home at noon. Her eyes were bloodshot; her eyelids, rimmed with red. Even the skin underneath her nostrils seemed raw.

"Rene, what happened?"

She sneezed. "It's my stupid allergies."

So much for her Benadryl strategy. "What are you doing here? I thought I was picking you and Bella up at your house?"

"We were worried about you. How did the meeting with Dharma go?"

I avoided her question by pretending to misunderstand it. "Dharma looks horrible, and I'm frustrated. So far, Dale's right. We haven't found a shred of evidence that proves her innocence."

Rene's response was characteristically blunt. "I wasn't referring to Dharma's case, and you know it. I meant that letter you found. Stop dodging my question."

I didn't reply.

Rene's voice grew softer. "You're not ready to talk about it, are you?"

"Not yet, Rene. But soon, I promise."

Rene's expression clearly indicated that she wasn't satisfied, but she stopped arguing. "Okay, for now. But I'm holding you to that. What else did you learn?"

"Nothing. At least nothing that proves Dharma didn't kill Raven."

"Maybe you're making this too hard. The system is 'innocent until proven guilty.' We don't have to prove that Dharma didn't kill

243

Raven; we simply have to come up with alternative suspects. All Dharma needs is reasonable doubt."

I shook my head. "That happens at trial, which could be a year from now. The way Dharma looks, she won't make it to the end of the month. That place she's stuck in is a prana-sucking vampire. Dharma's life force is being drained out of her, drop by drop."

Rene leaned back and scrutinized me, trying to decipher the truth. "I get that Dharma doesn't like being in prison. Who would? But why the sudden rush? Something changed when you met with her today, didn't it?"

Rene was right. The easiest explanation was that I was worried about Dharma's safety, which I was. But as I flashed on the bruise covering her left cheek, I realized that Dharma's health was only part of my new-found sense of urgency. The other part was completely selfish. For the first time in my adult life, I wanted to spend time with my mother.

Somehow, in today's brief thirty minutes with Dharma, my attitude toward her had changed. My childish beliefs about my father had, too. Dharma wasn't the black-suited villain I'd created in my imagination. Dad wasn't the white-hatted hero. They were simply two deeply flawed individuals who had made terrible mistakes.

I swallowed to clear the tightness out of my throat. "Yes, Rene, everything has changed. Dharma isn't who I thought she was." Tears threatened my eyes. "What if they take her away? I can't lose her before I have a chance to know her."

Rene stood up and grabbed my hand. "We won't let that happen. We'll figure out something."

I couldn't believe what I was about to say. "Actually, I have an idea."

I hated to involve Rene in my subterfuge, but I was running out of options. "I've been thinking about what you suggested last night.

Maybe you *should* go to DogMa—just to get a feel for the place and see if you can pick up on any gossip." I held up my index finger. "But I don't want you going alone. Sam can go with you when he gets back into town."

"Maybe…" Rene scrunched up her face and shifted left to right. At first I thought the twins were kicking her bladder again, but then I noticed that she was also avoiding eye contact. It was Rene's classic I'm-about-to-get-in-big-trouble dance.

"What have you done now?"

"You're not going to like it."

That was a safe bet. I didn't like it already. "Tell me."

"Bella and I went on a recon mission to DogMa today."

"You did *what*?" I wasn't sure which emotion was stronger: anger, frustration, or sheer incredulity. I peered at Rene through narrowed eyes. "We agreed that you weren't going to do that."

"No." Rene's reply was emphatic. "You and Dale agreed. You didn't give me any say in the matter. You both think I'm an incompetent boob, but I'm not. I want to help." She looked down at her fingers. "So while you were at the jail, Bella and I went on a field trip to DogMa."

That explained why she'd been so gracious about my going to the jail alone. She wanted me out of the way so she could go spying.

"I did exactly what you're suggesting. I dropped in at the shelter and told the woman at the front desk that I wanted to adopt a kitten." She pointed to her belly. "You know, for the girls."

"Rene, you're allergic to cats."

She rolled her eyes. "You act like I don't know that. I wasn't planning to take a cat home, just talk about one. I thought I could pop in, ask Maggie a few questions about their adoption procedures, and look around."

"Why didn't you say you wanted a dog?"

"I was afraid she'd show me a bunch of cute pictures like Betty did. I don't have your willpower, Kate. I could get suckered right in. With a cat, I knew I wouldn't end up taking it home. Honestly, I thought this plan through." She frowned. "Fine lot of good it did me. Maggie wasn't there. I got stuck talking to that assistant of hers, Sara or Sandra or whatever her name is."

"Sally?"

"Yeah, that's right. Sally. Evidently, she was the only person working this afternoon. She took me into an office, sat me at a desk, and made me fill out this humongous form, like I was adopting a kid or something. It was nothing like this morning with Betty. Seriously. That form was like five pages. Then she started the interrogation. Question after question after question. 'Will your cat be allowed outdoors? Have you ever declawed a cat? Have you ever owned an animal that was hit by a car? How much are you prepared to spend on your pet's health care?' Heck, how was I supposed to know the right answers? I don't even like cats!

"I kept waiting for her to leave me alone in the office, but she never did. I asked to go to the bathroom twice, hoping I could snoop around, but old Hawkeye Cat Lady never let me out of her sight. She even caught me peeking into the exam room." She shuddered. "Then it got worse."

"Worse?"

"Kate, she took me into a ... a *cat warehouse*. It was filled with the furry monsters. There were cages of them stacked on top of each other. My allergies went bonkers." She pointed to her face. "I mean, look at me! I sneezed so hard the twins probably have concussions."

I tried not to smile.

"The Cat Nazi wasn't impressed. She said I was—get this—*un-qualified* to adopt one of their animals. Then she added me to some sort of black list. She told me that she'd watched me drive up and that she'd seen the fighting dog in my car."

"Wait a minute. You let Bella ride in the Prius?"

"It was an emergency, Kate. I covered the back seat in blankets. Now are you going to listen to me or what?"

I nodded for her to continue.

"Anyway, that Cat Nazi thought I was gathering small animals to use as bait." Rene's hands formed tight fists. "Well, *that* made me angry. I've never harmed an animal in my life. And Bella may be big and unruly, but she's not vicious. I was about to tell Cat Woman where she could put her stupid list when her pocket started vibrating. She looked at her cell phone and pretended to have a family emergency." Rene placed her hands on her hips. "Kate, it was humiliating. She grabbed my elbow and walked me to the door like I was some sort of cat-hating con artist."

I suppressed a grin. "Well, you are."

"That's beside the point. She shuffled me outside and locked the door behind her, saying she had to leave because her husband was having some sort of health crisis. It was obviously an excuse to get rid of me. Then she gave me this flyer." Rene handed me a pamphlet titled *Why Spay and Neuter Your Pets?*

"She said that I should seriously consider sterilization, which doesn't make any sense, since she flat-out told me that she'd never give me an animal. How can I spay a cat if I don't own one?"

I didn't reply.

Rene's eyes grew wide. "You don't think she was referring to *me*?"

Rather than answer, I circled the conversation back to the case. "Rene, I know you were trying to help, but you were the one spy I had left. Why didn't you wait to visit DogMa until we had a chance to strategize?"

Rene's pretend indignation faded away. Her eyes grew watery. I had a feeling this time cat dander had nothing to do with it.

"I wanted to prove to you guys that I could help on my own."

My frustration melted. I'd known Rene over half of my life. Long enough to know she was a great actress. So great, in fact, that I sometimes forgot that her external bravado covered up inner vulnerability.

Dale's insensitivity toward her could be forgiven—he didn't know Rene, and his priority had to be Dharma, anyway. I had no such excuse.

I gave her a hug. "I'm sorry, sweetie. We shouldn't have dismissed you last night. But what do we do now?"

We stared at each other in silence for several long moments. Rene finally stood up and grabbed her purse from the bench.

"We go shopping."

Huh?

Rene was a huge fan of retail therapy, but the sudden change in focus seemed random, even for her.

"How on earth is shopping going to help?"

"Haven't I taught you anything? First we fuel, then we burn." She pointed down at her feet. "I need to waddle off these cankles. You need to come up with some creative ideas. Exercise solves both of our problems. We're taking Bella for a walk at Green Lake. Maybe being back at the crime scene will spark some ideas."

It wasn't the worst idea Rene had come up with. I certainly wasn't coming up with any solutions here.

"Okay, but what does that have to do with shopping?"

"I'm starving, and the PhinneyWood Market put their Easter candy on sale. The girls are about to eat their first marshmallow chicks.

Twenty minutes and two Cadbury eggs later, Rene and I pulled into the parking lot of the Green Lake Community Center. I parked the car, hooked on Bella's leash, and allowed her to pull me across the now-empty field that had housed last Saturday's event. Bella pranced happily at the end of her leash, occasionally coming back to sniff my jacket pocket, which held the last remaining goat-shaped cookies from Dale. Rene carried a reusable grocery bag in one hand and pulled bright yellow marshmallow chicks through her teeth with the other. Artificially colored sugar caked her lips and dusted her chin.

I knew my words were futile, but I said them anyway. "Rene, this junk food diet can't be good for you or the babies."

"Don't be silly," she replied. "Marshmallow chicks are an Easter tradition. Besides, everyone knows that you're supposed to eat a diet with a variety of colors." She pointed to the grocery bag. "I've got yellow, pink, and purple all covered in this one sack."

We walked past a woman holding a sign: *Homeless and hungry. Please help.* In an uncharacteristic demonstration of food-related generosity, Rene reached inside her bag and pulled out an unopened four-pack of bright pink marshmallow candies.

"Do you want some of my chicks?"

The homeless woman shook her head. "I don't eat that crap. It's pure poison."

I didn't hold back my snicker as I handed the woman a five-dollar bill. "You should be proud, Rene. A diet so bad the homeless prefer fasting."

"Keep walking, smart-ass."

We turned left at the trail and continued walking south. Bella and I normally avoided Green Lake's three-mile inner path and its hoard of canine-walking humans, but on this cool spring evening, the path was unusually empty.

For the first several minutes, the three of us walked in silence, only the soft crunch, crunch, crunch of gravel underneath our feet interrupting our reverie. The sweet smells of hyacinths and pink-blossoming trees tickled my nostrils.

Bella alternated between pulling me along the path and pausing to sniff the lake's shoreline, undoubtedly exploring the scent trail of one of Green Lake's many animal residents, which included rats, raccoons, herons, and a surprisingly large population of turtles.

Rene finished the last of her marshmallow chicks, crumpled the wrapper, and tossed it into a trash bin.

"Okay. Blood sugar catastrophe averted," she said. "Now I can think. Why don't you tell me what you've learned about Raven's murder so far? Maybe rehashing it will spark some ideas."

I started by listing the six people who I knew had conflicts with Raven: Maggie, Raven's grandmother, Goth Girl, Eduardo, Dharma, and Judith. Rene latched onto Judith.

"The bird lady? Betty didn't suspect her. Do you think she'd actually kill Raven because she threatened her bird business?"

"It's not a business to her, it's her lifework. Judith loves those animals like they're her children. She even calls herself 'Mommy.' I don't doubt for a second that she'd go after anyone who endangered her birds. I'd sure never let anyone harm Bella."

"You'd honestly kill someone to protect Bella?"

I thought for a moment. "Murder wouldn't be my first choice to solve any conflict. But I wouldn't kill for money, either, and people do that every day. Bella's a heck of a lot more important to me than material wealth."

"Good point."

"My biggest issue with Judith as a suspect isn't her motive; it's her age and physical ability. I'm not sure she's physically capable of overpowering someone as young and fit as Raven."

"Adrenaline makes people strong." Rene pointed at her feet. "You'd have been shocked at the old biddy I had to fight off to get these shoes at the Nordstrom Half-Yearly Sale. She tugged on that box harder than Bella going after a sirloin. Besides, Raven had hit her head the night she was drowned. She might have been dazed."

"It's certainly possible."

"Does the bird lady still have that pigeon of yours?"

"Mister Feathers? Yes, and she thinks he's going to make it. He'll be ready for release in a couple of weeks."

"Excellent. Call her tomorrow and tell her that you want to visit him. We'll go together and tag team."

"Okay, but let's make a list of questions tonight."

"No worries. I've learned my lesson. No more winging it for me."

Bella pulled me across the path and sniffed at something that looked so repulsive, I was afraid to guess what it was.

"Bella, leave it," I said. I tossed one of Dale's cookies a few feet away to distract her.

Rene kept talking. "So, that takes care of the bird lady. What about Maggie?"

"She'll never talk to me now, and Dale hasn't had any luck, either. Something was definitely going on with her, Raven, and DogMa. I'm not sorry Michael and I went to the wake, but I wish we hadn't made Maggie so mad. Interviewing her again would have given me the perfect excuse to snoop around at the rescue."

Rene pursed her lips and thought for a moment. "You know, I blew it with Sally, but Maggie doesn't know me. Maybe I can call her and pretend to be a telemarketer or something. Isn't that what you did with George's ex-wife last year?"

"I was pretending to be a reporter, not a—"

Something thumped the back of my head. I glanced behind me. Nothing was there. "Rene, did you hit me?"

Rene's look clearly implied that I'd gone insane. "Of course not."

I threw Bella another cookie and started walking again.

"Anyway," I continued, "I pretended to be a—ouch!" Something had thumped me again.

I whipped my head back and forth. "Did you see that?"

Rene furrowed her brow. "See what, Kate?"

A male voice yelled from behind us. "I think he wants one of those dog cookies."

Frustrated, confused, and a little concussed, I yelled back. "What are you talking about?"

The stranger pointed at a nearby tree. "That crow that keeps harassing you. I think he wants a cookie."

I peered up at the branches. On my best day I couldn't tell one corvid from another, but the crow staring back at me had to be Blackie.

"Bad crow," I said firmly. I held my palm forward, facing him. "Stay."

Bella looked confused, but she plopped her rear on the ground and waited for me to give her a cookie. Blackie dive-bombed me again.

"Knock it off!" I yelled.

The poorly trained crow landed on the ground next to me and stared. He had Blackie's unmistakable bald spot.

I pulled on Bella's leash. "Come on, you guys, let's go."

We took several steps forward. Blackie hopped the same number, tracking me.

"Okay, fine then," I grumbled. I pulled out a cookie and broke it in half. I fed one part to Bella and tossed the remainder to Blackie.

A smaller, more timid crow landed next to him. I smiled at Rene. "Isn't that cute? I think Blackie has a girlfriend." I broke another cookie in two and tossed half to each bird.

The man behind us shook his head. "You're going to regret that someday."

Evidently, someday was today.

Three loud caws later, the corvid volcano erupted. It was like a scene from an Alfred Hitchcock movie. Crows converged on us from all directions. They swooped overhead. They dive-bombed. They landed inches from our feet.

Bella glared at me, clearly saying, *Now look what you've done.*

Rene covered her head with her forearms and yelled, "Kate, get them away from me."

"They're not dangerous," I yelled back over the clamor. "They're hungry. Ignore them. They'll eventually give up."

I might as well have remained silent. Rene was overcome with bird-induced panic. She plunged her hand deeply into my pocket, grabbed everything inside of it, and threw.

I could see what was about to happen, but I was powerless to stop it. My house keys flew through the air, traveling farther and with much greater velocity than the cookies. Blackie's eyes seemed to sparkle. I would have sworn that he flashed me a feather-faced grin. He abandoned the cookies and took flight.

"Nooooo!" I yelled helplessly.

Blackie landed beside his new treasure, cocked his head to examine it, and picked it up in his beak. About a millisecond later, he'd transported it to its new home—fifteen feet off the ground, deep in the branches of a cedar tree.

His head—and my keys—disappeared into a hole inside the tree's trunk.

The rest of the murder—which, by the way, was the exact crime I planned to commit against my best friend—gathered their plunder and flew off to consume it.

Rene cringed and flashed her teeth in a submissive grin. "Oops."

"That's all you've got to say?"

She widened her eyes and held up her keys. "At least I drove."

"Lot of good that does us. My spare keys are jangling around in Michael's pocket somewhere in Oregon."

"Look on the bright side," she teased. "Maybe the contractors will leave the kitchen door open again."

"Cute, Rene. I'll bet it won't be so funny when Sam gets home. His car keys are on that ring, too."

Rene wasn't smiling anymore. She grabbed my arm. "Kate, we have to get them back. Sam will lop off my head if he finds out that I lent you his car."

I frowned up at the tree. Blackie cawed at me from the security of his bark-covered refuge.

"Don't look so smug." I pointed to Rene. "She's coming up there to get them."

Rene looked down at her belly. "Are you kidding me?"

Evidently, regaining access to Bella's and my abode would be up to me.

Between a feeble boost from Rene and the upper body strength born of hundreds of Sun Salutations, I managed to hoist myself up onto the lowest branch. From there, level by careful level, I climbed upward until I reached a branch one level below Blackie's. I glanced down.

Big mistake.

People didn't die from twelve-foot falls, did they?

Rene waved. "Hey up there. Good thing you're not afraid of heights."

I hadn't been, until now. Was that my imagination, or did I just hear a branch crack? I scooted closer to the trunk and wrapped my arm around it for balance.

Blackie cawed, clearly warning me away from his territory.

"Sorry, buddy, those keys are mine."

Rene yelled from below. "Do you see them?"

"Not yet."

Blackie's vocalizations became louder and more insistent.

"Oh, go caw yourself," I replied irritably. "I'll put everything except my keys back."

I tentatively reached my hand into the hollow, hoping that whatever lurked inside it wouldn't bite back. My fingers felt …

Lots of things.

At least my keys haven't been lonely.

Blackie had either been very busy since his return to Green Lake, or he'd started his collection long before he was injured. One by one, I pulled out a treasure trove of shiny corvid booty: a nail file, a metal barrette, two crumpled pieces of tinfoil, and enough quarters for bus fare to visit Judith on multiple occasions.

So far, no keys.

"Okay, buddy. Where did you put them?"

Blackie inched closer, as if he realized the significance of the final few objects. I reached my arm deeper into the hollow and felt around in the back, where Blackie obviously stored his most prized possessions. I pulled out keys.

Four sets of them.

I tucked my own keys inside my pocket, put sets two and three back in Blackie's hiding place, and examined the fourth set.

I glanced over at the curious corvid. "Sorry, bud. I lied. I'm keeping these, too."

Maggie's keys.

The same ones that Blackie had stolen on Saturday.

The same ones that opened the doors to DogMa.

The same ones I'd use for my next recon mission.

Blackie hopped on my shoulder and nuzzled my earlobe, as if asking, *Did I do good?*

"Yes, buddy. You did great. Gooooood bird."

TWENTY-THREE

I PARKED SAM'S CAMARO in a residential area a few blocks away from DogMa, pulled his recovered car keys out of the ignition, and cracked the windows and sun roof. Rene's grin was so wide I could see her back molars.

"Hey Kate, get this. We're about to break into an animal shelter."

"Hush, Rene. I know that." I glanced around to make sure no one was listening. "Do you have to alert the entire neighborhood?"

She burst into giggles. "But that makes us cat burglars!"

I slapped her arm. "Take this seriously, Rene, and keep your voice down. I know it's after ten, but people might still be up." I gave Bella a quick scratch behind the ears, opened my door, and then immediately closed it again. "Maybe this isn't such a great idea. Breaking and entering? If we get caught, we could be in serious trouble. Dale might get so mad that he won't bail us out."

Rene replied with her inimitable form of logic. "We're not really breaking, just entering. We have a set of keys, after all. Besides, we're not going to take anything—unless we have to, that is—so no one will even know that we've been there." She opened her door and heaved her body out of the seat. "Get off your butt and let's get going. It's past the twins' bedtime." She leaned inside and kissed Bella on the nose. "Don't worry, sweetie, we won't be gone long."

Bella sprawled on her side across the entire back seat, stretched out her legs, and closed her eyes for a late-evening nap. She showed no interest in joining our criminal excursion, which proved once again that Bella was significantly smarter than me.

I joined Rene on the sidewalk and checked my cell phone for the three-hundredth time since leaving a message for Dale two hours earlier. Still no return messages. "I wish I'd been able to talk to Dale. I'm not so sure he'd be happy with us if he knew what we were about to do."

"You *know* he won't be happy. Why did you even call him?"

"I was hoping he'd talk me out of this stupid idea. Besides, someone should know what we're up to." I pointed to the street sign near Sam's car. "Which reminds me, write down this address, just in case. If we get arrested, Dale will have to come and rescue Bella." As Rene rummaged in her purse, I frowned at my watch. "I thought he'd be packing to head back to Orcas by now, but maybe he decided to meet with Dharma. I left a message on his voicemail."

"You left a voicemail saying we were about to break and enter?"

"Not exactly. I said we were making an after-hours inspection of DogMa's facilities, and if we got detained, we might need his assistance. He'll figure it out."

"I'm glad he didn't answer the phone. He would have stopped us." Rene bounced on her heels in anticipation. "And that would have sucked, because we're going to have so much fun!"

At least someone was having a good time.

"Well, if he wanted to stop us, he missed his chance." I turned off my phone and slid it back into my pocket. "The last thing I need is for my phone to ring while we're prowling around trying to be inconspicuous."

Rene ripped off a page with the address and handed it to me. Then she put her notepad and phone in her purse, tossed it in the trunk, and started walking. "Come on, it's this way."

I pressed the lock button on the car's remote and followed her down the dimly lit sidewalk until we reached the rescue. Compared to Betty's place, DogMa looked like a professionally run paradise. The paved parking lot was lined with freshly cut grass, and each building's new-looking siding was decorated by colorful cutouts of playful-looking animals. A covered walkway between the two structures protected animals and their would-be owners from Seattle's infamous rain, should they be forced to walk from one space to the other.

Not that a homeless animal would care about any of that.

"This place is a lot nicer than Betty's," Rene said. "I could hardly tell that they have animals here until that woman took me into the cat dungeon." She pointed to the left. "That building is where they keep the cats and dogs—in separate rooms, of course. The building we want is the one on the right. That's where they have the office and all of the paperwork."

"What are we going to do if someone's inside?"

"Where would they be? The parking lot is completely empty and all of the windows are dark. Besides, when I was here earlier, that Sally chick claimed she was closing up shop for the rest of the day."

We slinked—well, I slinked, Rene plodded—across the darkened parking lot up to the door.

"Are you sure about this?" I whispered.

Rene snatched the key ring out of my hand and bumped me aside. "Oh, for goodness sake, Kate. What kind of lame super sleuth are you? Of course I'm sure."

"Wait." I pulled two pairs of rubber gloves out of my pocket. "Put these on."

Rene gave me an odd look. "Exam gloves? What are we, heart surgeons?"

"I learned my lesson on Orcas. This time, we're not leaving any fingerprints."

Rene sighed a bit more dramatically than was strictly necessary, but she put on the gloves. The second key she tried slid smoothly into the lock. She winked and elbowed me in the rib cage. "Here's hoping they don't have an alarm system."

The lock clicked open. Rene slowly opened the door.

Silence. No alarm. No animal sounds, either.

"Don't they have dogs here?" I asked. "Where's all of the barking? Bella would be having a fit."

"I told you. They keep the animals in the other building." Rene grabbed my gloved hand and pulled me through the door. "The Cat Nazi gave me a tour before she figured out that she hated me. This building houses the office, an exam room, and the training center. The room we're looking for is to the left."

We bumped our way through the darkened reception area to a small office. Rene opened the door and flipped on the lights.

"Rene, turn those off! Someone will see us!"

"We can't read paperwork in the dark, dummy."

"I know. That's why we brought flashlights."

Rene rolled her eyes. "Amateur. Flashlight beams will look suspicious from the outside. If we turn on the overhead lights, people in the neighborhood will assume someone is working late."

She had a point.

While Rene closed the blinds, I assessed the room's layout. A cluttered metal desk faced the back wall. A writing table and three chairs occupied the southwest corner. A four-drawer filing cabinet and a shelf containing a printer/fax/copier combination rounded out the rest of the office's decor.

"You take the desk," Rene said. "I've got the filing cabinet."

The desktop was covered with a large collection of notepads and pens, a computer monitor, and a towering stack of papers weighted down by a paperweight shaped like a golden retriever. I set the glass dog to the side and sorted through the papers, all of which were adoption applications in various stages of completion, including initial paperwork, home evaluations, and happily-ever-after reports of animals who had found their forever homes.

While Rene started on the second drawer of the filing cabinet, I tackled the desk drawers. The top one contained more pens, a dozen or so of the spay-and-neuter flyers that Sally had given Rene, and a smattering of stale-looking dog cookies. I was about to open the bottom drawer when Rene interrupted.

"Kate, I found a file with invoices here. Maggie said that DogMa's expenses have gone up recently, right?"

"Yes."

"Take a look at this." She handed me a thick folder. "Does anything stand out to you?"

I shuffled through the papers, looking for something out of the ordinary. I found receipts for a variety of animal-related expenditures: food, beds, toys, medications, and veterinarian fees. One of the receipts was an itemized record of pet foods purchased over the past three months from Pete's Pets.

"I'm a little surprised at the prices. I thought Michael was selling food to DogMa at cost. They're paying a lot more per bag than I used to pay for Bella's kibble. Is that what you mean?"

"No, but it makes me even more suspicious." She pointed to the bottom of the page. "Look at the signature line. "

"Sally signed for it. So?"

"Look at the rest. They were *all* signed by the Cat Nazi. Maggie doesn't seem to buy anything."

"That's not unusual. Sally is DogMa's office manager and book-keeper. Lots of businesses have an employee handle the day-to-day finances. I should do the same thing, but I'm afraid I'll lose track of my money. It's not like I have enough for anyone to steal, but ... "

That's when it hit me. I *hated* doing Serenity Yoga's bookkeeping. The only reason I hadn't hired it out was because I was a financial control freak. Maggie, however, had never been forced to clip cou-pons. It was natural for her to delegate DogMa's bookkeeping—like almost everything else—to Sally.

So when Maggie claimed that DogMa's expenses had skyrock-eted, how would she know? She'd never been in charge of the res-cue's day-to-day operations. That was Raven's job. Raven's job that Sally had been forced to assume more than a year ago.

Sally wrote the checks. Sally made the deposits. Sally was the per-son in charge of the money.

Sally also had a husband in an undoubtedly expensive rehab fa-cility. If Raven had somehow found out that Sally was embezzling money from DogMa ...

"Rene, I think we might have found our murderer."

"Maybe, but none of this proves anything."

"No, but it might point Dale in the right direction." I handed the file back to Rene. "Make a copy of this. Start with the receipts labeled as Pete's Pets. Michael will know if those have been forged. I'll see if I can get into the bookkeeping software. If Sally's been embezzling funds, she must have left a trail there somewhere."

I fired up the computer. Rene turned on the fax machine/copier, laid the file on the table next to it, and waddled to the door.

"Where are you going?"

It'll take a minute for everything to power up. I have to go to the bathroom."

"Now?"

"Yes, now. Unless you want me to piddle like a puppy in the middle of the floor. I'll be back before you know it." She took off her gloves.

"Hey, keep those on."

"They're making my hands sweat. My fingerprints are all over the bathroom from this afternoon, anyway. I'll put them on before I come back."

"Hurry up. This all makes me very nervous. Let's get what we need and get out of here."

While the copier warmed up and Rene emptied her bladder, I sat at the keyboard and tried to guess the computer's password. *DogMa*, *HEAT*, *PuppyLove*, *password1*, and *PasswordsSuck* all netted nothing. I picked up the dog-shaped paperweight and absently tossed it back and forth between my hands. Its eyes seemed to glitter.

Look at me, dummy!

Could it be that obvious?

I set the fake dog next to the keyboard and typed in several iterations of the words "golden retriever."

Nothing.

Well, it was worth a try.

I was trying various combinations of the names Maggie and Sally when the floor boards behind me creaked. I would have sworn that Rene had been gone less than two minutes.

"Wow, that was quick. You *do* have a small bladder."

Rene replied with a high-pitched squeak. The door clicked shut behind her.

"Raise your hands and don't make any fast moves."

Adrenaline jolted down my spine.

The voice didn't belong to Rene.

I slowly pushed back from the desk, lifted my fingers into the air, and tried to sound innocent.

"Sally, I'm glad you're—"

"Save it, Kate."

I turned around. Sally was holding a gun to Rene's temple.

"I knew this charlatan wasn't here today to rescue an animal, but I had no idea she was with you." Sally moved the gun away from Rene's scalp, pointed it at my chest, and shoved Rene toward me. "Get over there with your friend while I figure out what to do with the two of you."

I didn't take my eyes off the gun. "Are you okay, Rene?"

"I'm fine." Her voice sounded small. "I'm so sorry. She caught me on the way to the bathroom. She threatened to shoot me if I said anything. I didn't know how to warn you."

I tried to play dumb, which at the moment wasn't all that much of a stretch. "Sally, why are you pointing a gun at us? We're not burglars. My friend wanted to look at the cats again. We stopped by to see if you were still open. The door was unlocked, so we came inside."

Rene pasted on a fake smile. "That's right. I just wanted a kitten."

"Oh please. You're not fooling anyone. I overheard you two talking in here."

If playing dumb didn't work, maybe acting assertive would. I grabbed Rene's trembling hand, stood tall, and stiffened my body in pretend indignation.

"I have no idea what you're talking about, but Rene and I are leaving."

Sally shifted the gun's aim from my chest to Rene's belly. "You're not going anywhere. And if you don't shut up, I'll shoot your friend here in the stomach."

As threats went, it was surprisingly effective. Rene gasped and covered her belly with her hands. I pulled her behind me and backed us both into the desk.

Sally kept talking. "Looks like luck is finally with me. I'm not normally here this time of night, but my husband had a setback today. I had to spend most of the evening at the rehab center. I stopped by on my way home to check on the animals and saw that someone had turned on a light in the office. The volunteers never work afterhours, and Maggie barely stops by even when we're open. I thought we might have an intruder, so I decided I'd better be safe and bring in my gun. And wouldn't you know? I was right. I found you."

She held the gun alarmingly steady in one hand as she gestured with the other. "But what should I do now? One gunshot, I could explain. I could tell the cops that you were burglarizing the rescue and I shot in self defense. But two?" She paused as if considering it, then shook her head. "No, that will never work."

She started pacing. "This whole situation is Maggie's fault. If she had done right by me, no one would have been hurt. I've worked my butt off helping to set up and run DogMa. Maggie barely paid me half of what I was worth, but I didn't mind. My husband had a good job and rescue is love-work, you know?" She shrugged. "Then Frank got sick. I asked Maggie for a raise, but she wouldn't give it to me. She said that she needed all of the money to help the animals. I care about the animals, too, but shouldn't humans be more important?"

The question seemed absurd, coming from the lips of a murderer, but I didn't point that out. I bought time by stating the obvious.

"You stole money from DogMa to pay your husband's medical bills."

"It wasn't stealing. The money I took should have been mine in the first place. Most of it, anyway."

Rene shifted behind me. Sally kept talking.

"At first I only took a few hundred dollars. No one noticed, so I took a few hundred more. Then a few thousand ... " Her voice trailed off.

"How much have you taken?"

She shrugged. "Enough to make a difference, at least to me. The animals weren't hurt. It helped them, in a way. Every time I told Maggie that we were running out of money, she managed to find a creative way to get more. She never would have noticed the missing funds."

"But Raven did, and she blackmailed you." Granted, I was guessing, but what did I have to lose?

"Wrong answer, genius. Raven thought Maggie was taking the money—that she'd started gambling again. She figured all she needed to do to get back in her grandmother's good graces was find proof of it. She asked me to get it for her."

Rene poked me in the back. I ignored her and tried to keep Sally talking.

"How did Raven find out about the missing money in the first place?"

"It was so stupid. All of our electronic records are backed up online. I never thought about Raven still having the passwords. She'd been gone over a year when that awful old woman cut her out of the will. How was I supposed to know that Raven would blame Maggie for that?"

"So Raven snooped through DogMa's online records hoping to find dirt on Maggie?"

"Bingo. And she noticed my, shall we say, creative accounting. She called me a few weeks ago, convinced that Maggie was gambling again and I was covering it up. I denied it, of course. I thought I'd convinced her. Then she and her band of crazies showed up in Seattle."

"How did you get her to meet you at Green Lake that night?"

"I didn't. She called me Saturday afternoon and demanded that I meet her on that stupid dock at eleven-thirty. She had a big gash on her forehead when I got there, and she seemed a little dazed, but it sure didn't shut up her mouth any. She told me that if I wouldn't help her take down Maggie, she'd destroy DogMa. Turns out the protest was her way of threatening me. I realized that even if I refused to help her, she'd eventually find an auditor who would." Sally shrugged. "The real reason for the missing money would have come out. I couldn't let that happen."

She paused. When she spoke again, her voice sounded regretful. "Killing Raven was surprisingly easy. But you? I kind of liked you, Kate."

I had a very bad feeling about her use of the past tense.

"And I certainly never wanted to kill a pregnant woman."

I instinctively leaned into Rene, as if body contact would make me a more effective shield.

"You don't have to hurt us," I said. "This can end here."

"No, it can't. I can't go to prison. Who will take care of my husband when he gets out of rehab?" Her jaw hardened. "Sorry, ladies."

My mind spun, looking for options. There was no Bella locked in the bathroom to save us this time. Yoga might help keep me focused, but my fiercest Warrior Pose couldn't compete with a gun. I considered reaching for my cell phone to call 911, but there was no way I could get to it without Sally seeing.

I tried bargaining. "Sally, you've dedicated your life to taking care of the vulnerable. You don't want to harm Rene's babies. Let her go. She won't say anything." Rene squirmed behind me.

"Nice try, Kate. I'm sorry, but your friend has to die too. I promise, it will be euthanasia. Quick and painless."

Rene poked my low back with her index finger, over and over and over again. She wanted me to do something, but what?

"Kate, stop leaning on me. You're squishing my bladder." She looked up at Sally. "I really have to pee."

I had no idea what Rene was up to, but I assumed she wanted me to get out of her way. I took two steps forward, toward Sally. "Let her go to the bathroom."

Sally waved the gun at me and sneered. "Not a chance."

Which was precisely the distraction Rene had been waiting for.

She threw her gloves in Sally's face, screamed a primal "AAAGH," and charged her. I dove for the gun. Rene smashed Sally across the forehead with the golden-retriever-shaped paperweight she'd snagged from the desktop.

Sally staggered, but she managed to stay upright and hold onto the gun. She pushed me aside and shoved Rene into the desk—hard. Rene crashed into it, let out a gut-wrenching moan, and fell to the floor.

Everything next seemed to happen in an impossible fast-forward slow-motion.

Sally whipped around and pointed her gun at Rene's prostrate form. The door opened. The room went black. A body flew through the air. Screams, a sickening thud, and the sound of metal skidding across hardwood ripped through my eardrums.

I couldn't see what was happening—much less try to stop it—so I ran to the door and turned on the light. When my eyes adjusted, I saw Rene curled up in a side-lying fetal position next to the desk. A fierce-looking Dale pinned Sally to the ground. He gestured with his chin across the room.

"Pick up that gun. Now."

Surprise opened my mouth and spewed out a stupid question. "What are you doing here?"

"Apparently keeping you two idiots from getting killed. I called as soon as I got your message, but you didn't answer, so I came here to stop you before you did something stupid. Obviously, I didn't get here fast enough."

Rene groaned. Her face had turned an alarming shade of gray.

"Could you guys fight about this later? I might need an ambulance." I kneeled beside her. "Are you okay?"

"Something happened when I hit the desk." She curled into herself and groaned. "I think I'm having contractions."

My entire body flashed cold. "Hang on, sweetie. I'll be right back." I grabbed the phone off the desk and dialed 911. My best friend looked up at me with wild, frightened eyes.

"Kate, the girls. It's too early."

I stayed on the line long enough to make sure that both the police and an ambulance were coming, then dropped the receiver onto the desk, scrambled back to Rene, and waited for what felt like a thousand years for help to arrive. Dale restrained a vehemently swearing Sally; I huddled on the floor next to Rene. She squeezed my fingers so hard, I thought she might break them.

"Everything's going to be okay," I whispered. "I promise."

Sweat dotted Rene's forehead. "See, Kate. I'm not useless. I saved us."

I held back the tears threatening my eyes. "Yes, sweetie, you did. You saved us. And I swear, as soon as you're ready, I'm getting you a puppy."

Rene gave me a wan smile. "The girls would love a dog, but only if we find one that Bella likes. I'm her puppy sitter."

Sally stopped struggling long enough to snarl, "You're both nuts."

Rene groaned and hugged her belly again. "Please call Sam. I need him to come home now."

The police arrived first, followed a few seconds later by the paramedics. I stayed at Rene's side and muttered empty assurances while they hooked up an IV, lifted her onto a stretcher, and rolled her out to the ambulance. While they secured her inside of it, I gave Dale my house keys and the note with the car's location.

"Bella is inside a red Camaro at this address. Please go get her for me. I'm going to the hospital with Rene."

A uniformed police officer stopped me before I could climb in. "I'm sorry, ma'am. You'll have to stay here. I need to ask you some questions."

The growl that emerged from my throat was so fierce, I couldn't believe that it came from within me. "If you want to keep me out of that ambulance, you'd damned well better call the SWAT team."

A paramedic yelled from inside. "If you're coming with us, you ride up front. Either way, make up your mind. We're leaving. Now."

The officer hesitated a beat, then nodded. "I'll talk to you later."

I climbed into the ambulance, closed my eyes, and prayed for my friend. The sirens carried us into the darkness.

TWENTY-FOUR

THE NEXT TWO WEEKS passed in what felt like a heartbeat. In a weird series of events, the world changed, yet stayed oddly the same. Sally replaced Dharma in the King County Jail. Rene was checked into the hospital; Michael's father recovered enough to go home. I got my car back the same day Sam forbade me to drive his.

Who was I to question the laws of the universe? I was just happy we were all still alive.

Today was a new day. A day of beginnings.

The sun poured between white puffy clouds and melted my shoulders. Playground laughter drowned out the sounds of my inner demons. The smell of freshly cut grass evoked my favorite mantra: arriving home. I walked underneath the Greenwood Park sign, faced the wide expanse of green lawn, and lifted the small cardboard box as if offering its contents to the universe.

Dharma rubbed Bella's ears and smiled. "Are you ready?"

"Not yet. Give me a minute."

If the scratching and cooing coming from inside the box was any indication, Mister Feathers was eager to escape his dark prison. I knew I should simply release him and move on with my day, but letting that pigeon go seemed important. As if in liberating him, I would somehow free myself.

I closed my eyes, took a deep breath, and prepared to lift the lid. "Okay, buddy. Welcome to your new home."

Mister Feathers flapped his wings and was gone in an instant. He flew off into the distance, leaving the home I'd chosen for him far behind. I felt unaccountably sad. What had I expected? A thank you? A final circle overhead? A coo of farewell?

Dharma placed her hand on my shoulder. "Come on, let's head back."

We made small talk while Bella led us back to the yoga studio. "How was your visit today with your friend?" Dharma asked.

"Rene? She's feeling a lot better, especially now that the doctors got the contractions to stop. She's driving the nurses crazy, though. They've started a wager to see which of them quits first."

Dharma grinned. "She seems like quite a character."

"Believe me, there's no one else like her. I don't know how any of us will survive if she needs to be on bed rest much longer. The hospital food is killing her. She says if she doesn't get more sugar in her diet soon, her teeth will fall out. I smuggle in sweets when I can, but Sam's like the junk food police. He even searched my purse this morning."

"It could be worse."

"How's that?"

"You could both be eating jail food."

I smiled. "So true. Thank goodness Maggie didn't press burglary charges. With my luck, Rene would have been my cellmate. But at least she's found something to occupy her time in the hospital."

"What?"

"She's creating an infant accessory line. Some of her designs are truly awful, but the Baby Vampire line is kind of cute."

Dharma raised her eyebrows.

I shrugged. "I guess you have to see it. Nothing could be worse than her Baby Yogi line. I mean, really. Who puts the om symbol on diapers?"

We walked in silence to the end of the block before I said, "Hey, did I tell you that one of the nurses got approval for me to offer in-room yoga in the hospital's perinatal unit?"

"Can women on bed rest do yoga?"

"It has to be modified, but yes. Pranayama and meditation for sure. It helps keep hospitalized moms balanced and calm. Plus, it will give me an excuse to visit Rene."

We turned left and walked down 90th Street toward Greenwood Avenue.

"I have my own news," Dharma said. "You'll have one less house guest starting tomorrow."

I forced my expression to remain neutral. "You're leaving? It's only been two weeks. If the couch is too uncomfortable, Michael and I could invest in a guest bed."

"Where would you put it? Michael's junk is everywhere. I swear, Kate, I've seen mountain gorillas with better housekeeping skills than that man."

"I could ask him to clean up, but it wouldn't do much good." I shrugged. "We are who we are." Bella stopped to sniff the ground near a freshly composted pea patch.

"Honestly, Kate, that's not the problem," Dharma said. "I've loved the time I've spent with you two. But it's time for me to go."

The pain inside me felt deep, much deeper than warranted considering how little I knew Dharma. But like Michael—like me, for that matter—Dharma could only be who she was. Her leaving had very little to do with me and everything to do with her. Maybe that was why it hurt so much.

"Are you heading back to California?" I didn't want to get my hopes up, but if Dharma stayed in the States, we might strengthen the tenuous bond we were forming.

"No. There's nothing for me there. Not in Texas, either. There never was."

I looked away to hide my disappointment. "Out of the country again, then."

I heard a smile in Dharma's voice. "More like out *in* the country. I'm moving to Orcas Island to learn about goats."

I froze, feeling simultaneously confused, horrified, and—oddly enough—pleased.

"You and Dale? An item? When did that happen?"

Dharma shrugged. "I wouldn't call us an item. Dale has an empty room and he needs help. I need a fresh start." She wiggled her eyebrows. "I have to admit, though, he *is* kind of cute. I've always been attracted to men with facial hair."

I shuddered in spite of myself.

"Dale's a good man. Stable, yet uninhibited. After your father, I never thought I'd settle down with any man, much less some pretend country bumpkin. But who knows? At least with Dale, I'd be dating someone age-appropriate."

Now that I'd had a full twenty seconds to think about it, the match, if it happened, made a weird kind of sense. Dale had a habit of rescuing things, animals and people included. In this case, Dharma might rescue him back. Even better, Orcas was less than four hours away. Dharma and I could visit each other several times a year.

Bella abandoned her scent trail. We turned left and started walking the final four blocks down Greenwood Avenue.

"You're seeing a counselor now, right?" Dharma asked.

I nodded my head yes.

"Perhaps I will, too. I need to do something to help with the guilt."

"Guilt?"

"Over Raven's death."

"Dharma, you didn't kill her. Sally did."

Dharma shuddered, so subtly that I almost missed it. "I didn't hold Raven's head under the water, but I'm certainly not innocent. If I hadn't confronted her—if she hadn't hit her head when we fought—she might have been strong enough to fight off Sally."

I stopped walking and gripped Dharma's forearm. "You can't think that way. We don't control other people's actions. We are simply not that powerful."

Dharma stared at the ground in silence.

I wanted to say more, but I didn't know how. I had told my story once, but not to anyone who mattered. My counselor, after all, was paid to listen. Should I continue? *Could* I continue?

I kneeled next to Bella and gave her fur several long strokes. She nibbled my chin in return. Her deep brown eyes stared at me, clearly making a promise: *I will love you forever. No matter what.*

I believed her. Bella was family. So was Dharma, for that matter. Why did I expect so much less of her?

I kissed Bella's cool black nose and swallowed to clear the tightness from my throat. "For the past six months, I've tortured myself. I thought I caused someone's suicide. The police say his death was an accident; I think he jumped. We'll never know for sure."

"I'm so sorry."

"Me too, and it's been tearing me up inside. I pummeled myself with the 'maybes.' Maybe if I'd stayed out of the investigation. Maybe if I'd listened more carefully to his words. Maybe if I'd held onto his arm…" My voice caught. "Maybe I could have stopped him."

I paused for several long seconds. Bella leaned into me, as if offering me strength.

I took a deep breath and said the words I was finally beginning to believe. "And maybe I'd have ended up dead at the bottom of that cliff next to him."

I looked up and met Dharma's eyes. "I always knew that I didn't *physically* shove him off the cliff, but I'm beginning to realize that I didn't push him over the edge mentally, either. Whether he fell, jumped, or was gathered by Satan and yanked to his own private hell, *his* actions made it happen. Not mine."

I stood up again. "That's what my counselor says, anyway."

Dharma squeezed my hand and we started walking again. "Your father was right, you know."

"How's that?"

"You and I are a whole heck of a lot alike."

A few moments later, we entered the parking garage. There weren't any classes scheduled for the next hour, so we brought Bella with us to the studio's back door. The sound of contented cooing filtered from the alcove above.

I groaned. "You have got to be kidding me."

Mister Feathers was happily snuggled in his favorite roosting place on top of the chicken wire. A pile of wet bird waste had already begun to accumulate beneath him.

Dharma tried, unsuccessfully, to suppress a laugh. "Looks like you have a permanent guest after all."

I smiled ruefully. "It's okay. There's a bright side. Somebody's going to have to clean up his mess every few hours. I think I just found the perfect job for Tiffany."

I inserted my key into the door. Something warm, wet, and gooey fell onto the back of my head.

I looked up at the happy bird.

"Seriously?"

Dharma reached into her pocket. "Pigeons are perfectly awful, you know."

I took the tissue she handed me and wiped the bird gunk out of my hair. "Kind of like family, don't you think?" I grinned to let her know I was kidding.

Dharma's expression turned serious. The former stranger who was now my mother placed her hand on my arm. "I'm sorry."

"For a little bird poop?"

She opened her mouth, then closed it again. Her arm slowly floated back to her side. "For all of our lost time."

I waited a long time before answering, longer than was comfortable for either of us. But my words, when I spoke them, were true.

"It's okay, Dharma. We'll make up for it."

We had a beginning, and that was enough.

THE END

© Jason Meert

ABOUT THE AUTHOR

Tracy Weber is the author of the award-winning Downward Dog Mystery series. The first book, *Murder Strikes a Pose*, won the Maxwell Award for Fiction and was nominated for the Agatha Award for Best First Novel. *Karma's a Killer* is her third novel.

A certified yoga therapist, Tracy is the owner of Whole Life Yoga, a Seattle yoga studio, as well as the creator and director of Whole Life Yoga's teacher training program. She loves sharing her passion for yoga and animals in any way possible. Tracy and her husband, Marc, live in Seattle with their challenging yet amazing German shepherd, Tasha. When she's not writing, Tracy spends her time teaching yoga, walking Tasha, and sipping Blackthorn cider at her favorite ale house.

For more information on Tracy and the Downward Dog Mysteries, visit her author website at TracyWeberAuthor.com.